LOVE

MOTHER

LOVE

DAUGHTER

Other Books by Ellen Frazer-Jameson

LOVE MOTHER

LOVE DAUGHTER

ELLEN
FRAZER-JAMESON

Disclaimer: *Love Mother Love Daughter* is a work of fiction. Names, characters and incidents portrayed in this novel are the work of the author's imagination. Any resemblance to actual persons (living or dead) or specific events is entirely coincidental.

Published by
Fourth Dimension of South Beach
MIAMI, FLORIDA
www.ellenfrazerjameson.com

© 2020 Ellen Frazer-Jameson

The right of Ellen Frazer-Jameson to be identified as author of this Work has been asserted by her in accordance with sections 77 and 78 of the Copyright, Designs and Patents Act 1988

ISBN: 978-0-578-30894-4

Cover design and typesetting: Gary A. Rosenberg
www.thebookcouple.com

This novel is lovingly dedicated to my eternal husband,
Derek Jameson, my awesome family, and
a sacred circle of inspirational friends.

prologue

The picturesque Italianate graveyard was awash with summer sunshine. Marble monuments, copper crosses and alabaster angels cast noonday shadows on the hallowed ground. A place of peace, tranquillity and a satisfying finality.

No words were spoken but the breeze breathed the final farewell. 'Rot in hell, you bastard.' An open grave awaited its guest, a dark, silent resting place where a soul could pause on its journey homeward. By the grave, a mournful quartet watched as the coffin was lowered on silken red ropes into the ground.

Two grieving widows. Picture perfect, beautiful, statuesque honey-haired blondes dressed dramatically in matching jet black Versace ballerina-style net covered cocktail dresses; dangerously high Manolo Blahnik shiny pointed black court shoes and the outfit mysteriously topped off with dainty veiled pillbox hats.

The widows stood graveside. Stepping forward in turn, each dropped a single blood red rose onto the varnished black wood and gold handled coffin. Silently, motionless, beside their mothers stood two demure little girls dressed in matching black mourning outfits, ebony satin ribbons in their hair.

As the bored priest intoned the final words of the funeral service, 'Dust to dust, ashes to ashes…' the mournful group could contain their emotions no longer.

Suppressed sobs rose to the surface and became smiles then joyful laughter and the two small girls looked at each other and giggled. On an unspoken command, the matching blondes tore off their veiled headgear and threw them violently onto the coffin. As one they chanted, 'Adios, gypsy boy, not a tear will we shed.'

chapter one

'Nothing emboldens sin so much as mercy.'
Shakespeare's *Timon of Athens*

Julianne Faith Gordon suffered every day with the knowledge of her devastating secret. Sworn to silence, she was forced to deny the very truth of her existence.

Basking in the reflected spotlight of Julianne's successful career and high powered friends, her daughter, Kira Mae shared her mother's glamorous lifestyle of privilege, wealth and ease.

The two beautiful blondes were on the guest lists of all the top designers in the exciting world of London fashion, and prized guests on the international scene.

Soul sisters, blood relations, Julianne and Kira Mae were discreet enough to silence malicious rumours about their relationship.

Concealed in the mists of time, the truth of their family connection was denied, brought out and like the latest designer fashions ultimately declared 'to die for'.

Julianne trusted no one, always fearful that they would discover her shameful secret. The truth of her birthright that she had vowed to take to the grave.

Her silence had been bought – but she was the one who had paid that price. Julianne and Kira Mae were a formidable pair. Fiercely loyal to each other, driven by their personal demons and prepared to fight to the death to protect their gold-plated reputations – and their sanity.

★ ★ ★

Born in the 1970s in a small village in East Devon, Julianne's parents Alan and Martha Gordon were reserved, respectable and relatively unremarkable – except perhaps for their slavish devotion to the baby girl they had made together.

Her mother Martha treated Julianne as a beloved child. Cosseted, spoiled, she was not expected to help with chores or be concerned with matters connected with the running of their neat as a pin home. That was Martha's domain and she was more than capable of housekeeping for her husband, a classics scholar and public school headmaster, and her only child. She took great pride in overseeing a well regulated household while her husband prided himself on being a good provider, the breadwinner. No wife of his was going to work outside the home.

Not that Martha would have been particularly suited to finding a job, she had been brought up by immigrant parents who had fled from Italy during the war and as they worked to establish themselves in their new homeland, Great Britain, their only daughter Martha acted as an interpreter, companion and home help. She had not been expected to have a life outside the parental home until she married. In fact, she may have been destined to live her life as a spinster so sheltered and protected was she by her parents, Elsa and Abe, the quiet mannered Donattis who ran an Italian bakery in a small Devon village outside Exeter.

However, as a summer treat she had been sent to holiday with relatives in Italy and it was there that she met her future husband, Alan Gordon.

The two had begun conversing on the short ferry ride as he escorted a coach load of British public school boys on a trip to the island of Isola Bella, just off the shores of Lake Maggiore on the Italian Riviera.

'Please excuse the manners of my boys,' said Alan politely to the stylish, statuesque blonde as she basked in the sunshine and stood gazing out over the rail of the ferry, holding her long hair away from her face with one hand as a faint breeze ruffled her golden curls.

Martha smiled. She had already realised that the teenage boys naively thought that by speaking English they would not be understood by their fellow travellers.

'No need to apologise,' smiled Martha graciously. 'Compliments are always welcome – in whatever language.'

Joining an official sightseeing tour of the magnificent art filled palace of Isla Bella and touring its lavishly landscaped grounds complete with strutting peacocks, Alan and Martha exchanged interested glances and passing observations.

When Alan was not being interrupted with constant questions, '*Please, sir, can we go off and explore on our own? Please, sir, when are we leaving? Please, sir, what time is dinner?*' he managed to elicit the name of Martha's hotel, establish that she was travelling alone for this part of her trip and request that she meet him for a coffee the following day, before he and his class of students boarded a coach for the return journey to England.

Martha liked what she saw and she couldn't help speculating that a handsome, well-mannered school master was likely to find favour with the marriage expectations that her cautious and discriminating parents held for her.

She was right. Alan's education, respectability, earning potential and the fact that his parents too had fled a war-torn Europe, in their case coming from Poland, to find a better and safer life in Great Britain, made him an acceptable suitor when he began to court and later ask for the hand of their daughter in marriage.

Alan resigned his position in a prestigious Cambridge boys' public school soon after their wedding and accepted a headmastership at a modest rural school in Devon, close to Martha's parents. The birth of their own child, a beloved daughter, Julianne, made their lives complete.

Martha delighted in her role as a wife, mother and home-maker and her husband Alan, whose only fault was his moodiness which could sometimes tip into depression, always played his part as father, husband and protector.

Martha was a healthy, happy woman whose only daughter had just entered secondary school. She had no symptoms, no signs, no lumps. Nothing to suggest that she was about to be given perhaps the most devastating news a well woman can receive. After a routine mammogram performed as part of a new health screening programme, Martha was informed that a biopsy would be needed to further examine an irregularity in her breast.

The piece of tissue removed for biopsy was cancerous. It was to be the beginning of a harrowing two year journey in which Martha underwent multiple surgeries, including a double mastectomy and reconstructive breast surgery.

'I'm going to beat this,' she constantly reassured her daughter Julianne, who insisted on hearing every detail of what was happening, what might happen and what were the chances of her mother's survival.

'Don't treat me like a child,' she would plead, as she again sat at her mother's bedside, after yet more painful surgery. 'I'm here for you. I can help. Tell me what I can do to make you better.'

For hours Julianne held her mother's hand and read to her from self-healing books. One of her favourites was the *Gift from the Sea* by Anne Morrow Lindberg, which always seemed to deliver just the right measure of peace and serenity. The two developed a mantra which they would intone over and over again. 'No retreat, no defeat.'

Defiant in the face of her own mortality, Martha had read that 'what you resist persists', so she constantly talked to her daughter about what life would be like *After C*.

'We will come through this together,' she promised Julianne. 'What doesn't kill you makes you stronger.'

For a time it really did seem that Martha was getting stronger. In consultation with her medical team, it was agreed that she would be taken care of in the comfort of her own home, supported by her loving family and specially trained nurses who would visit to administer medication and help with her treatment.

Just one condition was imposed; the newly teenage Julianne, by now an experienced carer, was always to be listed on the charts as Team Leader. Julianne cast herself in the role of Florence Nightingale, the indefatigable and authority challenging nursing sister who had revolutionised the medical conditions of wounded soldiers at the time of the Crimean War.

A school essay on this feminist heroine had inspired Julianne and won her top marks in the class. Now she was on a mission to save the life of her darling mother. No child or adult could have offered more tender loving care and stoic devotion.

Issuing orders to the nurses and relaying reports to her ever more distant father became a daily occurrence. Julianne refused to be defeated; she assumed all the responsibility and all the concern for her mother, who even she could see was getting weaker by the day.

She prayed to a god in whom she was rapidly losing faith. 'Please God, don't let my mum die.'

Martha willingly indulged her daughter in a nightly ritual in which she had at first tried to believe, but which appeared more and more unlikely to be able to reverse the effects of the pain and lumps she was now finding on her own body.

To the accompaniment of bells and smells, Julianne would anoint her mother with holy water from Lourdes, smooth into her drying skin cream made from ingredients found on the banks of the Nile and massage her with oil recovered from the tomb of an ancient goddess, all the time playing healing spiritual music performed by Native American Indians.

'No defeat, no retreat,' they chanted together.

Martha and Julianne had attended several local Psychic Fairs together and they enjoyed learning about New Age beliefs and experimenting with oils and herbs promoting health and well being. They had even had their tarot cards read but chose not to impart that piece of information to a decidedly sceptical husband and father. The spiritual music selections that they had bought on these outings helped set the scene for their nightly meditation sessions.

Mother and daughter loved, supported and encouraged

each other. They laughed together and shared family stories of their joint lives and made elaborate plans for all the adventures they would share when Martha recovered.

Martha navigated her way through the painful dilemma of on the one hand allowing Julianne to believe that a miracle would occur and she would be cured; and an obligation to prepare her for the worst. The bond between mother and daughter was so strong that it was difficult for anyone else to find a way into their sacred circle, even Martha's husband, the father of her blessed child.

'It's women's business,' he explained when forced to discuss his discomfort with the situation. 'I can't be dragged into those emotional swamps of the sick room.'

Julianne did not voice to her mother concerns that her father was seething with anger and somehow blaming both of them for destroying the happy family with their 'women's problems' of diseased breasts, bloody surgery and brutal chemotherapy. He seemed to want to run as far away as possible. His beautiful, perfect wife was mutilated, he refused to deal with the emotions and realities he was being forced to face. If he was hurting, he certainly was not about to confess that to the woman who had caused the pain.

The end for Martha came swiftly. Yet another biopsy had identified cancerous cells, this time in the lymph nodes. She did not reveal the full results of the tests to her daughter. Instead, she tenderly explained that they were both to prepare themselves for an unwelcome and unexpected parting.

'We don't know when it will come,' she told a crying Julianne. 'You don't even have to try to be brave; just know that I had a happy and blessed life – because I had you. I could not have asked for a better daughter.'

Julianne wanted to scream and shout and rail against the unfairness of it all, but she kept quiet and retained her dignity for her mother's sake.

Using a psychological technique that she would use every day for the foreseeable years of her existence, Julianne choked back her very breath. She swallowed down her feelings, shut her mind to the reality and made herself very small. Shoulders hunched, hands made into silent fists and teeth clenched, Julianne forced herself to close down emotionally, physically and spiritually.

In the darkness of the early hours of the morning, by the flickering light of a scented candle, Julianne held her mother's hand and watched and prayed as the powerful prescription pain medication allowed her to sink into a coma and breathe her last.

Martha's husband had left the room and gone to sit in his favourite armchair, drinking whisky and staring morosely into the distance while playing mournful Wagnerian music.

'Mum's gone,' said Julianne, as the visiting nurses set about their final duties and she took on the task of informing her father.

'You are my wife now,' he slurred ominously.

chapter two

'By the pricking of my thumbs,
Something wicked this way comes.
Open, locks,
Whoever knocks!'
Shakespeare's *Macbeth*

Nothing would ever be the same again. Alan did not consult his daughter about his decision that they should move from the picturesque, thatched roof cottage that had been his wife's pride and joy. He cared nothing for the colourful, lovingly tended flower beds, neatly trimmed lawn and moss free driveway.

While his wife was alive he willingly provided her enough housekeeping to ensure that decoration, furnishing and jobs around the house were kept in good order. After her death and a well-attended funeral, which he grudgingly paid for, complaining all the time about what he saw as unnecessary expense, it seemed that his wallet had become frozen along with his heart.

Julianne had persuaded her father that it was only fitting that they should give her mother a good send off and invitations had to be issued even to relatives who had not bothered to come and visit during her illness.

Only a handful turned up – one couple travelled all the way from Italy – and Alan may have been right that they came only for a good meal, free drink and to see if Martha had left them anything. After all these years, it was unlikely that close relationships would become established.

However, they made the appropriate noises and told young Julianne, 'Let us know if we can do anything. After all we are family.'

Martha's parents had died young, a result, she was convinced, of the strain of their early war time lives and too much hard work trying to make up for all they had been forced to leave behind. Their daughter had often expressed how thankful she was that they were not alive to know of her own medical condition.

Knowing that his drinking had escalated during the two years of her mother's diagnosis and treatment, Julianne was fearful that her father might make an exhibition of himself at the funeral. Hate and animosity for the world in general and everyone in it, had become her father's default position. He blamed everyone and everything for his wife's death.

The once fiercely conscientious headmaster now decided to take an extended leave of absence from school on compassionate grounds. Released from the obligation to be close by the premises in case of emergencies, he relocated himself and Julianne to an isolated cottage on the moors, some miles from the village they had previously called home. Julianne changed schools, having been coerced into believing that it would be better for her and her studies if she took the opportunity to move to a new senior school in an environment where she was not known and people would not be aware of the heartache she had endured losing her mother. Crucially there would also be fewer daily reminders of the life they had known when her mother was alive and Julianne was still able to enjoy a happy childhood with two parents who loved her.

★ ★ ★

Alone, just the two of them in a new and strange location, Alan told his daughter again that she had now become his 'wife' and out of respect for her dead mother she should be willing to take over all the wifely duties. For a short time Julianne was mercifully unaware of exactly what that would mean – but the evil day loomed.

One night as Julianne lay in bed reading, her father knocked on her door and asked permission to come in. She agreed for as usual he had been drinking and she did not want to do or say anything to provoke him. His ferocious temper could be sparked at the slightest suggestion of opposition. It was not unusual for him to push, slap or manhandle his daughter, though he generally made a big deal of finding an excuse for his behaviour – or apologising after the event.

On this occasion he appeared to be in a conciliatory mood as he sat beside her on the bed and in a morose voice admitted how much he missed Martha.

'I loved your mother,' he told her earnestly. 'My life is not worth living without her. Sometimes I think it should have been me who died, not her.'

Julianne had never heard her father speak like this before; he was usually so controlled, secretive, not given to talking about feelings or showing his emotions. Where previously she had felt contempt for what she perceived as his heartless treatment of her mother, she now began to see her father in a different light. He was hurting and she felt empathy and sorrow for him. She did not object when he reached out and stroked her hair and then her face.

Still sitting alongside her on the edge of the bed he moved his body further up the bed and continued to stroke her hair with his right hand and ran his left finger hesitantly over her lips. They sat like that for what seemed an eternity, as Julianne became more and more uncomfortable with the intimacy.

She pulled the bedclothes closer to her and flinched as her father reached over and turned off the bedside light. Abruptly he stood up and left the room, saying only a brusque, 'Goodnight.'

Much relieved, Julianne decided against turning the light back on and tentatively settled down to sleep. Drifting in and out of consciousness, a couple of times she awoke and sat up, thinking she had heard movement in the bedroom. She tried to get back to sleep but there was no denying it. Someone was in her bedroom. She could hear their breathing. The covers were thrown back and she felt her father get into her bed.

He lay alongside her and shushed her saying, 'You're all right, go back to sleep, it's only me.'

Holding her breath to prevent a sound escaping from her lips, Julianne pretended to be asleep. She lay rigid but cried out involuntarily as she felt the weight of her father's body manoeuvre on top of hers. This time he put his hand over her mouth as he said, 'Be quiet. I'm not going to hurt you. I love you.'

Julianne was paralysed with fear and she felt hot, helpless tears sting her eyes. In the darkness she looked up to see the bloodshot eyes of her father gazing into hers.

She was pinned under his body and tried wildly to appeal

to him with desperate tears, as he roughly pulled up her nightdress and forced her legs apart. A red hot pain exploded through her body and she felt like her insides were being torn apart, as a bone hard object was forced into her virgin body.

Whisky fumes filled her mouth and lungs and heavy raspy breathing punctuated, as sickening snorts like a pig filled her ears. Julianne felt she was being suffocated and screamed in pain as she tried to struggle out from under her attacker. His weight was too great. At the moment, when Julianne felt that she would surely die of pain and shame, the heaving beast expelled a guttural shout and collapsed in a heap – all primordial energy spent.

Lying awkwardly on top of his daughter, Alan Gordon, widower and rapist hauled himself off her trembling body and sat again on the side off the bed, adjusting his pyjama trousers. He hung his head in what might have passed for mortification before offering his justification.

'You made me do that,' he told his innocent child. 'Now go and wash yourself clean.' Julianne obeyed, she saw no alternative.

Julianne never knew when she would be subjected to her father's sickening sexual demands. There might be weeks in between the frightening incidents and sometimes he seemed to ignore her, losing all interest in even talking to her. In vain she tried to convince herself that she had imagined the night time violations and they were not going to recur again. Then, like a thief in the night, he would be back in her bed, sneaking under the covers, brutally yanking her nightdress up or her pyjamas down and raping her. The sticky white mess that he left behind between her legs repulsed her and she would scrub herself for hours to try and rid herself of the sight and smell.

To anyone who knew what she was suffering, it would not have come as a surprise that Julianne was a solitary child who did not make friends easily or communicate well with those around her. She was respectful of her elders and teachers but also wary. She did not confide in anyone. Her demeanour drove away many who might have befriended her and she was subject to a subtle form of bullying in which she was ostracised by her peers for being haughty, standoffish, aloof. They perceived her as an outsider – not one of the crowd – and she did nothing to change their opinion of her. Julianne was a swot who always had her head stuck in a book. Just one girl managed to penetrate her shell, Annabelle Anstruther. The two shared a love of horses and worked together at the local stables where they helped with mucking out to offset some of the costs of stabling their own horses.

Riding provided Julianne with the desperate relief she needed away from the house of shame and her soul destroying secret. She rode like the wind, jumping fences, galloping across the moors and finding a kinship with one other living creature. Her beloved horse, Rocket.

She and Annabelle competed in gymkhanas and boasted to each other about how many rosettes and cups they had with their names engraved on them. Julianne's father used the horse as a threat and often claimed he would take it away. Cruelly he suggested that if Julianne did not do as he demanded, he would ensure that Rocket was made to make the final journey to the 'glue factory'. Strangely though, his threats never carried real weight and Julianne refused to believe that Rocket was in mortal danger.

If he was, she would defend her equine friend to the death and even her father was shocked when after one baiting session in which he threatened to sell the horse, Julianne confronted him. Eyes blazing, hands on hips, she faced him down and yelled.

'Don't even think about it – or you'll live to regret it.'

Perhaps he sensed his daughter's steely reserve and realised that it would be the straw that broke the camel's back. To preserve Rocket she would have done anything – even jeopardising her own safety to finally break out of the shameful collusion and tell on her father.

Aside from Annabelle whose company she enjoyed, Julianne was reconciled to being the most unpopular girl in school. It did not help that she was extremely beautiful, with poise unusual in one so young. She had inherited her mother's natural grace and stylishness. Her heart shaped face was enhanced with flattering dimples, well defined rosy coloured lips and large unfathomable baby blue eyes, framed with jet black lashes.

Her skin was pale to the point of being almost translucent. Julianne was a beauty but that beauty carried an unspoken warning, 'Don't get too close'. From behind an impenetrable barrier exuded an aura of sadness as she looked out at the world with a questioning that could have been contempt or shyness. Most people did not stop to question which. They knew her mother had died and perhaps could be forgiven for thinking that this was the cause of her deep grief, lack of laughter and refusal to engage emotionally or form friendships.

Julianne kept herself to herself. If she was lonely, she did not allow those around her to know or encourage any intimacy that would have necessitated her opening up or sharing secrets. Julianne did not even cry openly the day a cruel classmate wrote on the blackboard, 'Everyone hates, Julianne-No-Mates.'

chapter three

'A wretched soul bruised with adversity,
We bid be quiet when we hear it cry.'
Shakespeare's *Comedy of Errors*

Living like a prisoner alone with her father in their isolated and cheerless cottage behind high hedges out on the moors, far from neighbours and prying strangers, Julianne won admiration from the few people with whom they did engage, for the way she had taken over the duties of housekeeping, cooking and cleaning since her mother had died.

That she had also taken over night-time duties and was now forced to share a marital bed with her father would have scandalised the small close-knit community.

But no one ever asked the questions and behind closed doors the abuse and agony continued all through Julianne's senior school life.

One other area in which her father gave her the benefit of his undivided attention was academically and Julianne had become a high achiever, passing all her examinations and gaining a coveted place in the local college where she would go after leaving school at sixteen.

Reading, researching and keeping up her grades provided

Julianne some release and escape from her desperate home situation. Apart from horse riding, only her school work provided the opportunity to show any real conscious involvement in life. Here Julianne did not need to react on a personal level – she could keep tutors at arm's length by hiding behind her books and intellect. Her superior demeanour and unsmiling countenance discouraged friendship and frivolity. No teacher ever needed to cajole her to do her homework; Julianne took herself and her studies very seriously.

So seriously that she had identified the only way to relieve the pressure of her miserable life – alone in her room she would cut herself and allow the pain to flow out with the blood. Then she would punish herself further by striving for ever better grades. Perhaps one day her academic achievements would be enough for her rage filled, overbearing father to praise her for her scholarship – not her sexuality.

No family members intervened, though they had been solicitous enough when her mother died, promising to be there for the motherless young girl.

No teachers intervened. Presumably they thought that the respectable, scholastic headmaster they had known before the tragedy of losing his wife to breast cancer, was a loving and thoughtful father. Someone who would be a pillar of strength and admirable role model to his grieving daughter.

No social workers intervened. In fact a case worker visited the remote family home just once. She was so impressed by the articulate, caring father act that she never visited again – but did leave a calling card and telephone number, 'in case we can be of assistance'.

Julianne suffered in silence and her withdrawn, sad demeanour was, not surprisingly, attributed to the fact that she had lost her beloved mother. No one ever took the time to question the melancholy young girl who played alone and looked out from bewildered eyes at a world that valued adult needs over those of a child. A child who had become a woman before her time.

Not that she would have told them the reason for her sadness – even if they had asked. She hid her shameful secret and blamed herself for the squalid life she led. A woman child who knew too much – and understood nothing.

Julianne continued to excel at school and her being reserved was accepted as the personality of a shy but gifted child.

Her father made lots of promises to his darling daughter, including the oft-repeated one that he would kill her if she breathed a word of their secret relationship to anyone. He continued to drown his sorrows in whisky and as he descended further into alcoholic depression and morbid self-introspection, he lived a half-life, cutting himself off from people and life in general. Medically retired he claimed a good pension and was financially secure on the proceeds of his wife's early death insurance pay-out.

When she was a 'good girl for daddy', Julianne was spoiled, indulged and rewarded with presents. Any sign of resistance led to punishment. Julianne was bright enough to know what course of action was in her best interests. Shutting down emotionally and learning not to cry, not to show her emotions, not to feel her feelings, Julianne accepted her lot and dreamed of the day when she could escape and be free.

★ ★ ★

At the age of sixteen, Julianne, whose menstrual cycle had never been regular, stopped having periods. She had no close female friends or relatives to confide her fears, but gradually she came to the realisation that she was having a baby.

A child, pregnant with a child, Julianne resorted to the only cure that she knew made her transcend her fear. She took a kitchen knife into the bathroom and cut her arms, her legs, her thighs, and her stomach. The red flow of blood that had stopped from her vagina and acted like a betrayal, flowed from her wounds. The pain outside surpassed the pain inside.

In a drunken rage her father accused her of trying to trap him by deliberately getting pregnant. If only he knew how far from the truth that was, the suggestion that Julianne would do anything to sacrifice herself to her tormentor and abuser for one minute longer than necessary was unthinkable.

As the school holidays approached in the summer of 1986, her father revealed that he had plans for her. This involved shipping her far away from the only people who knew her – and could possibly start asking awkward questions.

Julianne was to stay with relatives in Scotland until she had the baby – she had never even met any of her Scottish relatives and knew only that her father's family had come from Europe – and he had spent some time in Scotland before pursuing his teaching career down south. One Scottish legacy he did retain was an acquired surname – Gordon. Julianne chose not to ask further questions about his Celtic heritage, but she acknowledged to herself that anywhere had to be better than where she was now. Anywhere where he was not, would be a welcome relief. Alan Gordon had thought of everything, immediately after birth the child – whose father had done everything in his power to ensure that he would not be named or shamed – was to be adopted.

chapter four

'And thus I clothe my naked villainy,
With odd old ends stolen out of Holy Writ,
And seem a saint when most I play the devil.'
Shakespeare's *Richard III*

Ida Mitchell was a God-fearing woman of unsophisticated intelligence and simple tastes. She was a relative who lived in the same Scottish village where Julianne's father had been born and raised.

The widow of a miner who had been more than a decade older than her on their marriage, she had led a sheltered existence, moving house only once – that being on her wedding day – from No.19 to No.17 Main Road in a small erstwhile mining village equidistant from Glasgow and Edinburgh.

The couple never had any children of their own and Mr William Mitchell had died in his early fifties from a respiratory disease, caused by all his years working as a lift operator travelling all day – and many night shifts – to the deepest levels of seams in the coal producing mine.

Mrs Mitchell survived on a small pension from the Coal Board and a handful of memories. Her most prized possession hung proudly on the living room wall, a hand engraved certificate presented to her husband 'in recognition of thirty years' service to the Coal Board'.

Beside that hung an impressionist painting of a renaissance garden scene, painted by the son of a miner friend of her husband. Ida's husband was proud of his friend's talented son Jack and had always declared, 'One day he will be famous.'

Since investing in the luxury of having central heating installed some years before, Ida had no need of the other gift from a grateful Coal Board. One ton of coal per quarter – delivered to the door.

Mrs Mitchell did not really know her husband's brother Alan who had left the village before her marriage to go and study in England. Bill generally described him as being 'too big for his own boots'. He called him a snob who took for granted the privileges he had been given to pursue further education and who could not wait to put hundreds of miles between himself and his more working class family members. Until he needed them.

Needing to resolve the dilemma of a pregnant daughter who with each passing week had the potential to provoke a huge scandal, Alan Gordon saw a use for his far distant and mostly forgotten sister-in-law.

Ida Mitchell was well aware of the stigma attached to being pregnant and unmarried, even at a time when the pill was widely available and enlightened organisations such as the Marie Stopes clinics no longer expected women to be married before contraception could be prescribed, as they had done a decade earlier.

Ida Mitchell had seen at first hand the demeaning and often cruel way that unmarried mothers were treated in some church welfare homes. The nuns who so often ran such homes under the guise of social welfare had little sympathy for 'fallen women'. Indeed it was received wisdom to set the unmarried mothers, often young and vulnerable girls, to work scrubbing floors and washing windows. Such back breaking chores were meant to concentrate the mind on the wickedness of their past actions and the unholy consequences. It was also supposed to help bring about a swift confinement.

The Catholic Church was known to run a secretive commercial organisation called The Magdalene Laundry Girls, where young unmarried mothers were exploited to work in the laundry factories and, after giving birth, give up their babies. Many of these girls stayed in the system for years after their initial incarceration, unwanted by family and forgotten by society.

'Hard labour never hurt anyone, especially a sinner,' one battle-axe nun, Sister Margaret, had told a crying young girl on whose behalf Mrs Mitchell, a friend of the church and volunteer, had tried to intervene.

She had handed in her apron that day and never returned to her tea making and library duties at the bleak Victorian convent on the edge of town.

When she was approached, after many years of silence, by her husband's younger brother who sadly recounted the tale of his errant daughter, Mrs Mitchell had agreed to take her in as an act of human compassion. Here was one young girl who, whatever her foolish behaviour, would not be washing windows or scrubbing floors.

Mrs Mitchell began to look forward to welcoming her young visitor, the niece she had never met. Julianne would come to stay at the neat little whitewashed pebbledash cottage in the heart of the village, with a small stream running along the end of the garden.

Ida Mitchell hummed happily as she prepared the small guest bedroom that overlooked a tiny garden, with weed free flower beds and a doll's house sized piece of lawn. The first floor guest room was already painted a cheerful buttercup yellow and had china blue frilly curtains, with white tie backs at the small leaded window. More years before than Ida permitted herself to remember, the room had been planned as a nursery. Now it would indeed be needed for its original purpose.

One small single bed was covered with a hand crocheted cream eiderdown and snowy white sheets and pillowcase that offered a soft place to lay a weary head. On the bedside table were a miniature electric replica of an old oil lamp and a thoughtfully chosen selection of books. *The Country Diary of an Edwardian Lady, Scottish Country Life* and *Charles Edward Stuart: Life and Times of Bonnie Prince Charlie.*

An iris blue glass water holder and matching glass competed for space on the dressing table top. On the walls, were several small prints of flowers and heather in white frames and one gold framed showpiece of the local ruined castle, Auld Castle Campbell.

Down the hallway, the bathroom was painted a pastel blue shade with white paintwork, net curtains over the mottled opaque windows and a crocheted blue crinoline lady delicately concealing the spare toilet roll on top of the cistern. Fluffy white towels were neatly stacked in a white basketware storage box.

Everything was spick and span. A place for everything and everything in its place. Warm and cosy and designed to say 'Welcome. You will be safe here'.

★ ★ ★

Alan Gordon, who used his second Christian name of Gordon instead of the more homely Mitchell that his brother was known by, arrived with his pretty daughter, Julianne, on a bitterly cold afternoon in February.

Snow had been threatening all day and as father and daughter knocked on the door of the tiny cottage flakes of snow fell from the sky. Ida, wearing a pale blue pinafore dress over a crisp, white blouse, her thick chestnut hair pinned up in a loose bun, opened the door at the first knock and fussed them all the way inside.

'Come in, come in, you'll catch your death of cold. The kettle is on – come in, come in.'

The wooden stable style front door led directly into the main downstairs room. The artificial log fire burned brightly – fuelled by North Sea Gas – and there was a delicious smell of freshly baked bread.

Like the upstairs, downstairs was simply but comfortably decorated and furnished. The walls were a very pale bluebell blue and the lights were of the same electric powered, faux antique oil lamps as in the bedrooms. There was a bright chintz covered settee directly in front of the brass surround fireplace, one velveteen wing armchair with a tartan covered footstool and a freestanding wooden sewing box to the side. Behind the settee, there was a small round dining table covered with a white lace tablecloth. The wall-to-wall carpeting was of a flowered pattern that almost, but not quite, clashed horribly with the flower pattern in the settee covering. One small runner in front of the hearth provided a buffer – probably more by luck than good judgement.

The table was set for afternoon tea. A pretty, delicately patterned, china tea service was laid out at three places round the table. On the table, with not a spare inch of space, there were newly baked and buttered white crusty farmhouse sandwiches. A plateful of delicious smelling hot scones awaited the addition of smooth country butter, home-made strawberry jam and clotted cream, which were all tastefully arranged in glass dishes with little silver serving spoons. Snowy white napkins with lace edges were laid at the three places beside the silver cutlery of teatime knives and forks.

In the centre was a Dundee cake, a Scottish speciality, a fruit cake packed with juicy sultanas and candied peel, decorated with whole almonds. Julianne looked appreciatively around the cosy room. Its friendliness seemed to envelop her, even though she felt shy in front of the aunt she had not previously known. She was hungry, too. Her father had stopped just once on the eight-hour journey from Devon and they had eaten at a fast food counter in the service station, after he had filled the car with petrol.

If Julianne was shy, her father seemed positively unnerved. He answered his sister-in-law's polite questions about the journey curtly and seemed determined to avoid any questions that could lead to complicated explanations. When Julianne accepted her aunt's offer to go upstairs to freshen up after the journey, Alan made a point of explaining that, as Julianne had already turned sixteen the previous October, she was no longer legally required to attend school.

He lowered his voice – in case she was already on her way back downstairs – as he sadly told his long lost but now very useful relative, of the shame he felt and how he blamed himself for not taking better care of his daughter.

'I blame myself,' he said apologetically. 'After my wife died I just couldn't cope. I'm not proud of it but I fell apart and maybe I neglected my daughter. She had always been a mummy's girl and I didn't know how to communicate with an uncommunicative young girl. She became a teenager soon after her mum died and I just lost all control.'

He gave a rare laugh. 'How was I supposed to know how to deal with a girl – my speciality was teaching boys. Women are a bit of a mystery to me,' he explained, attempting to turn on the charm and illicit sympathy from Ida. 'I did my best but obviously it wasn't good enough. Yes, I blame myself but it's too late now to change things.'

Ida listened carefully but said nothing. Her brother-in-law's protestations of guilt felt rehearsed, unreal. She didn't know the man but already she knew she did not like him much. Alan was warming to his theme and he leaned forward and in a conspiratorial gesture covered Ida's hand with his.

'Martha, Julianne's mother, my wife – you never met her did you? She was a lovely woman – will never forgive me if I don't at least try to do the right thing by her.'

His voice now was small, sad and pleading. As she appeared in the doorway of the living room, Julianne recognised that voice as the one he used to garner sympathy and deflect criticism, whenever anyone tried to probe too deeply into private affairs. He avoided Julianne's accusing stare as he continued his sorry tale.

'I am so grateful that you have agreed to look after my daughter,' he said as Ida disentangled her hand from his and moved her body position in her chair so that he was not within easy reach of her. 'This way she will be spared the shame of people knowing about her pregnancy. You know how gossip spreads in a small village.'

Julianne thought she might throw up. 'Isn't it time you were leaving?' she said boldly. 'You've got a long journey back to Devon. I'll be all right here.' She threw a look at Ida, hoping the older woman would back her up.

Alan looked relieved, he would soon be able to get out of there, but first he had to show his newly found relative that he was indeed a loving father trying to do his best for his wayward daughter.

'She,' he pointed at her, 'will have a good allowance. I don't want her or her bastard child to be a burden on you.'

Anger barely hidden behind his seemingly reasonable exterior, Alan Gordon had almost spat out the words, now he chose to ignore the effect his use of the word 'bastard' had on Ida and his daughter who had both flinched.

'There's no need for that kind of language,' said Ida quietly. 'I will look after your daughter and her baby when it comes. She and I will get along just fine. I think it's time you were on your way.'

Julianne gave a barely concealed smile, she was not used to having anyone defend her or her father being chided, and she knew how much he hated any kind of criticism. Aunt Ida was turning out to be quite a champion. As if prepared for flight her father had remained standing for most of the visit and now he stood in front of the fire holding a teacup in one hand and a cigarette in the other. Ida bustled about making much show of finding an ashtray and then explained that no one had smoked in the house since her husband had died some ten years before.

Almost before he had finished his tea, Alan declared that

indeed it was time for him to get back on the road. He wanted to start his journey before it got dark, even though his intention was to drive through the night. Julianne was not sorry to see him go and did not even go to the door to see him off. As Ida politely walked her brother-in-law to his car, she again assured him that she would take good care of his daughter and keep him informed of developments. Alan thanked him profusely and beat a hasty retreat. The sooner he was away from there the better.

After her father had left, Julianne and her aunt drank more tea and cautiously started getting to know each other. Sensing Julianne's discomfort, Ida attempted to put her at ease.

'You will be safe here; I'll look after you,' she told her new young charge. 'You are not the first girl to make a mistake and you won't be the last. It can get lonely here on my own, you will be company for me and we will have plenty of time to get to know each other.'

Julianne wanted to throw herself into the older woman's arms and weep like a baby. She would have given anything to blurt out the whole sordid story and unburden herself, but she did not. Her father had threatened her so many times that if she told anyone she would be taken away and he would go to jail, now she was terrified that she would be expelled from the place of sanctuary she had found.

Already she feared for her beloved horse Rocket. She had no alternative but to trust that her father would keep his word to have the animal stabled and cared for in a place where they knew and loved him. He had so often used the horse as a threat she certainly knew he would not keep paying the yard fees if he was in jail.

If he did go to jail, what would become of her, where would

she go? Would his family still want her or would they blame her for his troubles? Even from hundreds of miles away she knew he would be able to exert a malevolent influence and she couldn't trust anyone to know the true circumstances of her predicament.

'We'll become friends,' said Ida cheerfully, 'don't you worry about a thing.'

Julianne said a silent prayer that she would not be let down again and in her heart she felt the beginnings of a belief that she had found a true friend.

'Thank you for having me,' she said shyly.

Tea over and the washing up done, Julianne unpacked and began to make herself at home in her new bedroom. She had a bath, powdered herself with sweet smelling talcum powder and wrapped herself in a large white bathrobe.

Even though it was still early, after her long car ride – having left Devon just after dawn – Julianne looked forward to snuggling down between the snowy white sheets.

Mrs Mitchell – 'My name is Isabella but everyone calls me Ida' – insisted on bringing Julianne a cup of tea and a hot water bottle. As she set the tea on the bedside table and busied herself pushing the covered hot water bottle down to the foot of the bed, Ida said kindly, 'You will be safe here. No one will harm you.'

Julianne looked at her and choked back a sudden sob as tears sprang to her eyes. It was the first time she had cried in front of another person since her mother had died six years before.

'We'll get along just fine,' said her aunt, taking her niece's hand in hers. 'After all, you're family.'

★ ★ ★

Julianne was grateful for all the loving fussing. It reminded her of the time before her mother became ill when she insisted on babying her. However, she remained wary and never let her guard down. She avoided questions about her father and their relationship and Ida did not press her. One great improvement was that Julianne was able to admit to herself that she no longer hurt so badly that she felt the need to harm herself. She felt protective of her growing baby and a strange calm had settled over her.

'No defeat, no retreat,' she would chant to herself as she lay in her comfortable, safe bed. Sometimes she cried herself to sleep and even though she felt sure Ida heard her, her kindly aunt never forced the issue.

'I am sure you must miss your mother,' she would say softly. 'Let the tears out, they wash the windows of the soul. I'm here for you. I can never replace her, but I do have a heart full of love to share.'

Julianne bitterly regretted that she could not be honest with her aunt. On the verge of letting the whole story flood out she would bite her lip, pinch herself, threaten herself and much to her shame find herself reacting badly when her aunt asked a perfectly normal question.

'Leave me alone, you're not my mother,' she blurted out when Ida asked about inviting her father to visit. 'Why can't you just mind your own business?

As the words left her lips and she saw the hurt in Ida's eyes, Julianne wanted to bite off her own tongue. The tears flowed and she ran to Ida and hugged her, 'I'm sorry, I'm sorry, I didn't mean it,' she sobbed.

'No bother,' Ida responded, brushing aside the hurt. 'It's your hormones, it happens to all women in your condition. You'll be back to your own sweet self when that wee baby is born.'

Ida's understanding and Julianne's genuine growing love and respect for her, ensured that emotional upsets rarely lasted long. Both accepted that there were some wounds that would not heal. With empathy and compassion they learned to work their way around them and not attempt to pull off the sticking plasters.

Mostly they were best of friends. They shopped together, looked after the small spotless cottage together and in the evening the older lady delighted in showing the younger one how to knit beautiful doll sized baby clothes for the coming arrival. Under the protection and care of her aunt, Julianne was growing strong emotionally and she had made the decision to have nothing to do with her own father since coming to live in Scotland.

'Please just trust me,' she pleaded with Ida. 'I have my reasons, maybe one day I will be able to tell you. Maybe not.'

In her own mind, Julianne had tried to expunge the horrific memories. She did what she had trained herself to do when the abuse was happening. Rise above it, leave her body, and refuse to feel or think or react. On occasion the nightmares still surfaced in her dreams and after a series of sleepwalking incidents, she confided to Ida that she was worried about having the baby and Ida believed her. The doctor prescribed plenty of rest, hot milk and no television before bed. Ida was not about to add to Julianne's obvious discomfort and prenatal stress by forcing the situation.

Periodically letters were delivered and the monthly allowance he had promised was dutifully paid into a bank account – but her father never attempted to visit. From the safety of her new home seven hundred miles away, Julianne had issued an ultimatum. She had written it just two days after she moved to Scotland.

'I am keeping the baby. If you ever attempt to come near me or the baby, I will go straight to the police. This is not an idle threat, I mean it.'

Fortunately he seemed to have no intention of testing her resolve. The odd card and letter continued to arrive but Julianne did not respond. Instead she ripped them into shreds and threw them out unopened.

She had more important things to think about now, like her new baby. She would not allow thoughts of her hated father to contaminate the love she felt for the new life she was bringing into the world.

It was on the hand knitted white quilt in the small upstairs bedroom that Julianne gave birth to her own little baby girl. Ida Mitchell, aunt and now great auntie, assisted the local midwife at the birth.

The love that bound them helped obliterate the past.

chapter five

'And thy fair virtue's force perforce doth move me,
On the first view to say, to swear, I love thee.'
Shakespeare's *A Midsummer Night's Dream*

Kira Mae Gordon was born at Midsummer's on June 21st, in the year of our Lord, 1987.

The sunshine of the day and the happiness she brought to her small family was to be reflected in her sunny disposition. It could have been a cause for sadness that there was no large gathering of the clan to welcome the new baby. However, Aunt Ida and proud mum Julianne made sure that the new arrival was greeted royally.

'My beautiful baby will never want for anything,' declared Julianne. 'I don't care what I have to do to get it, but this child will be treated like a princess.'

Smiling indulgently, Ida gently rocked the child in her arms.

Julianne was still but a child herself, she'd never even had a job and though she had been academically advanced, with no training her career prospects were severely limited. However, Ida was more than willing to contribute her small widow's pension to the household budget and her rent was modest thanks to a Coal Board subsidy. She actually prided herself on being frugal.

'I don't need much,' she said. 'I've never been one for splashing money around.' Then she laughed at herself, 'Not that I've ever had any to splash around.'

Fortunately the three of them were able to live quite comfortably, if simply, on the allowance that Julianne's father continued to send every month. Even Julianne had to concede that without that income they would be struggling financially. On many occasions Julianne had been determined that she would refuse to accept another penny from him but her aunt astutely prevailed upon her to allow him to continue to support them.

She had wisely never questioned beyond the guilt and remorse that he had admitted to about having failed Julianne after her mother died. If she suspected anything she never voiced her doubts.

'Let him pay,' she told Julianne. 'He needs to – your mother would have wanted it.'

During her secluded and tranquil confinement, Julianne lived her teenage life through magazines, novels and the illusionary world of television.

Her aunt had always kept herself to herself, so during her daily trip to the local shops, when neighbours would politely nod and say, 'Good morning, Mrs Mitchell – and how are you today?' No one expected more than a courteous nod and, 'Aye, fine, thank you.'

On the occasions when it had been necessary to introduce her young visitor, she did so divulging a minimum of information. 'My young niece,' she would say. 'Visiting from down south.'

The small Scottish village had no cinema so the local youngsters hung out at the old-fashioned Italian ice cream parlour in the high street. Not having gone to school there, Julianne really had no friends of her own in the area but she would push Kira Mae in her pram to the ice cream parlour.

During the warm summer months, she would sit outside, lingering over a strawberry sundae or a double-sided chocolate oyster shell wafer. She came to know some of the local girls by sight and she exchanged pleasantries with them as they cooed over her beautiful baby girl.

Julianne hardly dared admit it even to herself but she had been dreading the possibility that her daughter would look like her father.

'Please, God,' she had prayed, kneeling on the floor beside her bed. 'Let me love my baby. Let it be a girl – not a boy. A boy might remind me of him. Don't let me spend my whole life having to hate my baby's face. Let me not see his face when I look at my baby. It's not my baby's fault any more than it was my fault.'

After her beloved baby girl was born Julianne came to treasure the gift of her child and she even began to lose some of the shame. When she looked at Kira Mae she only saw her own face reflected back at her – she refused to acknowledge or even think that there may be another's features also lurking there.

'Kira Mae looks just like you,' everybody told her. Holding the tiny bundle tight she thanked the God to whom she had prayed. 'I wish your grandma was here to see you.'

But as quickly as the thought came, Julianne pushed it away. Even imagining the pride her own mother would have felt in her first grandchild, Julianne was aware that her father had stolen even that joy from her. Cuddling her baby fiercely, she told her, 'He poisoned my life, I'm damned if he will ever get the chance to poison you.'

She never discussed the circumstances of the baby's parentage with anyone. If her aunt suspected that there was more to the story than she had been told, she never attempted to unearth the truth. When she and Julianne and baby Kira Mae had taken the local bus into the nearest town to register the birth, they had left the space for the father's name blank. He had been well and truly written out of the family history. The three of them made up their own complete family circle. They neither wanted nor needed anyone else.

Though he had been reluctant at first, the local priest agreed, for his long-standing and faithful parishioner, the dear widow Mitchell, who was to be godmother, to baptise baby Kira Mae in a private christening ceremony.

Church law did not forbid the giving of the Holy Sacrament though it did look less than favourably on single motherhood. But he took the Christian view that it was better that the child be baptised than left to the perils of perpetual purgatory; the fate that befell those who did not have the blessing of being baptised in the eyes of God.

Forming their own sacred circle of three graces, Kira Mae was dressed in a long white lace christening robe, her mother Julianne wore a dove grey dress and her great aunt, Ida who was now also the godmother, had chosen pale blue for the church ceremony. The photograph capturing that blessed day would take pride of place on the living room wall of the cottage. Picture perfect.

'Girls are God's way of giving us all an excuse to dress up,' said Aunt Ida happily.

chapter six

'We are such stuff. As dreams are made on.'
Shakespeare's *The Tempest*

Despite her sheltered upbringing, through her love of magazines, Julianne had developed an encyclopaedic knowledge of fashion. As well as teaching her to knit, her beloved aunt was also a dab hand with the sewing machine.

With baby Kira Mae tucked up safely in bed, Aunt Ida taught Julianne how to cut out patterns and make clothes. Sometimes they used the shop bought 'Simplicity' paper patterns but more often than not, with a steady hand and foot long pair of dressmaking scissors, together they cut out brown paper, traced and marked the material with blue chalk and did the cutting freehand as they tailored to their own designs.

Before the days of mass produced and cheap high street fashion chains nearly all women – except the very wealthy – made their own clothes. The clothes rationing of World War II had meant that the more a woman could make for her family from shop bought fabric, the more precious clothing coupons she could save for more hard to replicate items like a gent's suit.

In the village shop, the selection of stylish clothes was

severely limited and although Ida and her niece Julianne were far from poor, it made sound economic sense for the two seamstresses to make their own clothes. And for Kira Mae they knitted and crocheted and sewed.

Kira Mae was a happy child, filled with curiosity and the ability to make people laugh. She was a pretty little thing, with luminous cornflower blue eyes and silky buttercup blonde hair. Everything about her was delicate, her sweet little mouth was a cute baby pink and her delicately flushed cheeks had tiny little indented dimples.

Her godmother delighted in telling her, 'That's the mark of the angels. You will always be loved.'

Kira Mae was nurtured and protected like a rare exotic plant; she grew tall and strong, enveloped in the love and constant praise of the two women who adored her. When Kira Mae danced, they clapped, when she laughed, they laughed with her, when she cried, they kissed away her tears.

Demanding attention, Kira Mae would call, 'Jo Jo,' to attract Julianne. Kira Mae never called Julianne 'mummy', that honour was reserved for Mummy Mitchell, the same name that Julianne had given the wonderful woman who had provided her refuge and her salvation.

Mummy Mitchell wrapped her family in a cocoon of love and devotion. She was fierce as a tiger in protecting the well-being and happiness of her young charges.

'Family is the most important thing in the world,' she never tired of telling her darling 'daughters'. 'Together we are strong – no harm can befall us. We are three that is the Holy Trinity.'

It was Mummy Mitchell who first came up with the idea. Julianne resisted though she couldn't deny that the idea appealed.

'Leave Kira Mae here with me and go to London, pursue your dream, make a life and career for yourself.'

The decision was not easy. Julianne resisted, she felt she needed to sacrifice herself for her beloved daughter. At night she would toss and turn trying to find an answer to the dilemma.

'Should I do it? Why don't I take Kira Mae with me? But then I won't be able to work – perhaps I need to stay here until she is grown up – I can still make a life for myself.'

But in truth she knew she was stifled, a small town, a small baby when there was a big wide world to explore out there. Eventually she agreed to consider some of the options and see if her previous good grades might get her into a college programme. At the local library she found lists of London colleges and further education establishments where she might be able to continue her education as a mature student. 'Mature?' Ida looked puzzled. 'You're not yet twenty-one.'

★ ★ ★

For her coming of age, Ida proposed that she give Julianne a return train ticket to London – and a small monthly allowance to cover living expenses.

'Go,' she urged her. 'You can always come back home if you don't like it.' It was shaping up to be an offer too good to refuse. What was there to hold her back?

Student accommodation was on offer at one of the sixth form colleges to which Julianne decided to apply. They invited her to London to sit an entrance exam and if successful, she would be offered a place to start that autumn right before her twenty-first birthday. Kira Mae was just four years old.

Julianne would have trusted Mummy Mitchell with her life and now into her care she entrusted her most precious possession – her baby girl. All three of them were in tears as they said goodbye at the railway station. So sad and bereft did Julianne feel that she almost turned around there and then and abandoned all hopes of a life away from her daughter and the woman they called 'Mum'.

A six hour journey from Glasgow to London gave Julianne the opportunity to examine all her life choices and study her reflection in the window of the speeding train. At almost twenty-one she had her life ahead of her and she so longed to achieve something, to put her education to good use, to challenge herself and see what she was capable of, to find out if she did she have gifts, talents.

Julianne had lived a half-life for so long; she honestly felt she owed it to herself to find out what the big wide world had to offer. She had promised herself long ago that she would not be a victim all her life, that the cruel father who had stolen her childhood would not steal the rest of her growing up. The sound of the train wheels clacking on the rails seemed to beat out a familiar rhythm, 'No defeat, no retreat. No defeat, no retreat.'

Filled with a huge burst of energy and resolve, Julianne promised the women who loved her, her dead mother, Martha; Ida Mitchell and her baby girl that she would be strong and with their unstinting support and blessings, follow her dream. For her, and for them.

'Girl Power,' she smiled. 'Bring on the adventure.'

chapter seven

'Good night, good night. Parting is such sweet sorrow,
That I shall say good night till it be morrow.'
Shakespeare's *Romeo and Juliet*

It was at college in London that Julianne created for herself a shiny new personal history and persona. Shy, quiet Julianne was left in the past and from her chrysalis emerged transformed Julianne – a beautiful, colourful, talented butterfly.

Annabelle Anstruther, her friend from Devon was also at college in London and the two teamed up to share a flat after becoming disillusioned with student accommodation.

Both girls still loved riding and they soon discovered the joys of hiring horses from the stables in Rotten Row and trotting out in London's Hyde Park. They made a striking pair as they rode their majestic beasts around the bridleways dressed in their black twill jackets, tight fitting camel coloured jodhpurs, shiny black boots and their silk covered hard hats – blonde hair clearly visible under the hats, streaming down their backs.

'Wait up,' called a handsome horseman in soldier's uniform, as Julianne exited the stable block. 'I haven't seen you here before. What's your name? Where do you live? What do you do? Can I have your phone number?'

Julianne quickened her pace, rushing away from him and almost slipping on a big mound of manure that one of the horses had deposited in the stable yard.

'Got to go,' she called over her shoulder, pulling off her hard hat and unbuttoning her jacket. Roughly shoving the jacket and hat into her large travelling case, Julianne frantically looked around for Annabelle. She'd seen her horse inside its stall happily munching hay, so she knew she had to be close by.

Many of the capital's eligible bachelors enjoyed a daily canter through the park and at mounting and dismounting time, requests for dates were often made.

Annabelle was inclined to accept, Julianne demurred. A boyfriend was not on her agenda. Still in her early twenties she guarded the secret that she had never dated a boy, never been kissed or even been alone with a male. 'Not since…' her mind started to say but she immediately cut off the thought. 'Don't even go there,' she warned herself.

Spying Annabelle talking to a good looking dark haired man who she knew worked at the stables, Julianne rushed over. 'I'm off,' she said. 'See you at home,' and she made a dash for the gates.

From past experience, she knew it might be several hours before Annabelle followed her home to the small, unpretentious attic flat they shared in Fitrovia, an up and coming part of central London, ripe for gentrification and ever increasing rents. Dodging her admirer, Julianne hurried from the park and swiftly made her way into Hyde Park underground for the journey home. But she did not go straight home. Jumping off the tube before her home stop, Julianne made her way to the secret meeting she had been attending since she moved to London from Scotland at the beginning of her college course. Once a week Julianne met up with her friends and support network in a self-help group of survivors of incest and rape. Julianne had been scared the first time she entered the grand portico of white columns at the entrance to the impressive church, within sight of London's Regent Park. Now she ran confidently down the stairs to the small basement meeting room with the sign 'Counselling and Pastoral Services', on the door.

Inside, half a dozen women sat in a semi-circle and Julianne acknowledged them – she already knew all of them. 'We thought you weren't coming,' said the grey haired woman sitting in a chair at the apex of the circle. She had papers on her lap, a pen in hand and appeared to be the group leader or facilitator.

'I think you know everyone,' she said kindly, 'but introduce yourself anyway and then grab a coffee.'

Julianne claimed an empty chair in the semi-circle and arranged her belongings underneath, as confidently she looked around at the expectant faces and smiled as she said in a clear voice, 'My name is Julianne – and I am an incest survivor.'

There was a small round of applause and she then apologised for being late, saying, 'Life is so busy these days, if you'd known me when I first came here two years ago you wouldn't believe that I would be having a social life, mixing with people, going to college and enjoying myself. Most of the time, I'm pretty good.'

She pulled a face, 'Well, I don't wake up in the middle of the night any more terrified, sweating and suffering from a huge anxiety attack.'

Julianne surprised even herself that she could now be so

comfortable tallking about her traumatic past in a room full of people. Fact was, these women and others like them, all also survivors of incest or sexual abuse, had saved her life.

Living at home with Mummy Mitchell, Julianne had felt safe and protected and she had colluded in suppressing her feelings and the torturous memories. She had lived in a state of denial and was thankful that the blocks she had put in place meant she had refused to acknowledge reality. Moving to London and starting to live independently, she had gone through a really scary time, as she began to unravel emotionally and mentally.

Reading self-help books like her long-time favourite by the inspirational Louise Hay, *You Can Heal Your Life*, did help somewhat but the results she was able to achieve alone were a far cry from allowing her to live a normal life.

Rape Crisis Centre stories featured regularly in the women's magazines she read all the time. Screwing up her courage, she had called their helpline number. In that first phone call to an anonymous voice on the other end of the line, she had poured out the painful story of the incestuous home situation she had endured.

Sensing that for once she would be understood and believed, Julianne had told the patient, caring woman who had answered the phone, about her anger, shame, guilt, and the murderous and suicidal thoughts she was suffering from on a daily basis.

'I've never told anyone before,' Julianne had admitted. 'I was scared and ashamed. Now I've told you, but I don't know what I expect you to do.'

'Well for one thing I can call you back, save you having to keep putting money in the payphone.'

In that first ever telephone conversation, standing alone in the deserted corridor of her student accommodation, Julianne had surprised herself at how she had unburdened herself to a complete stranger. Her intention had been to just make contact perhaps, even receive a referral to someone else. It was a breakthrough and her call for help was answered.

'Is it safe for me to send information out to you?' asked the woman who Julianne had already begun to call Carole. The bond had been established when Carole told her, 'I am a volunteer, I am also a survivor of incest.'

Having plucked up the courage to make the call, Julianne had embraced the full range of services the organisation was able to offer. Knowing she would be listened to and respected, she had made regular phone calls to the helpline and after a few weeks had started to attend sessions with other members of the team.

The trained counsellors and her new friends in the group had explained to Julianne that she was suffering from a form of Post-Traumatic Stress Syndrome. A result of her incestuous upbringing and the sexual, mental and physical abuse.

'It was not your fault,' she was assured again and again. 'HE is the aggressor, you were the victim, but now you can make the journey from victim to survivor. You can reclaim your power, you can use the courage and endurance that got you through the initial horrific experience to grow beyond it. It will take time. The shocking memories may never completely go away, but you will learn to live with yourself again, and forgive yourself and love yourself – and one day, God willing, love someone else.'

Even as she healed and worked through the after effects of the complex feelings, emotional and physical, with professional help and loving support, Julianne had dreaded exposing the last devastating piece of the secret. Her teenage pregnancy and the daughter who knew nothing of her defiled parentage.

However, gradually she relinquished even that painful secret and Julianne came to learn through the years of her attendance at the support group that there were women who had gone through what she considered even worse scenarios than her own, and they had recovered.

Becoming familiar with the four stages of grief after rape and incest, Julianne learned to be compassionate with herself and not to deny or minimise what had happened. She was to trust and honour her own feelings and history. Julianne came to identify with the complex psychological recovery process, like that used in grief counselling. Denial, anger, bargaining, depression and finally acceptance.

Using the tools and psychological healing techniques the Rape Crisis Centre provided, Julianne learned to journal, to express her feelings, to talk about her anxieties and to gradually recover.

'Be kind to yourself,' said one of the other survivors, giving Julianne a tentative hug as she had left her first meeting. 'It will take time, and there will be days when you feel like you are going backwards, but day by day, you are on the path to recovery, and we are all here to love and support you.'

Julianne had looked with gratitude at the strong, powerful women, knowing that next time she would tell them about her mum's motto, 'No defeat, no retreat.'

★ ★ ★

After her meeting, Julianne looked forward to arriving at the safe haven of her small home. Emotions were always stirred up by the meeting but she would not swap for the world the level of wellness she was achieving by her attendance.

'I have been restored,' she told herself.

Climbing four flights of stairs to the small flat, Julianne was relieved to reach the top and insert her key in the lock. Everything was neat and tidy, it had to be with two girls living in such a confined space. Contemplating flopping out on the couch for an evening in front of the television, Julianne took herself to task and quickly settled down at the small desk she shared with Annabelle.

Julianne was a conscientious student and her academic record showed that she was still achieving A grades and was on course for a first class degree. Before opening her school books, she made her nightly phone call to Scotland to check on Ida and Kira Mae, who was now at primary school. Kira Mae loved to talk on the phone and tell all about her day. She refused to go to bed until she had heard her mama say, 'Goodnight and God Bless, Kira Mae, be a good girl for Mummy Mitchell.'

Kira responded with numerous requests for kisses, all designed to prolong the telephone call and bedtime. 'Blow me a kiss, blow me another kiss, another kiss. See you soon. Love you.'

'Love you too Kira, night night. God bless.'

Julianne had taken the decision not to tell anyone about her child and although she bitterly regretted that she now needed to live another lie, she did not want to face the questioning and consequences of admitting that she was a mother. And one who had willingly left her child behind to pursue a career at that. She was not about to defend her choices to anyone – not even her friend, and flatmate Annabelle.

In her own mind she re-wrote the script and if forced to offer an explanation, Kira Mae now became her niece, the child of Ida Mitchell. So well-practised was Julianne at keeping secrets, she sometimes even believed her own lie.

In term time, Julianne lived the life of a student, attending lectures, meeting with her tutors, writing essays and burning the midnight oil in the library while researching her specialist subjects and preparing for examinations. Her social life revolved around a couple of carefully chosen student clubs, one being the Friends of the Victoria and Albert Museum and the other the amateur dramatics club. She also volunteered at a local school overseeing a children's art class.

Holiday times and term breaks were spent at home in her adopted village in Scotland, being a mum and a daughter and delighting in the company of her small family and living the simple life far away from the bustling academic world of London. Julianne's heart overflowed with gratitude to Ida for enabling her to live two lives in one. They never ever mentioned Julianne's father and it seemed they had almost forgotten how they came to be family in the first place.

'You are not just Kira Mae's godmother,' she told her, 'you are my fairy godmother. You waved your magic wand and transformed my life. There will be a special place for you in heaven – alongside my other mother.'

★ ★ ★

School holidays provided the perfect opportunity for Julianne to spend extra quality time with her daughter. She never missed the chance to travel to be with her daughter in Scotland or to bring her to London to spend time with her. However, no trip generated as much excitement or provoked more animated conversations than their Easter trip to Disneyland, Paris. Kira was seven years old.

The pair had flown out from Glasgow airport on a special four-day weekend excursion. They had tried to persuade Mummy Mitchell to accompany them. She had never been out of the country and she claimed that the thought of how awful she would look in a passport photo was reason enough to refuse. They all knew that the real reason had been because she wanted mother and daughter to enjoy the magical trip alone, together.

Making her first trip to an international airport, she had waved them off. Trouble was, just being in the bustling, noisy airport had been enough to make her nervous and uncomfortable. Not to mention tearful. She was definitely a woman who liked to keep her feet on the ground.

Kira Mae had had no such worries – she had been high as a kite with excitement and couldn't wait to get into the air. Fellow passengers had stopped and smiled at the beautiful blonde child dressed in a frilly pink dress and wearing a matching straw hat with a pink ribbon.

Kira Mae had once asked her mother, 'Do people look at me because I am beautiful, like you?'

Kira Mae had proudly wheeled her new pink suitcase through the busy airport. She had walked confidently up the stairs of the plane, as though she had been an international traveller all her life. It was after all her second flight – the first one had been when Julianne had taken her daughter to

London previously for a birthday treat when she was just six years old.

On the two hour flight from Glasgow to Paris, Kira Mae had proceeded to work her usual magic and charm the flight attendants.

'I'm going to Disneyland Paris,' she told the flight attendant who asked what she wanted to drink. 'Only good girls are allowed to go to Disneyland,' she continued, 'and I am a good girl. I'll have an orange juice, please, on the rocks.'

The trip to Disneyland had been a joy for both Kira Mae and Julianne. They had stayed in the Disneyland Hotel, a pink fairytale castle and Kira Mae had insisted on wearing a tiara and her best princess dress with plastic high heels for the whole trip.

She had danced in the street with the carnival animals, begged to be allowed to stay up to see the illuminated Disney parade and giggled with delight as she saw a twinkling fairy Tinker Bell flying across the night sky. No treat had been denied and no rides were dismissed – except those for which Kira Mae was judged too small when she was measured at the entrance and did not quite meet the height requirement.

The music that had played in the street through loud speakers had fascinated Kira Mae and she had asked her mother, 'Why don't they play music in the streets everywhere, then everyone could be happy all the time?'

But the favourite story of all was the one that had happened on the trip back through security at the Paris airport.

Kira Mae had pushed the Mickey Mouse balloon she was carrying into the x-ray machine. The French security guard who was monitoring the machine nearly jumped out of his skin as he looked at the screen to see a big Mickey face grinning at him. He had not been amused – unlike Kira Mae and Julianne who had hardly stopped laughing all the way back to Scotland.

'Tell me again about the Mickey balloon,' she would squeal with delight and the two of them would immediately go into a fit of giggles, helpless with laughter, holding on to each other.

Mother and daughter delighted in each other and over the years they built up a bank of happy memories centred around holidays and special treats. Trips to the theatre, the ballet, pantomimes and visits to art galleries, museums, river boat rides and long happy car journeys.

Julianne used her artistic skills to create albums and journals to remind them of all the places they had been and the things they had done. She encouraged Kira Mae to always collect photos, programmes, pamphlets, tickets, postcards and all manner of memorabilia. They worked together on their albums or made special gifts to send to each other, sharing their scrapbook memories. Dozens of albums and framed photographs lined the walls of the cottage and Julianne's London home, mother and daughter surrounded themselves with treasured memories and mementoes of each other. Julianne, with the help of Aunt Ida, ensured that their love link could never be broken – or forgotten.

chapter eight

'Never fortune did play a subtler game.'
Shakespeare's *Two Noble Kinsmen*

Julianne graduated from St. Martin's College of Art and Design in 1994, at the age of twenty-four, the world at her fashionably shod feet. Beating off stiff competition for a coveted graduate position, she took a job as a showroom model in the prestigious Italian fashion house, *Angeles of Mayfair.*

Julianne was one of the bright young things living a life of glamour, adventure and romantic abundance in a London that was still enjoying international acclaim as Cool Britannia from the Swinging Sixties.

'Drugs, sex and rock 'n' roll' was the rallying call for the youth of the day – and a way of life. But none of that would impact or interfere with the fierce ambition that Julianne had developed.

Although her job was to model the new designs in-house for buyers, Julianne was determined to learn as much as she could about all aspects of the haute couture business.

She sat at the feet and worshipped the design skill of one of the iconic fashion designers Maria de Angeles, a legend second only to her mentor Mary Quant who had led the British fashion revolution through the late sixties and into the seventies. Her appeal was timeless.

Quant's trademark black and white daisy geometric designs had been one of the first universally recognisable symbols of the pop art culture that fused art and fashion. Maria had her own trademark – a vibrant purple six sided star, edged in silver. This was a starting point for all her original fabric designs and appeared on belts, bags and hair accessories. Julianne persuaded the head of the showroom to let her work in the development department when she was not needed to model for the mostly international clientele.

One aspect of the job was the modelling that she had at first embraced as a chance to show off wonderful garments and then come to see as simply being a clothes horse. Julianne craved to be an innovator learning her craft nearer to the creative process.

She delighted in discovering the history of the company and familiarising herself with the hundreds of items in the Maria de Angeles fashions, cosmetics and skin care range.

Maria was an enthusiast, tireless in her quest for perfection in fashion, a hands-on designer who made it her business to welcome and monitor the progress of every new member of the team.

Walking into the company's headquarters, off Park Lane in London, an elite suite of offices above a private bank, Julianne was determined to make a name for herself in this most prestigious of companies.

'Welcome, Julianne,' said her new boss, extending a firm handshake and flashing a beaming smile, showing off whiter than white teeth and flashing green eyes. Wild red curls cascaded down her back and were caught up with one of her signature bejewelled hair clasps. Maria de Angeles' magnetic energy hid the fact that she was tiny, a real pocket Venus, small but perfectly formed.

Balanced atop five-inch stiletto heels, she drew herself up to her fullest height. No one ever claimed to have seen her without her shoes – the joke in the company was that she probably wore them in bed.

'If you give one hundred per cent to this job,' she warned, 'you will be falling short by at least ten per cent on what I demand. Give me one hundred and ten per cent and I will reward you one hundred and ten per cent. Now let's get to work.'

Julianne had much to prove – and two very special people to whom she wanted to prove herself – she would never have admitted it to her boss, but Maria de Angeles came third on the list. Kira Mae and Ida came first and second.

A diligent worker and quick learner, Julianne gave the one hundred and ten per cent that was expected and, in what others in the company considered a relatively short period of time, less than a decade, she had progressed through the development department and landed the coveted position of personal assistant to Maria herself.

Maria was a fiery Latin, with a temper to match her blazing copper red hair but she was also warm, generous, funny and burning with creative energy and joie de vivre. Julianne made herself indispensable, and work and her social life took off into the stratosphere. Doors opened that she had not even knocked upon.

The Angeles name was a passport to every fashion show, party and media event in town. She travelled, first class to all the international fashion shows and buyers' fairs. The iconic fashion designer Gianni Versace and his muse, sister Donatella were close friends of Maria and Julianne was often invited to join them for business events or social occasions. Julianne never ceased giving praise for the glamorous and exciting world she had been transported to, a galaxy away from her bleak childhood existence.

Princess Diana and Madonna had previously slept in the trademark red, gold and black guest bedroom that Julianne was assigned when invited with her boss to the Versace oceanfront mansion in Miami Beach.

An opulent three story, ten bedroom palazzo, known as Casa Casuarina, the former Amsterdam Palace was built in the 1930s on Ocean Drive. Julianne was in seventh heaven from the moment she arrived, accompanying Maria to a grand house party in the fabulous home. Never before had she seen such wealth and luxury and she marvelled at the genius of the global branding Versace had created.

During her stay, taking notes, seeking inspiration and learning from the master, she could only dream that one day the name of Maria de Angeles would become such a towering international brand in the world of design, marketing and retail.

Refusing to be intimidated, she challenged herself, 'Never limit your dreams. The universe will deliver your greatest desires.'

Each exquisite room in the breathtaking building was designed and commissioned by Versace himself to showcase his love of fine art, marble statues, antiques, rich tapestries, crystal lighting, gold ceilings, stained glass windows, brocade drapes, luxurious velvet bedcoverings, Persian carpets, carved doors and oversized headboards, gilt furniture, animal prints, chandeliers, mosaics, venetian mirrors and plants, ferns and palm trees.

The courtyard pool and fountain hidden behind cathedral sized wooden doors was decorated with one hundred million Italian mosaic tiles. Marble statues overlooking the sparkling azure-blue pool and gushing fountains were imported from a sixteenth century chateau in France. Julianne had never felt herself so overwhelmed by beauty, artistry and a divine presence.

Basking in the warm sunshine while standing bewitched by the cool blue water pool which was lined in twenty-four carat gold, Julianne heard someone approach. Her host, the wonderfully handsome Gianni Versace himself, had come to share a secret with his young guest.

'Do you believe in magic?'

Julianne nodded in reply.

He dropped his voice to just above a whisper. 'Only magic will solve the mystery of the motif on the mosaic tiles here in the courtyard. A cryptic code is claimed to be secreted in the design. No one has yet been able to decipher that sacred code.'

Versace smiled and then admitted, 'However, I did incorporate the design in a scarf in my South Beach collection. It is too good a story – and too alluring a design to not deserve a wider audience.'

Versace laughed and began to walk away, but not before asking Julianne, 'Have you read Truman Capote? I come here to read his books. At my house on Lake Como I read Proust, here in Miami, it is Capote. Miami suits him, Miami is simple, beautiful, fantastic. I am serene here. Ciao, see you at dinner.'

If ever there was a perfect day, Julianne decided this was it, and she couldn't wait to tell Kira Mae all about it.

★ ★ ★

Julianne embraced her new lifestyle and was convinced she'd died and gone to heaven the day she became the proud owner of a warehouse conversion apartment overlooking the river in London's regenerated and now super trendy Docklands. The docks which had been operating since the 1600s had almost ceased to exist two decades before, but now billions of pounds had been spent in developing the old sailors' town into spectacular riverside houses and apartment blocks.

The waterside village of narrow cobbled streets and high walled warehouses had come back to life with bars, restaurants and continental style cafés on leafy squares and water-filled spaces.

Julianne's north bank, river walk apartment in the historic Docklands district was just a mile east of Tower Bridge and the Tower of London. Overlooking the widest part of the river, it offered an excellent vantage point for watching Thames cruisers, working barges and pleasure craft as they turned to face the direction of the current – either on entering or leaving the waterway.

The des res former trading district was the height of fashionable London living and the fifty-five miles of restored waterside wharves and warehousing attracted young professionals, creatives and large volumes of tourists to the trendy wine bars, London's oldest riverside pub, The Prospect of Whitby, and the picturesque boutique area of St. Katharine's Dock. Julianne loved living right in the heart of this vibrant community.

In addition to her coveted job working for one of the great names in a legendary fashion dynasty, Julianne's own strong statement clothing meant she attracted attention everywhere she went in the image obsessed world of fashion and pop culture.

Julianne had learned early in her career that to make an impact, colour and an individual style was essential. She had her hair coloured at the Kensington salon of one Kevin Shanley who had achieved worldwide fame as the personal hairdresser to Princess Diana, the ultimate trendsetter. Kevin blended his colour palette to produce a vibrant burnished gold colour for Julianne that perfectly complemented her pale, ivory skin and her striking sky blue eyes. Her naturally ultra wavy hair was cut in a pageboy style, framing her lovely face, high cheekbones and heart shaped jaw line. Her colleagues in the fashion house named her look, contemporary renaissance.

Life was so good; Julianne had taken to lighting a candle in the morning and offering up a prayer to the universe for protection.

'With all my heart, I thank you for the blessings bestowed upon me – I pray you to keep the ones I love under your divine protection. And for all the abundance I have received – don't forget…' At this point Julianne always smiled as she ended her made up prayer, 'I am ready and willing to receive lots more.'

chapter nine

'I must be cruel only to be kind.
Thus bad begins and worse remains behind.'
Shakespeare's *Hamlet*

As she woke early on the first Saturday morning in her new home, Julianne's prayer was especially heartfelt. She had planned a wonderful weekend to celebrate moving into her new apartment.

Although she was considered something of a mystery woman and the girls at work teased her about having a secret lover, Julianne smiled to herself and went ahead with the plans for her own special housewarming party. As she showered, Julianne mentally made notes of the new range of products she was testing. Maria de Angeles was passionate about the signature range of beauty products she had developed. The collection contained green tea and ginseng – and Maria had given Julianne the task of coming up with a name that would encapsulate the company's new policy of natural ingredients, not created in the laboratory. A green policy that had been started and developed by beauty innovator, Anita Roddick in her Body Shop empire when the idea was still avant-garde.

Now the boundaries needed to be pushed further using sustainable products and packaging that was eco-friendly. The company had signed up to a concept of worldwide responsibility and accountability *Go Green – T – The New Radical Traditional.*

Julianne's personal fashion philosophy had long been 'Dress to Impress' and today was no exception. Attired in her trademark effortlessly elegant style, Julianne had chosen a pair of super soft linen, Fendi, tailored, high waisted, wide legged trousers in a slate grey shade. This she teamed with a turtleneck cashmere sweater in pale lilac. She slipped her bare feet into a pair of Gucci loafers, with the mandatory entwined gold Gs on the front. Keeping jewellery to a minimum, Julianne inserted small diamond studs into her pierced ears, on her right arm a thin white Cartier bracelet – a present to herself – and on her left wrist a gold and silver Rolex on which she had blown a month's wages in Hong Kong on a company buying trip the year before.

Her shining golden hair she clipped at the nape of her neck with a silver clasp displaying the signature MDA motif picked out in diamante.

Julianne took one last look in the full length mirror, as she picked up a vibrant violet cashmere pashmina from the bedside chair, arranged it artfully around her shoulders and checked the contents of her Gucci clutch bag, which matched her grey leather slip-ons. Satisfied with the image reflecting back at her, she let the excitement that had been building inside her all day, spill over.

Must make a good impression on my VIP guests, she thought, smiling to herself. A well-practised visual once over, assured her that everything was in place. The walls of the living room were painted a light reflecting shade of ice white, the perfect canvas for the uncompromising bold splashes of colour in the expensive but tasteful furniture.

A white box-shaped five-piece corner unit dominated the living area, and in front of it a glass oblong occasional table that seemed to be suspended in space covered by glossy hard backed coffee table collections of *Vogue* and *Marie Claire* and imposing glass sculptures. In a circular alcove, there was a round glass coffee table with white leather chairs and overhead lighting from recessed silver-backed micro spotlights.

The seating was grouped together and strategically placed on a fluffy white wall to wall carpet. Surprising splashes of colour captured the attention in silk cushions, hand stitched in vibrant shades of magenta, purple and Prussian blue. Floor to ceiling windows in the converted Docklands loft boasted a breathtaking view of the River Thames, so close that it almost seemed to be flowing through the apartment. A double length balcony with wrought iron furniture could be accessed from the lounge or the master bedroom.

Julianne never stopped marvelling at her good fortune to have bought the million pound property at mate's rates in partnership with a model girlfriend who was never home. Like Julianne, her work took her all over the world – and on her infrequent trips home there was plenty of room in the two bedroom, two bathroom home for both of them.

The apartment had an entry phone security system and secure underground parking. Thanks to her absentee housemate, Julianne was able to afford this luxury penthouse apartment for a manageable mortgage that wasn't much more than she had previously paid to rent in London's hot property market.

The open plan living area was divided from the kitchen by a low wall that doubled as a breaker counter. Two black and silver stools were neatly tucked under the counter. For someone who did minimal cooking the kitchen was the perfect size. Clinical white with a black and white diamond-patterned floor, the appliances were pristine white. Colour was provided through bold shades of red in the teapot, ceramic coffee jars and geometric-patterned china mugs hanging on small silver hooks under the overhead cupboards and above the stainless steel double sink.

Julianne completed her final once over. Lastly she opened the fridge door and checked that the glass bottle on the top shelf was reaching the perfect temperature. Chocolate milk should always be served chilled.

She clapped her hands in delight and, quickening her pace, smiled to herself and headed out the door after one last check that the apartment looked perfect in every detail.

She cast a quick glance at her watch, speeded up her departure, changed the radio music channel from Classic FM to Kiss FM and hurried through the apartment out of the front door, pausing only to collect her Alexander McQueen double breasted dark grey wool jacket and Gucci clutch bag.

Hurrying down to the street three floors below she looked around anxiously, willing a black taxi cab to appear. At that moment, a black London cab came crunching around the corner, yellow for hire light illuminated. Raising a hand, Julianne took a half step into the street and the vehicle came to a halt beside her.

'Euston station, please,' she told the driver and, as she settled herself into the back seat she added, 'I'm running late to meet a train, could you step on it, please?'

She needn't have worried; the station clock showed just two o'clock as she paid the cab and hurried inside. The

Glasgow train was due at 14.12 p.m. After checking the arrivals board, she made her way to platform two, through the busy London mainline station.

A knot formed in her stomach as she waited at the barrier, she strained to catch the first glimpse of the headlights of the incoming train. Around her a heaving mass of people also waited at the barrier – most of them attempting to get an early position in the queue for when the train completed its turnaround process and was ready to leave again – homebound for the north of England and central Scotland.

As the train came to an orderly stop, hundreds of passengers began to disembark. A sea of passengers, pushing, pulling and struggling with luggage, pushchairs, wheelchairs, bicycles and wheeled cases, came crushing towards her.

Julianne stood her ground and searched each new face hopefully, every second expecting to find the ones she longed to see. For a dreadful moment, she panicked that they had missed the train. They had been scheduled to be picked up by the local taxi service from their modest home before dawn to catch the train from Glasgow.

Then she saw them – they must have been almost the last travellers off the train – coming down the platform towards her. Two small figures carrying between them one huge suitcase.

Julianne rushed to greet the two people she loved above life itself. She hardly knew whether to laugh or cry as she pulled her beloved daughter into her arms and held her as if she would never let her go.

'Mother,' said seventeen-year-old Kira Mae in a mock severe tone, the one teenagers reserve for telling off embarrassing parents, 'You'll squeeze me to death.' Then she grinned from ear to ear and returned the bone-crushing embrace.

All this time Mummy Mitchell stood quietly on the side-lines, happily observing the joyous reunion between mother and daughter. Whether there had been just a few weeks or several months between visits, mother and daughter always displayed genuine, total joy at being back together again.

Tears came to her eyes and she wished, as so many times before, that their lives had been different. Those two needed to be together. All their lives had been lived in a series of goodbyes and counting days until the next meeting.

The ritual of their night-time, 'Goodnight, God bless,' had never altered and wherever she was in the world Julianne always made time to call her daughter. However, like most other working mothers, she still suffered terrible guilt at putting her career before her daughter and Kira Mae knew just how to press her maternal buttons and bring on a major guilt trip.

'When are you coming home? Why can't you come to visit? Why can't I stay with you? How long will you be gone?'

Even though she had a happy and busy school and social life, she was always happiest when her mother was at home too. 'Why do you have to go to work?' she would say sadly. 'I miss you. Why can't I come to work with you? When will you be home? Please come home soon.'

It broke Julianne's heart yet according to Aunt Ida, as soon as she hung up, Kira Mae would happily get on with watching her favourite television show or talking for hours on the phone to her friends.

As the platform emptied around them, Julianne eventually let go of her daughter and turned to her own beloved surrogate mother.

'Oh my, oh my, it's so good to see you,' she told Mummy Mitchell, wrapping her arms tightly round her and giving her a bear hug. 'I've missed you so much. More than ever.'

At the same time as she complimented her on how well she looked, Julianne couldn't help noticing that Mummy Mitchell was beginning to show her age. It must be hard for a middle-aged woman to be bringing up a teenage girl on her own. Julianne had no doubt that her daughter could be a handful, though she was usually on her best behaviour when mama was around.

Realising that they were the only people left on the platform – the barriers not yet having been opened to allow the incoming passengers access – the two mothers and daughter hurriedly made their way out to the taxi rank, with all three now lugging the giant case between them.

The trio did not stop chattering, even long enough to take in the sights of London on a gloriously bright and sunny spring day, as they made their way from Euston in the north of the city to the East End.

Their journey, by request, took them past some of the best-loved tourist sights: Big Ben, Buckingham Palace, and the Tower of London. It took the best part of an hour through the Saturday lunchtime shoppers to reach Docklands – an area that had benefited from a massive regeneration programme aimed at improving the poor housing and down at heel image of this area.

As the taxi pulled up outside the converted tobacco warehouse that Julianne now called home, Kira Mae was first to come rushing out. She could barely contain her excitement at being back in London and about to see the new home that she had heard so much about. At first she looked dismayed at the towering, industrial, red brick building. Having been brought up in the Scottish countryside, Kira Mae loved open spaces, trees, flowers, streams – and above all fresh air. However, curiosity overcame her and her disappointment did not last long. She propelled herself up the stairs to the third floor apartment, delighted just to be stepping in her mother's footsteps up the steep, winding staircase. Now all three of them were positioned outside the front door, suitcase deposited between them by the cab driver, who was still mumbling under his breath and complaining of a bad back as he started to descend the stairs. They were not to know they were lucky, tip or no tip, that he, an East Ender, was a gentleman or he would have made them carry the suitcase themselves.

'Not so much a suitcase, more a week's work,' he had ruefully joked, as he heaved the heavy suitcase out of the small luggage compartment beside his driver's seat.

With the driver out of earshot, Julianne commanded, 'Close your eyes. Both of you.'

She quickly inserted the Yale key into the lock and swung the door open. Kira Mae and Mummy Mitchell gasped with delight as they opened their eyes and saw the spectacular view of Old Father Thames through the floor to ceiling windows.

'Welcome home,' cried Julianne excitedly as she bundled them inside before closing and locking the door.

The trio of females spent most of the first day home sitting side by side on the white settee. Mummy Mitchell claimed the reclining seat at the end and sat with her tired legs comfortably elevated, as she sipped tea, Julianne sipped white wine and Kira Mae slurped her chocolate milk.

A study in domestic bliss, Julianne sat in the middle with one arm around her beloved daughter's strong adolescent shoulders and the other stroking her adopted mother's work worn hand.

'How many times have I told you to wear rubber gloves when you are washing up or doing housework?' Julianne asked solicitously.

The only reply she received was a quizzically raised eyebrow and a dismissive, 'Yes, I hear you.'

They talked and laughed and swapped stories, they provided updates of their separate lives and basked in the warmth of their combined love. The perfect background to their happiness was the constantly changing outside slide show, projecting the ebbing and flowing tidal water of the Thames and the kaleidoscope of colours in the sky above London.

Afternoon sunlight and a bright blue cloud-free sky deepened into the warning shades of dusk and the sun prepared to dazzle with a well-rehearsed performance of softly streaked pale rose pink sky, morphing into purple and navy blue and finally into the inky colours of night-time. Stars became visible and a sliver of new moon illuminated the sky.

'Make a wish on the new moon,' said Julianne, at which all three burst out laughing. 'I know, I know,' she said gaily. 'We mustn't tempt fate – we already have all we could possibly need or want.'

'Well, I wouldn't mind a new school bag,' said Kira Mae, at which they all laughed even more.

After a light supper of smoked salmon with scrambled eggs on granary toast, followed by death by chocolate cheesecake, the oldest member of the little family went for a well-earned early night.

Mummy Mitchell kissed her darling daughters and held

them tight as she said, 'Goodnight, God bless – see you in the morning. Not too early mind.'

Kira Mae swanked around the apartment looking like she owned it; she certainly approved of this lifestyle. Her mother had great taste and she hoped that she had inherited her style and fashion sense. She eeny meeny miny moe-d to choose her favourite bathroom and indulged herself by luxuriating in a bath lovingly scented with the new MDA Green Tea bubble beads.

She gave her considered opinion, based on many years of sharing her mother's professional interests and pride in the evolving and socially aware MDA brand. She declared the Green Tea range, 'adequate'.

Sensing Julianne's disappointment at this lack of enthusiasm, Kira Mae assured her mother, 'Adequate is what you older people call ab fab.'

Julianne lovingly helped her daughter wash her waist length blonde hair. Kira Mae's hair was still a golden Nordic blonde, in glorious defiance of her Celtic ancestors and their traditional black or darkest brown hair.

Just as she had when she was a baby Julianne helped her daughter wrap up warm and cosy, this time in a large white towelling bathrobe – with tartan piping on the collar.

Kira Mae sat like a contented cat on the comfortable woollen rug in front of the settee, while her mother brushed and dried her hair. This satisfying bedtime ritual complete, Kira Mae snuggled into her pretty pink silk pyjamas and mother and daughter cuddled up on the settee. For many hours they sat delighting in each other's company and talked late into the night.

As they sat curled up together Kira Mae went into her old

refrain, 'Tell me again about our Disneyland trip and the Mickey Mouse balloon – and the security guard – was he going to arrest us?'

Julianne was firm. 'I am not telling the story again tonight, my darling daughter. It's bedtime for you, we've got a busy day tomorrow – and lots of surprises in store. Time to say goodnight. God bless.'

Julianne took her daughter's hand and walked her towards the bedroom. After tucking her up in bed and kissing her goodnight, she looked in on her other special house guest.

Peering into the darkened room she noticed that the bed clothes were slipping from the bed – she crept closer to cover up the sleeping form of her beloved mother – she didn't want her to get cold in the night.

She leaned over the bed to straighten the bedclothes and softly kissed her mother's cheek.

'We love you, Mummy,' she whispered. 'Goodnight and God bless.'

Julianne said a prayer as she drifted off to sleep, thanking God for all the wonderful gifts he bestowed upon her – and the love of her daughter and mother.

★ ★ ★

The next morning, waking early, she went into the bedroom with a cup of tea for her most welcome house guest.

Julianne's happy secure world was shattered. Ida was lying, pale and still – and did not appear to be breathing.

Julianne was distraught. She held her hand up to her mother's mouth to try to confirm whether she was breathing. She felt for a pulse on her wrist, not really knowing what she was doing. Then she anxiously tried to administer CPR. She held her mother's mouth open, covered her nose and attempted to force her own breath into the lifeless body.

Over and over again, she repeated, 'Oh, my God, oh my God, oh my God, don't let her die. Please don't let her die.'

Kira Mae appeared in the doorway yawning. 'What's happening?' she asked.

'Go back to bed, please just go back to bed.' Julianne tried to force herself not to shout. She knew her voice was on the verge of being hysterical. 'I'll call you if there is anything you can do.'

Kira reluctantly turned to go and her mother called her back. 'Call an ambulance,' she said. 'Phone 999. Quick. I think she's had a heart attack.'

Kira ran to the phone in the living room and called the emergency services. As she tried to give an address and phone number for her mother's new home she realised she didn't know it.

'Ambulance, we need an ambulance,' she screamed. 'Please hurry.'

Julianne heard the phone call above the noise in her head as she frantically prayed that her mother would not die. She called out the address and phone number to her now sobbing daughter.

'Hurry,' she said as she slowed her own breath in an attempt to stop herself from panicking, trying to urge Kira to convey to the operator the seriousness of the situation. 'I think she's dying. Please help.'

Ida Mitchell had never spent one day in hospital and avoided doctors like the plague. In her lilting Scottish accent she had explained her morbid fear. Her own highly superstitious mother had warned her, 'If they take you out of the house on a stretcher, they'll bring you back in a box.' That had come to pass.

Ida's mother had suffered a heart attack from which she never recovered and having been removed from her home by ambulance, came back in a coffin. At the age of fifty-one.

Ida Mitchell had been determined that fate was not going to befall her. However, she was just sixty years of age when she too passed away. Not quite as young as her mother but a full ten years before what she had always believed would be her allotted three score years and ten.

'I've had a good life,' she had often told her daughters. 'I have nothing to fear from the hereafter. Don't mourn me when I am gone, celebrate the life I had – and get on with enjoying your own.'

The ambulance crew were marvellous. They arrived within minutes and took control. They made only minimal attempts at CPR before pronouncing the patient dead at the scene.

Julianne could hear her mother's matter of fact voice in her head and she was shocked that she should at this moment remember the words her mother often quoted. 'Death is not the worst thing that can happen to a decent person.'

The paramedics said they would arrange for the removal of the body and when Julianne asked if she should follow the ambulance to the hospital, they looked at her sadly. 'No need for that, miss,' said one of the green uniformed medics gently. 'The hospital will contact you. I have all your details.'

There was to be an inquest because Ida was not known to the medical team and no doctor had examined her in the days before her death, however they were not treating her death as suspicious. Like her mother before her she had died of a sudden and massive heart attack.

The doctor declared, 'She would have felt nothing. Not even known it was happening. It is just like a light switch being flicked off. One minute they are here, the next they are gone.'

Julianne could only hope and pray he was right. She couldn't bear to think of the wonderful kind lady who had given her a second chance in life, suffering.

Kira Mae kept questioning why and Julianne could only tell her, 'To go to sleep in your own bed and not wake up is a peaceful, painless way to go. She is blessed. It's the ones who are left behind who suffer.'

Later Julianne would make the arrangements to carry out what she knew would be her mother's last wishes. The local funeral home would transport her body back to her homeland. Ida Mitchell's place in the family plot had been reserved and paid for decades before. Now she would rejoin her long dead husband.

chapter ten

'The evil that men do, lives after them,
The good is oft interred with their bones.'
Shakespeare's *Julius Caesar*

Julianne and Kira Mae supported each other in their grief. A song, a word, a smell, an object could set one or the other off sobbing and generally it would not be long before they were both in emotional meltdown.

'When will it stop hurting?' wailed Kira Mae. 'Why didn't I spend more time with her? I was always promising we would do something together, go out for tea, go shopping but I was always too busy with my friends. Now it's too late.'

Julianne knew all about the guilt of not having done enough, not having been there enough, not being good enough. Still, she tried not to voice these feelings to her daughter, as the mother it was her job to stay strong.

For long hours they sat together and cried together and made a conscious effort to remember the good times and the laughter, and know beyond doubt that not for one single minute would darling Ida have blamed them for anything. As far as she was concerned her girls were perfect and she couldn't have loved them more.

'The best way we can honour her memory is to plan a beautiful memorial with all her favourite people, flowers, hymns, prayers and readings,' announced Julianne, knowing that she had to keep herself active and focused on something other than the searing pain in her heart.

'You can choose something special to read for her in church and help me decide on some treasured mementos to put in the coffin,' she promised Kira Mae. 'We can help speed her on her way to heaven.'

Only with each other could they find some relief from their heartbreak. They did not have to explain their feelings or make excuses for emotional outbursts or try to put on a brave face. Only those who have lost a loved one know the bleakness that settles like a depressing fog over everything when it seems that life will never again be worth living. All joy and hope for the future is extinguished.

Ida's death reawakened all the hurt and anger and painful memories of her own mother's death. Julianne repeated her mantra, 'No defeat, no retreat,' and remembered what her own mother had told her.

'You don't have to be brave. Just know that I love you and will be in heaven watching over you.'

Julianne and Kira Mae made the journey back to Scotland together. Their destination was the Mitchell cottage, where they would begin the painful job of sorting and disposing of her belongings.

Ida had lived simply and they did not think there would be too many difficult decisions to be made. If asked it would probably have been a good bet that most of the furniture and clothing and ornaments would be donated to the church and the local charity shop. However, they had no idea of the shock that was in store. Opening the Highland Shortbread biscuit tin in which Ida had always kept her important papers, Julianne found a will.

Attached to the will, an insurance policy in the joint names Julianne and Kira Mae Gordon, an insurance policy worth the staggering amount of over £100,000.

What Mummy Mitchell always referred to as her 'penny policy' had grown into a small fortune – reading through ancillary documents in the tin box, they were able to piece together the fragments and discover that the policy had been the legacy of a life policy paid out on the death of her long dead miner husband.

Back in the fifties, when the Prudential insurance company ran a home collection service going door to door selling policies and making weekly collections on their penny policies, Mrs Mitchell's husband had taken out the life policy, which on his death had been transferred to his widow.

Having no need of the money and more likely having no idea of just how substantial the sum had now become, when her husband died she had not taken the death benefit that was payable. Instead she had continued to pay the premiums and in later years would assure Julianne that, 'I've left enough money for you to bury me. You won't be out of pocket when I've gone. There might even be a wee bit left over. That's for you and the girl. You and Kira Mae can have a holiday.'

The man from the Prudential came round two days before the funeral to deliver a cheque to the joint beneficiaries. In full and final settlement the amount in words read 'One Hundred Thousand and Seventy Six Pounds Only'.

Kira Mae was fascinated by the word 'only'. She questioned Julianne, 'Do you think it's because it's not a lot of money to a big insurance company?'

The insurance man displayed a great deal of interest in the oil painting that hung on the living room wall. 'I could take that off your hands,' he said.

'No thank you it has sentimental value. It was painted by a miner – the son of a friend of my honorary grandfather,' said Kira Mae who had heard the story many times, of how sure her grandfather was that the painter would become famous one day. But so far no one seemed to have heard of Jack Hoggan.

Still, the insurance money was way beyond anything they had dreamt would be a legacy from the unassuming miner's widow.

Before returning to London Julianne made arrangements to have the lease and keys of the cottage returned to the local council who were now the legal owners of the property. Happiness at their financial good fortune was overshadowed by the sadness of the loss of their mother figure and protector.

'Who will look after us now?' asked Kira sadly. Julianne and Kira Mae had not been the only mourners to attend the simple funeral service, when they laid to rest the lady they both so loved and to whom they owed so much. They had respected her wishes to be buried in the tranquil, well-tended Scottish graveyard at the foot of the Ochil Hills.

With the hills that she had looked out on through her living room window for over thirty years to the west, and a small waterfall and free flowing burn to the east, surrounded by the bonny blooming heather, Mummy Mitchell rested in peace.

In the small graveyard Julianne and Kira Mae were surrounded by mourners. Mrs Isabella Mitchell had been a stalwart of the local church community and her devotion was remembered by a sizeable group of fellow worshippers. She would have been humbled at how many people took the time to say that she had touched their lives over the years with acts of random kindness.

Ida would have known every person at the graveside. Julianne scanned the congregation. She was looking for one person – a sceptre at the feast – one individual who would definitely not be welcome at the internment – or indeed at any other time or place. Her biggest dread, that her father would somehow find out and show up was not realised. Fact was the family ties had always been tenuous and now all these years later, connections were almost non-existent.

The mourners were all welcomed and respected guests. The ladies, with whom Ida had shared church flower arranging duties, mostly made up the small but sincere group of worshippers and ensured that their faithful fellow churchgoer was laid to rest with dignity.

Members of the choir who had regularly sung with her took pride in providing the music at the funeral service of their friend. Julianne invited the mourners to a small lunch party after the church service.

In the village's best hotel, she and Kira Mae received guests and then sat down, as waitresses served a traditional meal of steak pie, mashed potatoes and peas. A selection of fresh cream cakes – ordered and delivered from the co-op that morning – were also offered along with cups of tea and small glasses of sherry. The officiating priest, a genial Scotsman with snow-white hair complimenting his starched white dog collar, attended the small gathering. He declined the sherry and a waitress immediately appeared asking but not needing to wait for an answer to the question.

'You'll have your usual, a whisky, Father?'

Father McKearney had known the departed parishioner

for many years and he assured Julianne and Kira Mae that their beloved Mummy Mitchell would be sadly missed. Somehow they had never realised the extent to which she been a part of her community – so preoccupied had they been with the knowledge that she was the centre of their world.

'And what plans do you have now?' he asked Kira Mae kindly, knowing already that she had lived with her grandmother and attended the local senior high school – an internationally recognised academy.

The academy had been founded in 1818 and held the distinction of being the oldest co-educational school in Britain. The esteemed educational establishment held the accolade as Scotland's highest performing public school academically, as well as being acknowledged as a centre for excellence in sporting achievement. A high proportion of the one thousand, three hundred students were international students and the school accommodated day girls as well as boarders. Housed in a neo-classical Greek façade building set in some forty acres of its own grounds, the international academy had its own playing fields, tennis courts and an indoor swimming pool. Kira Mae had been a pupil there since kindergarten and had been a straight A student and a formidable player in the league topping hockey team.

'I'm going to live with my mother in London,' replied Kira Mae to the priest's question.

Much to her mother's discomfort. Julianne had already talked to the academy's headmaster and told him that Kira Mae would be continuing her education at the school. She had proposed that Kira Mae become a boarder like so many of the other one thousand, three hundred pupils – most of whom did not have family living in the village.

'And,' added Kira Mae, watching her mother's face closely to see how she responded. 'I'm leaving school. I'm going to St. Martin's College of Art and Design. I've already sent off for the prospectus – my grades are good enough to get in. I just have to have an interview and pass an entrance examination.'

Julianne was reeling. All of this was news to her. She thought she knew her daughter so well and never dreamed that on such a major decision she would not have consulted her.

Kira Mae stared at her mother and defied her to challenge her in front of the priest, who was already picking up the sense that things were not all that they seemed. Julianne had been rendered almost speechless with shock and anger. Kira Mae defiantly stuck out her chin and, turning away from her mother, excused herself and walked purposefully towards the exit doors of the hotel.

'She was very close to her grandmother,' Julianne heard herself explaining. 'Her sudden death was a great shock. We haven't made any decision about what will happen next. We will have to wait and see. It is my hope and intention that Kira Mae will finish her schooling here in Scotland. She only has another year to go. Then she can start thinking about moving to London.'

The priest, acutely aware of the embarrassment of the scene that had just taken place, nodded kindly.

'Children today,' he said. 'They have minds of their own. Kira Mae is a good girl and I am sure she will see the sense of what you are proposing. Please let me know if I can be of any assistance.'

The two shook hands and Julianne made her escape from the funeral party, after thanking the manager of the hotel for the splendid meal and service his team had laid on.

Her head was reeling as she walked purposefully from the hotel, determined to find Kira Mae and confront her.

Kira Mae, little girl that she still was, hadn't gone far. She was sitting on a bench outside the hotel, contemplating the stream that wound its way down from the high hills and rushed over the boulders and rocks. At this passing place on its journey, as it meandered past the hotel, it was little more than a few inches deep.

Julianne walked towards her daughter. Kira Mae stood up, kicked off her heels and walked the few feet down the gently sloping riverbank to the water's edge. Dipping her feet in the cooling, crystal clear water, she didn't notice Julianne approaching.

Julianne was in no mood to be ignored, but even in her anger she couldn't help noticing how beautiful and how grown up her daughter looked. Right up to the morning of the funeral Kira had insisted that she was not wearing boring black. Instead she wore a stylish white and navy blue suit – skirt not too short, Julianne had noted with relief – and a white blouse with a Peter Pan colour. Her long blonde hair was held back from her face with a navy Alice band. Her navy blue shoes had a pretty gold buckle and a demure heel. These shoes now lay abandoned by the bench – Kira Mae was bare legged.

Julianne strode purposefully to the water's edge and in a tone as icy as the water at her feet; she put on her parent voice to address Kira Mae.

'You cannot drop a bombshell like that, and then try to ignore me. I am your mother, I have a right to be consulted on something as important as this – it's your entire future and career we are talking about here.'

Then in a more conciliatory tone, she added, 'You do get some funny ideas. Whoever put this daft one into your head?'

Kira Mae was not to be placated.

'Don't treat me like a child,' she snapped. 'I've made up my mind. I'm going back to London with you and I am going to become a world famous fashion designer, so there!'

With all the confidence of her seventeen years, Kira Mae had delivered her intentions. Julianne looked at her headstrong young daughter and realised with a jolt that the two had a lot of adjusting to do.

For all of Kira Mae's life she had had two mothers. Julianne had been a Sunday best mother. She had left the day-to-day parenting duties to Mummy Mitchell.

She had always been the treat, holiday time part of Kira Mae's life. There was much that she did not know about the young woman who now confronted her. Kira Mae obviously knew her own mind. She was strong, assured and stubborn. Mummy Mitchell would have been proud of her.

Julianne reached out and took her daughter's hand. With her other hand she flicked open the clasp on her handbag and checked that the cheque was safe. One hundred thousand pounds just waiting to be deposited into her account, Julianne silently thanked her lucky stars. She and her daughter were well blessed.

The decision had been made – no point in resisting – Kira Mae would return to London with Julianne.

chapter eleven

'Now does my project gather to a head,
My charms crack not, my spirits obey.'
Shakespeare's *The Tempest*

Tears stung her eyes as Kira Mae turned the key in the lock of Mummy Mitchell's cottage home for the last time. It had been a long time since the heavy wooden door had received a coat of varnish but the brass knocker with the thistle emblem shone bright and proud. Kira Mae looked forlornly at the familiar threshold beyond which she had lived all of her short life. Although she could not quite name the feelings, it was obvious that this was to be some sort of defining moment. A transition.

Is this what they call a rite of passage? Kira Mae wondered, briefly remembering a school lesson in which her form teacher, Miss Cameron, an Australian of Scottish stock, had talked about these life changing moments.

'This is my walkabout,' Kira Mae declared aloud, 'just like the Aborigines have in the outback.' Inwardly she admitted that she was part scared, part excited. Sternly she told herself, 'There is no going back.' At this realisation she started to cry real tears, deep sobs, for herself, for her missing mother and for the life that she had already left behind.

'Goodbye, Mummy Mitchell and thank you,' she whispered. Putting on a brave face, she wiped away her tears and blew her nose on a clean white handkerchief. Under her arm she carried the painting of a woodland scene that would always stimulate evocative memories of her happy childhood home.

Taking one last look at the country garden, a riot of colour and dahlia blooms in the afternoon sunshine, Kira Mae picked up what remained of her luggage – the rest already having been packed up and shipped down to London – and walked slowly down the cobbled path, out of the small wooden gate, down the achingly familiar village street towards the taxi cab where her mother was already standing waiting. They had a long journey ahead of them.

The cab had been booked well in advance and was driven by a neighbour who was secretly excited to be doing 'an airport run'. These long distance journeys were few and far between in a small village. Although by a strange irony, only a few weeks earlier he had driven Kira and Mummy Mitchell to Glasgow for the train journey to London. Journey time would be some two hours to Glasgow airport and from there they would fly to London Heathrow.

Julianne had diplomatically left Kira Mae alone to say goodbye to the house and garden where she'd lived all her life. She had already said her own private goodbyes. It had been many years since she had called this cosy cottage home, but, apart from the all too short time she had shared with her birth mother, Julianne knew deep in her heart that this was the only real home she had ever known.

As long as she lived, she would never lose her gratitude for the sanctuary she had been granted.

Julianne had many misgivings about the life she and Kira

Mae were about to embark on, but she kept those pessimistic thoughts to herself. Squeezing her daughter's arm, she reassured her. 'Everything will work out just fine, darling. I will look after you.'

Kira Mae gave a small nod of acknowledgement but she continued to stare out of the window, lamenting the fast disappearing countryside of her homeland. Like many an only child before her, Kira questioned her place in society. Much as she had been spoiled and sheltered during her upbringing, she was aware that her ability to understand or relate to more traditional family set ups was limited. There had never been a male role model in her life aside from the occasional teacher whom she would either hero worship or fear. She envied girls who had fathers or even grandfathers and without any information about her own father, she had begun to glamorise this mythical figure. Her mother reacted badly whenever Kira raised the question and refused to tell her about her father, even to say who he was and Mummy Mitchell would have sworn on the Bible that she did not know.

Left with this void to fill and a vivid imagination, Kira had concocted all kinds of stories and scenarios. The one constant was the belief that her mother was to blame for sending or driving him away. But now Kira Mae had made a discovery and she was ready to track down her father. She fantasised that he would welcome his little girl with open arms and she would become an adored child, perhaps even in a new family. That way she would not need to depend solely on her mother, whom she had long since convinced herself cared more for her career than she did for her daughter.

Kira played loud music through her headphones all the way to the airport.

'Kira, I am talking to you,' she sensed rather than heard her mother say, as the cab turned off the highway and entered the terminal roadway.

Reluctantly Kira turned down the music and put her headphones around her neck. 'Sorry, what were you saying?'

'I just wanted to know if you want to eat before we get on the plane. We'll be lucky if they give us more than a couple of biscuits and a coffee on the in-flight service. The flying time is only just over an hour,' explained Julianne. 'Or we can wait until we get home and I'll order in pizza.'

'Pizza is good.' Kira smiled.

Julianne reached out her hand to her daughter and admitted, 'I won't pretend that I am happy about your decision to leave your school to come and live with me in London, but I will do everything I can to try to make this work for us.'

Kira Mae too had her misgivings, but she wasn't about to show that she was already worrying about whether she had made the right decision. No longer would her mother be able to walk away from her at the end of a visit. Now Kira Mae was determined to ensure that she was no longer a guilty secret. Imprisoned in her ivory tower, isolated and excluded from her mother's real world, Kira Mae was ready to assert herself. She was determined to make good on the promise she had already made; she vowed that she would do everything in her power to make her mother's life hell.

chapter twelve

'Hell is empty and all the devils are here.'
Shakespeare's *The Tempest*

Julianne had no idea of the cauldron of insecurity and hate that was boiling inside her daughter as they started their new life together in London. To Kira Mae's outbursts of bad temper and downright rudeness she responded with understanding, attributing the bad behaviour to the pain of her grandmother's death. Her own heart was breaking but she tried to blot out the grief by working harder than ever.

Kira Mae spent long hours alone in the Docklands apartment, very quickly losing any enjoyment in the ever changing view, the uniqueness of the location or even the wonderful lifestyle on offer. The newly up and coming area of London was still undergoing a gentrification process – cafés, bistros, boutiques and galleries were adventurously opening up in the former run down harbour area.

Kira Mae was desperately unhappy and she was determined that someone was going to pay for her pain. Her mother was her chosen target and, in her mind, not without just cause.

While clearing the belongings from Mummy Mitchell's

Scottish home, Kira Mae had unknowingly opened the Pandora's Box out of which would escape the secrets, lies and family shame from which her mother and grandmother had so long shielded her.

At the bottom of her grandmother's wardrobe, under a cream crocheted woollen bedspread, Kira Mae had unearthed a shoebox filled with old paper sewing patterns – and a letter.

The letter was addressed to Miss Julianne Gordon c/o Mrs Isabella Mitchell, Glen Cottage, Main Road, Campbelltoun. Inside the envelope was a letter written on blue lined notepaper, in a strong firm hand, the writing was clear and concise, though the message was long and rambling.

Begging forgiveness for the past and pleading for a chance to make it up to her, the writer Alan had sounded like a man who was desperate. He had one request, that Julianne allow him to see his daughter.

'She deserves to know that she is loved,' he had written.

The letter had been written and was postmarked from Devon, with a date shortly after Kira Mae's birth. Recognising the handwriting Ida Mitchell had taken it upon herself to open and read it. Studying and re-reading the letter she attempted to read between the lines. There was an implication that was too horrible for her to contemplate. Although it was not spelled out she had the reprehensible thought that her brother-in-law was admitting he was the father of her darling Julianne's baby.

She had known that it was pointless to tell her charge Julianne that yet another letter had arrived and instead after reading it, she struggled with whether to destroy it or not. On so many occasions she had suggested that Julianne at least open a dialogue with her father. Now a chill ran through her body and telling herself that she would attempt to talk to Julianne about it, she hid the letter away. Stuffing it in the old shoebox at the bottom of the wardrobe, Ida was careful to push it to the bottom of the pile of old paper patterns that were already in the box. It would be many a year before anyone had any need of these out of date discarded patterns. Life had moved on.

Kira Mae had, not unreasonably, expected to find old shoes in the box at the bottom of the wardrobe – instead she had been fascinated by the documentary record of fashion styles that were preserved in all the envelope covers of dozens of Simplicity patterns. Seeing the letter at the bottom of the box, she had fantasised that it would be a love letter from a secret admirer to her grandmother. A treasured memento that she could not bear to have made public. Kira Mae had been on the verge of throwing the letter away when she realised it was addressed to her own mother. Asking herself the question, of why it was hidden in her grandmother's wardrobe, Kira Mae had opened the letter and read it.

Reeling from the shock of the contents, she had taken the letter and put it in a safe place – with some of her own papers. It was hidden but close to hand for her to read and re-read in secret.

The subject of her parentage was a closed book, Kira Mae had often tried to get an answer but her mother resolutely refused to engage in the conversation. Who was her father? Who was Alan? Why was she being kept away from people who loved her? Kira Mae struggled with trying to work out the tangled family history.

Since moving to London and starting her own university life, Kira Mae had felt herself more and more alienated. Time was not healing the hurt inside or the chaotic emotions that made her so unsettled and unhappy.

During yet another high volume row with her mother she had screamed out the pain of the secret and constant questions that had been eating away at her.

'I found his letter,' she shouted at her mother. 'You've kept me away from my family. Why can't I see them? What are you afraid of? Why wouldn't you tell me the name of my father? I hate you.'

Julianne had broken down in tears, sobbing and had tried to explain to Kira Mae that the situation was not as she thought.

'Please trust me,' she had entreated. 'I would never do anything to hurt you. This is for your own good. Please, do not pursue this; no good can come of it.'

★ ★ ★

Always an earlier riser – unlike her daughter – Julianne made it a habit to be at her desk at 6.30 a.m. At that time there were no distractions from phones or colleagues, so she achieved a great deal before the office began to come to life.

Kira Mae lay in bed waiting as she heard her mother leave the apartment and the soft click of the front door. She quickly got up, showered and left the apartment, walking the short distance to Canary Wharf and the Docklands Light Railway. From there she travelled into Central London and on by coach to Exeter.

Kira Mae took just a small overnight case. Returning to an empty home, Julianne feared the worst. She was convinced her daughter had gone to the source of the newly discovered letter and dreaded that there she would discover the information she craved.

Kira Mae did not get in touch for three long days.

Julianne stayed off work, pacing the floor, staying close by the phone, willing it to ring, willing her daughter to get in touch. She was heartsick. In their row, Kira Mae had spat out the fact that she knew where the sender of the letter, Alan lived and that she was determined to go and find him. It broke her heart that her daughter was about to discover the true identity of the writer of the letter. She struggled with the dilemma, Should I go after her? What if I do manage to stop her this time? I can't keep her under lock and key forever. What will he tell her?

Julianne had shed so many tears, she was exhausted and all cried out. Lying on her bed trying to take an afternoon nap, she heard the front door open and jumped to her feet, running into the living room.

Kira Mae put down the holdall she was carrying and shot her mother a look filled with pure hatred.

'You whore,' she said. 'No wonder you didn't want me to know who he was. He's a bloody old man. What was he, your sugar daddy?'

Julianne felt a knife go into her heart as her beloved daughter looked at her in disgust. She responded softly, 'No, not *sugar* daddy.' She deliberately stressed the word *sugar*, but the subtlety of her mother's reply was lost on the young girl. 'It wasn't just one; I found loads of letters,' admitted Kira Mae. 'When we were clearing out Mummy Mitchell's house. He asked you again and again if he could come and see me. Why wouldn't you let him?'

Kira Mae triumphantly declared the extent of her

knowledge. Having found one letter she had gone on searching in the bedroom until she found another stash of envelopes containing cards and letters.

Kira Mae had in her possession every birthday and Christmas card that her father had sent to her for almost her entire life.

'How dare you keep him from me?' Kira Mae was perched on the edge of the white settee now, crying hard. 'You're selfish and manipulative and horrible. You wanted me all for yourself. Oh, God, I wish I was dead.'

Julianne sat next to her heartbroken daughter on the settee and cradled her in her arms. Smoothing her daughter's hair and stroking her hand, she made soft shushing noises.

Tears burned her eyes and she refused to take her hands from her daughter to brush them away. Soothing her like a baby, the two sat together as daylight became twilight and Kira Mae lay down on the settee, her head in her mother's lap and fell into an exhausted sleep. Her darling little girl was quiet at last, but as she drifted off to sleep she looked up at Julianne and said, 'Sorry, Mummy. Sorry.'

'There, there,' said Julianne softly. 'It's okay. It will be okay.'

Kira Mae replied, even more softly. 'But I told him where we lived.'

Julianne felt the fear grip her stomach. She thought that she might just pass out. The horror of what her daughter had just revealed opened the floodgates of her every waking night. Laying Kira Mae's head gently on a cushion, Julianne got up and walked into the bedroom returning with a blanket that she tenderly tucked around the sleeping girl.

Without turning on a light, she moved herself to the

opposite settee and sat in the dark, staring at the river as its tide swelled and the current changed course. Storm clouds were visible over the tops of the buildings on the far bank. Julianne wept.

chapter thirteen

'O weary night, O long and tedious night,
Abate thy hours, Shine comforts from the East.'
Shakespeare's *A Midsummer Night's Dream*

Julianne dragged herself reluctantly through the next few days. She lived in dread that her father would knock on the door. She forbade Kira Mae to open the door while she was at home alone during the day.

When she later recalled the day her father did come knocking on the door, Julianne thanked her lucky stars for just one blessing. Kira Mae was not at home. In a rare excursion she had taken herself off to a new fashion exhibition at the Victoria and Albert Museum.

Finding her father had been a turning point for Kira Mae. She now knew she had a father and she knew she had no intention of pursuing any relationship with him.

Their meeting in Devon had been brief and strangely formal. Kira Mae had knocked on the door at the address she had taken from the letters – a small town half an hour outside of Exeter surrounded by the wild, rural beauty of the Dartmoor countryside – and a grey haired man had answered.

He was tall and looked rather forbidding – he presented

to her the stern, unsmiling face that so many pupils had feared through his long career as a headmaster at the local school. He had demanded respect and had not asked for or wanted to be liked. Now he had stood wordlessly waiting for Kira Mae to state the nature of her business. Although she had rehearsed the words over and over again, as she had made the long coach ride from London to Exeter, then taken a local bus to a village on the outskirts of the town and walked nervously down the one track lane with the high hedges on either side, Kira Mae did not know what to say when the door was opened and there stood the man she believed was her father.

'I think you know my mother,' she had said. 'Her name is Julianne.'

'You had better come in,' he had said, still with no warmth in his voice. The pair had sat awkwardly, facing each other in armchairs on each side of the unlit fire. Kira Mae had told him about the letters and the fact that she had longed to know who her father was. It had been her decision to follow up the letter and her mother did not know she had come. She also told him that Mummy Mitchell had passed away. At the last minute she had averted herself from telling him about the inheritance of over one hundred thousand pounds that she had left in her will. However, she had gladly gone on to tell him about herself, her upbringing, her life to date and her plans for the future.

The father she had fantasised about for so long had said little. He certainly did not tell her all the things she had longed to hear, about how happy he was to see her, or how lovely she was and how proud he was to have a daughter like her. He had told her nothing about himself, he was still a complete stranger. There were even more questions than answers now. He had not even seemed to be all that interested in any information she had wanted to pass on about her mother – but he had asked for her address so he could write to her. Even Kira Mae could see now that this had been no lost teenage love affair, something sinister was afoot, but she could not fathom out what it was. Her sheltered life experience had not given her the insight to unravel this complicated relationship.

When she had finished her tea, the man she had hoped would turn out to be her father had checked the time on the mantelpiece clock and told Kira Mae, 'The last bus leaves in half an hour, you can't stay here. Get yourself on the bus and back to Exeter. You know where you are going from there, don't you? You have got a return ticket?'

'Yes,' she told him.

Alan Gordon had walked his young visitor a little way down the lane; far enough to be able to point to the small crossroads, a place where it was claimed that over a thousand years before slaves had been freed and allowed to decide their destiny by the direction they chose to take. Under the wooden sign at the crossroads at the bottom of the lane, the man on whom she had pinned her hopes had given her no such choice, but had directed her to board the bus opposite to where she had alighted.

There had been no warmth in his goodbye and Kira Mae was rather glad to be back on the bus heading away from the cheerless cottage, the unsmiling man and the uncertainty of many still unanswered questions.

Kira Mae hadn't been able to face the humiliation of going straight back to her mother, so on arriving back in London she had gone and stayed with a friend for a couple of days. A male friend from college. Her mother did not know that she was no longer a virgin.

'But what business is it of hers?' Kira Mae had asked the young man, with whom she had previously only shared a college refectory lunch – now she shared his bed. She added him to an elite list of her 'friends with benefits'.

Truth was she had been rather scared to go home. She would have had good reason to be scared had she known that she had set in motion a terrifying stream of events. Following her visit, Alan Gordon was already planning to follow her to London. But not to see Kira Mae who he had long since ceased caring about. No, his mission was to avenge the indignity of a daughter who had cut him off and dared to threaten him with the police all those years ago.

Julianne answered the entry phone and pressed the button to allow access to the owner of the male voice who said curtly, 'Delivery for No.5!'

As she opened the door to accept the package, her father forced his way into her apartment.

Without a word of greeting, he grabbed her by the throat and slapped her. His eyes blazed with the pent up aggression and rage of nearly twenty years and he slammed her against the back of the door.

'Bitch,' he said, as his huge fist smashed into her face. He pushed and pulled her and threw her to the floor. As Julianne lay there on her pristine white carpet, she felt a boot slam into her side and saw the trickle of blood from her nose. Fervently she prayed that she would black out, that she would not have to face what was coming next, but she knew only too well from all her childhood years of humiliation, where this was heading.

Shouting, threatening and swearing, he punched and slapped as he had done so many times before, to teach her a lesson. Powerless to fight the huge, hulking male presence that had already weakened her physically, Julianne closed her eyes and tried to escape out of her body, far away as she had done for all those childhood years.

He grabbed the waistband of the loose white cotton trousers she was wearing and started to manhandle them over her hips exposing her naked private parts. Julianne struggled and tried to pull the trousers up again, while forcing her legs together in an attempt to deny him entry.

'No, no, please stop,' she cried. Showing no mercy he straddled her, facing her feet and while she beat her hands on his back he yanked the trousers from her hands and over her bare feet holding her trapped with the full force of his weight. He threw the trousers across the room and as Julianne tried to struggle upright and get away, he climbed back on top of her facing her directly and penetrated her as she screamed out in agony.

Julianne was completely inexperienced sexually, like a born again virgin she had allowed no man to touch her since that day almost two decades before when she realised that she was carrying a baby. Now she felt the physical pain as excruciating as the first time he had raped her and she endeavoured with all her might to push him off. A boiling rage erupted in her as she remembered the hurt, the shame, the humiliation.

'I hate you,' she said in a low menacing voice and taking the phlegm of fear and adrenaline that had accumulated in her mouth, she spat full in his face.

'Bitch,' he said and hit her hard across the face, before dismissively wiping the saliva from his own cheek and resuming the heaving and grunting on top of her.

For what seemed like hours but was likely minutes, Julianne tried hard not to breathe and tried to disconnect her mind from her body as she prayed for the degrading act to be over.

He can violate my body, she told herself – remembering an insight that she had read in a book about survivors of rape and incest – but he can't touch the *me* inside.

Julianne began to pray with every ounce of her being. Dear God, please don't let Kira Mae come home. Keep her away. Keep her safe. Please, please let this nightmare end.

Her prayers went unanswered. Kira Mae was hurrying home, happy and excited, eager to tell her mother all about her visit to the fashion exhibition. The spectacular fashions had breathed new life into her. She felt inspired, energised and enthusiastic.

In a small gold and black V&A carrier bag, Kira Mae carried the present she had lovingly selected as a 'sorry' gift. A pair of diamante bow earrings.

Opening the street door to the flats, she made her way up the stairs. The sound of angry voices rose to greet her. Kira Mae froze, rooted to the spot; she recognised the sound of the male voice as that of her father. Filled with guilt, she realised that she had known he would come, that by giving her address she had betrayed her mother.

Kira Mae started to pray. Please God, don't let anything bad happen to my mother. Let her be okay.

Her prayer too went unanswered. Between the shouts and slaps, Kira Mae heard her mother sobbing. 'Go away, leave me alone. I promise I won't tell Kira Mae your dirty little secret. Please, please I beg you.'

Kira Mae could bear to hear no more. She put her key in

the lock and pushed against the door. Using more force than was needed, the door gave way and Kira Mae almost fell into the room.

The scene that greeted her was one that would stay in her worst nightmares forever. Pandora's Box was opened and she was powerless to reverse the scene that now played out before her horrified eyes.

Her mother was on the floor on her knees in front of the man Kira Mae had so newly come to call her father. He towered over her frightened mother, he held the shoulder length blonde hair in a cruel twist; his fist clenched. Julianne was trying desperately not to struggle against the brute force, which had forced her into a position of submission. A position she had been forced into so many times before, the demeaning position that confirmed what she had always known, that she was totally in his power. Julianne was defeated.

Kira Mae crashed into the room and ran towards her mother crying – even as she struggled to work out the implications of what she had just so graphically heard and seen. Her mother's trousers lay in the middle of the floor where they had been ripped from her. Kira Mae felt bile rise in her stomach and she thought she might throw up. Instead she was filled with a murderous rage.

'Get out,' she screamed hysterically, at her mother's attacker. 'Leave her alone, leave her alone.'

For a split second it seemed that he would continue with what had plainly been an intention to force himself into Julianne's mouth but now he pushed her roughly away. His rage and sexual aggression having already been spent, she was spared the final indignity as he unhurriedly zipped his trousers and walked towards the front door.

Without even acknowledging the presence of his younger daughter, the rapist turned and issued a warning, 'I am not finished with you yet, bitch.' His tone aggressive and menacing he said, 'I will be back. What did I do to get a whore of a daughter like you? I swear to God I will kill you one day.'

As he stormed out of the apartment, Kira Mae rushed to the door, slammed it violently and locked it.

Julianne slumped further down on her knees rolled on to her side in the foetal position, covered her bloody face and head with her hands and cried deep, wailing sobs.

Kira Mae cradled her mother's head and tried to stroke and comfort her. Together they wept. Julianne raised her swollen and battered face to her daughter. The beating her father had inflicted was brutal and merciless.

'I'm calling the police,' said Kira Mae, desperate at least to try to make some kind of restitution.

'No, no, please don't, I can't bear it, please, Kira Mae, listen to me. You mustn't call the police. We mustn't tell. Next time he *will* kill me.'

Kira Mae did not call the police; instead she helped her distraught mother to the settee and covered her with a blanket, as her mother had done for her so many times before. She bathed the poor, swollen face and, following her mother's direction, found in the bathroom cabinet arnica ointment to put on the bruises. Finally, exhausted, her mother fell asleep.

Kira Mae sat all night in an armchair watching over her mother, sleeping herself only fitfully and cursing the betrayal that had brought this cruelty to her mother's door.

The dark shameful family secret was now in the open. No words needed to be said, Kira Mae knew without doubt that the last taboo had been broken. The secret shamed all of them. The man she had thought was her father was in fact her grandfather as well. Her mother had been raped and made pregnant by her own father. They were both victims of his incestuous lust.

They could not put the genie back in the bottle. Nothing could ever be the same again.

Kira Mae could not still the demons. When she closed her eyes she saw the devastating scene replayed again and again. The furies tormented her. This is your fault, you brought this upon yourself, and you deserve to be punished. On and on the merciless voices mocked her. Accusations, revelations, questions going round in her head, the pieces of the jigsaw falling into place. As dawn broke, a terrible painful realisation forced itself into Kira Mae's consciousness. My mother is my sister. We have the same father.

The sins of the father had been visited on both of them and the blood they shared was now spilled.

How would they ever survive the shock and shame of this most heinous of crimes? Her mum would know what to do. Her mum would make it all right.

Julianne was sleeping, drained and ashamed. She did not want ever to open her eyes again. She whimpered in her sleep and Kira Mae's heart was breaking. She pulled the cover over her mother's shoulders and kissed her on the forehead.

'I'm sorry, Mummy,' she said tearfully.

Julianne reached out and gently touched her daughter's hand.

'Don't worry, my baby. We've got each other. I'll take care of you. It will be okay. Trust me.'

The next day Julianne sent a message to her housemate

offering to sell her half share of the house, resigned from her job and booked two one-way tickets to Spain. They would run far away from their problems and start a new life.

That was the plan.

chapter fourteen

'The devil hath power to assume a pleasing shape.'
Shakepeare's *Hamlet*

Striding through Alicante airport, the two tall beautiful blondes turned heads as, arm in arm; they made their way to the luggage carousel.

Confidently reclaiming their new Louis Vuitton luggage with the iconic logo in chocolate brown and burnished orange – two pieces each – they effortlessly released the small base wheels and pulled the travel cases behind them as they exited towards the taxi rank.

Dressed in figure hugging skinny jeans with pale pink low cut tops, the two looked like sisters. No one would have guessed they were also mother and daughter.

Julianne topped off her outfit with a white tailored Armani jacket and minimal jewellery. A small white gold cross on a chain around her neck, tiny diamond studs and a white gold Cartier watch. Combining comfort and style, her favourite Gucci loafers in dove grey.

Reflecting the fashion sense of a younger set, Kira Mae wore a short denim Abercrombie & Fitch jacket with a few strategically placed rhinestone appliqués. Her jewellery was big and bold. She sported a set of designer jewellery from the graduation collection of one of her friends at St. Martin's College of Art and Design. Chunks of white-washed alabaster on a silver chain with ancient script fired into it. Her earrings were super-size hoops and she wore a dozen razor thin silver bangles.

To keep time, Kira Mae favoured a marquisette lapel watch, worn like a nurse, suspended from the front stud fastened pocket of her denim jacket. On her feet, canvas wedges from Miu Miu with white laces. Both women carried their signature summer collection Louis Vuitton carry on travel bags.

They walked quickly, with confidence and a sure sense of direction. These two certainly knew their way around. Flying British Airways club class, not chartered tourist airlines, they had retrieved their luggage and were on their way out of the one storey airport building before the over exited and already partying British holidaymakers, heading for the over populated resort of Benidorm, had managed to heave all their duty-free bags out of the overhead lockers.

A frantic gaggle of holiday company reps, trying hard to look enthusiastic as they welcomed yet another bunch of tourists, held up clip-boards declaring Thomsons, Global, SunTours. Lined up outside, were a long suffering band of taxi drivers – also holding up placards bearing the names of hotels and individual holidaymakers and battalions of seasonally weary coaches and their even more weary drivers.

Julianne and Kira Mae walked quickly past all the noisy, expectant activity and straight to the front of the queue of waiting airport taxis.

'Long term car park,' Julianne instructed the smiling

driver, his toothless smile revealed that out of all the holidaymakers emerging from the teeming airport, his first choice of passengers were this delicious duo of classy English blondes. However, his smile quickly became a sneer when he realised that their fare would only pay him the cost of a trip to the airport perimeter.

At the long stay car park, Julianne paid off the driver, with a smile and a large tip, and watched as he transferred mounds of Vuitton luggage from the trunk of his cab to the pre-ordered top of the range red Alpha Romeo cabriolet.

With the top down and their expensive luggage overflowing from the small passenger parcel seat, Julianne slipped into the driver's seat and drove out of the airport.

The late afternoon sun was still high in the sky, the temperature a body-warming seventy and the cloudless sky a glorious shade of rich peacock blue – this region of Spain boasted more than three hundred days of sunshine a year and almost three thousand hours of sunshine. Julianne made a mental note to tell her daughter the myth of the Puig Campana Mountain that magnificently dominated the landscape of this coastal region.

Locals told the story that the wife of the giant Roldán was dying – physicians predicted she would not last beyond the setting of that day's sun. Mad with grief, her heartbroken husband ordered stonemasons to carve a deep crevice from the top of the mountain to capture every last ray of the departing sun and delay the death of his beloved. The power of love.

Julianne turned to Kira Mae and smiled happily. They had made their escape and their fear-filled lives were now many miles away. Light and hope were again shining in their lives –

they had delayed the setting of the sun – and it was a perfect day for a high-speed drive through the Valencian countryside.

Julianne and Kira Mae spoke little, not that conversation was really an option over the noise of the racing engine and the exhilarating wind, and instead they drank in the sights and sounds of the Mediterranean paradise.

Delighted, they pointed out to each other the vineyards on either side of the road, the lemon grasses, and the wide avenues of olive groves. The major road out of the airport took them through several sprawling urban towns, before leading further into the country and a succession of pretty, whitewashed Spanish villages. Flowers cascaded from the iron window grills and terraces or were simply clustered around every front door. The most common plants used to provide a riot of colour were geraniums, petunias, marigolds and begonias. Their scents so strong they perfumed the village streets and permeated the warm air outside the car. Sun ripened Spanish farm workers toiled in the fields, spurning mechanised farming methods for the more traditional ploughs pulled by bored looking donkeys. Though large billboards boasted of Spain's participation in the technological revolution with ads for Sony, Ericsson and Apple, a slower more ancient slice of life was being played out in the countryside far below the self-glorifying road signs.

Julianne had no need of a map or directions; she knew exactly where she was heading. She had visited this area of Spain many times to spend chill out time with her old school friend, Annabelle Anstruther, who had moved to Spain to set up an English language newspaper, *Costa Blanca Tourist Times*. The paper had not succeeded in attracting circulation, competing as it was against more established opposition expertly run by former Fleet Street journalists. The publication had been bought out in a small blaze of publicity and abruptly closed down. However, Annabelle had developed a taste for the hedonistic lifestyle of an expat in Spain. Needs must and so although she returned to London to work when necessary, she refused to give up her lifestyle and beloved villa.

Now on an extended stay in England, trying desperately to find a rich husband who would keep her in the lifestyle to which she had become accustomed, Annabelle had graciously invited Julianne and her daughter to be her houseguests. Annabelle and Julianne had shared a flat in London and, for a time, been colleagues in the couture house. They shared a love of fashion, beauty products and luxury brands, and had both counted themselves blessed to be working at the prestigious de Angeles empire. Listening intently as Julianne had explained her dilemma – leaving out the more sordid details but revealing that a traumatic relationship break-up was forcing her to flee London without delay – Annabelle had immediately recognised the gravity of the situation and had offered her home as refuge.

'The villa is yours for as long as you and Kira Mae need it,' she had said. 'One phone call will arrange for the maid, Maria, to open up the house for you. She knows all the ropes. She will take care of everything. Anything you need, just ask her.'

Julianne had been anxious to discuss payment for the holiday accommodation, but her dear friend would not hear of it.

'You are my most welcome guests,' she had insisted. 'Enjoy – and don't forget to check out the most wonderful Spanish restaurant right there in the village.'

Smiling saucily, she had added, 'Give my love to Romero

– one of the star attractions of the restaurant – and give my love to darling Pepe, the owner.'

Even as she drove, Julianne was already planning a first night dinner at the restaurant; she did not want to be cooking after their journey.

'Are we there yet?' Kira Mae asked in a little girl voice, making a joke while also making a point. 'How much longer?'

Barely an hour had passed since they left the airport, now they were following a narrow road up into the mountains.

If she had not needed all her attention to concentrate on the hairpin bends over the hidden valleys and deep gorges, Julianne would have been able to marvel at the breathtaking view sweeping over the countryside and out to the ocean in the distance.

Kira Mae had her headphones on and music turned up though she kept her eyes closed – it could have been either through fear of the treacherous road conditions or to indulge in a little nap to help pass the time. Julianne was grateful that the area had been developed enough to provide high-class facilities in the way of services and amenities, thanks to the huge potential of the growing trend away from the packaged holidays of the tourist trade. However, the out of the way location and absence of booze-driven nightlife meant that the outlying area breathed a life of its own, a million miles away from the hot spots of Benidorm and its surrounding towns.

★ ★ ★

Choosing her moment to wake her sleeping daughter, Julianne judged that the start of the unmade road leading to the elegant white-washed villa would give her a chance to gather her thoughts, before Kira Mae was awakened by the suspension of the car protesting about the rock strewn, hole filled track.

A high wooden fence with white entryway columns marked the boundary of the Villa Verecchi. A paved courtyard provided parking spaces and, through open wrought iron gates, their eyes were drawn to a shimmering blue-tiled swimming pool. Crawling all over the villa, was a profusion of trailing vermilion bougainvillea and Chinese yellow jasmine, their heady perfume delighting at least half the senses while holding the promise of more sensual treats in store. See it, smell it, touch it. The wooden shutters at the windows of the long low building were painted a deep azure blue. The rustic wooden door stood welcomingly ajar.

Julianne was parking the car under the small carport to the right hand side of the building when Maria, a petite, olive-skinned, dark-eyed Spanish dynamo dressed in an unpretentious white cotton dress that perfectly complimented her tanned limbs and perfect ten figure, appeared.

'*Buenos días, hola, hola*, hello, hello, *cómo estás*?' she re-acquainted herself with Julianne, whom she had met briefly on other visits and busied herself helping with the luggage. Kira Mae nodded politely and walked past her into the villa.

Julianne wasn't sure where Kira Mae gained the assurance and entitled attitude of her right to servants, but she wasn't about to start a row this early on their trip. Maria had prepared the house beautifully and the inside of the villa, shuttered as it was against the sun, was cool and comfortable. The marble floors were covered with woven rugs and the huge, squashy settees were designed more for ease than fashion.

In the small old-fashioned white enamel fridge there was

milk, crusty bread and crisp salad vegetables, including fist-sized beef tomatoes and crisp purple onions with two bottles of olive oil – one virgin for the salads and one every day for cooking. Stored in the kitchen cupboards, Maria had stocked up with basic provisions. Coffee, sugar and a selection of herbs in small glass bottles. In earthenware bowls she had piled up colourful pyramids of fresh fruit – oranges, lemons, mandarins, nectarines and grapefruit.

Beds had been made up in two of the bedrooms – both double and en suite – their interiors shuttered and airy with faux marble floors and overhead wooden paddle fans. Black wrought iron bedsteads were complimented with snowy white sheets and lace bedspreads.

Assured that she had carried out her duties to the satisfaction of the owner's guests, and after even Kira Mae had declined an offer to have help unpacking the luggage, Maria took her leave, promising to return the next morning.

Julianne was pleasantly surprised by the new power shower in the bathroom but reminded herself that this had been the home of her friend, the high maintenance, and luxury loving Annabelle.

Kira Mae had rushed out through the French doors leading from the lounge to the terrace and beyond to a palm shaded rectangular pool, with its Roman steps leading into the azure blue waters. She stripped off her clothes and jumped straight into the pool – without even waiting to unpack her bikini.

Under the shade of a flourishing pink oleander plant – the wild bush of Spain – the enchanting gazebo by the poolside had a changing room and shower; under a small side terrace that led down a blue gravel path to an enclosed garden filled with fruit trees and a one hundred year old grapevine, there stood an inviting white wrought iron garden furniture set. Maria had placed fruit-filled blushed red sangria in a multi-coloured glass jug with matching tumblers alongside an overflowing silver ice bucket. Suitably refreshed after their journey, and eager to explore the neighbourhood, the new girls in town agreed to an early dinner – followed, if Julianne had anything to do with it, by an early night.

★ ★ ★

The restaurant was a short stroll down the hill from the villa. Pepe, the owner, greeted his new customers like long lost friends, as did the two large dogs of indeterminate pedigree that jumped and played around his feet. Pepe could have been sent from Central Casting as a bonhomie innkeeper. Small, almost as round as he was tall with black hair, a pencil moustache and a bellowing, jovial manner. His wife, a long thin woman dressed in mourning black, smiled less – but to give her the benefit of the doubt, maybe she was shy, and she could not speak English like Pepe.

He ushered the two women into the large restaurant and insisted on joining them in a house drink of Jerez Spanish sherry, while he enquired about their good friend the lady Annabelle.

Few diners were yet in the restaurant but in the corner of the room a gypsy guitarist was setting up his black leather stool and silver music stand, as his lovely assistant set up the microphones amplifiers and wire network of the sound system. Later the flamenco would start with the combined *personal fandango – the torque –* playing of the guitar – *the cante –* the singing and *the baile –* the dance.

Julianne and Kira Mae looked forward to being serenaded as they enjoyed their delicious meal, starting with oven hot seeded bread drizzled in warm olive oil – followed by *datiles con beicon* – dates stuffed with almonds and wrapped in crispy bacon. The main course of *salmonete et aubergines*– red mullet and aubergines – was washed down with a full bodied fine red Rioja wine, all personally selected by Pepe.

The warm welcome, good food and fine red wine combined perfectly to entice Julianne and Kira Mae to relax. They stretched out their long legs, sat back in red velvet padded black wood chairs and sipped strong espresso coffee and liqueurs.

Pepe had insisted on pouring for Kira Mae a creamy chocolate-based liqueur and Julianne sipped the local Spanish orange-based liqueur. Almost empty when they had arrived, many Spaniards do not eat before 10 p.m., the bar had now taken on a lively though not too busy atmosphere. Many of the customers appeared to be locals, stopping by for their nightly drink and tapas. Pepe had lined the small dishes up on the bar, bite-sized appetisers of his most preferred main dishes. Simple fare of plump spiced olives, toasted almonds and tiny prawns in their shells were supplemented by a cooked tapas feast that included croquettes of cheese and ham, goujons of crisply fried fish, meatballs in tomato sauce, roasted peppers and salads from the simple to the exotic. Julianne and Kira Mae commented to each other – but not in the hearing of Pepe – that they would have been as satisfied to dine on the tapas dishes as a full three-course meal.

Flushed with the wine, satiated with the nourishing food and reluctant to leave the restaurant, the two visitors turned their full attention to the entertainers. Equipment set up and tested, the strolling minstrels had disappeared only now to reappear in colourful flamenco costumes. Sporting a tight black bolero, black trousers and a red shirt, the male of the species was at least as finely feathered as the lady in a scarlet and black flounced dress with a short black mantilla veil.

With a rhythmic stomp of her black shiny high heels and a sweeping flourish of her arms, the haughty female dancer stamped to signal that the performance was about to start. With a dramatic answering chord the gypsy guitarist demanded attention as he powerfully played into life the traditional music, dance and poetry that fused to tell the forlorn tale of a gypsy love affair. The green wind, the green branches, the boat on the sea, the house on the mountain, a song of longing, bitterness, danger and regret. A story told with passion, strength and daring.

Pepe responded to the fire coursing through his own gypsy veins and added his own accompaniment, cheering, stamping and clapping. Bending low to whisper in Julianne's ear, the pungent smell of garlic hot on his breath, he shouted the title of the song 'Broken Love'.

'Broken Love brings only pain,' he translated the words for them. 'They are singing the story of a gypsy curse when the woman is betrayed by her lover and she vows to bring pain to anyone he dares to love ever after.

'Romero, the gypsy, all the women fall in love with him,' Pepe explained with a deep belly laugh, during a lull in the music when the entertainers next disappeared to take a rest break – and soothe their raging emotions.

Undeniably, Romero was more handsome than any man had a right to be. He resembled the silent movie star, Valentino. His chiselled features were aggressively, undoubtedly masculine but softened by the smoothness of his skin, the almond shaped eyes and sculpted jet black eyebrows. Tall and muscular, he walked with the arrogant swagger of a bullfighter. Black curly hair untamed and uncut, falling just below the collar of his shirt. Coal black unreadable eyes with long lashes were enhanced with just enough mascara to be acceptable on a man and framed in kohl eyeliner. He had a cruel mouth with full lips that rationed smiles, but made the smile, when it came, all the more devastating. A red ruby earring flashed like a warning light in his left ear.

Pepe played a game of cat and mouse with Julianne and Kira Mae, as they feigned disinterest and pretended not to have noticed the brazen flamenco player. Certainly Romero had given no indication of having noticed them. On several occasions he had strode past their table looking deliberately ahead and not even acknowledging their enthusiastic applause for the playing and dancing of him and his partner.

Surely he was not expected to acknowledge every attractive patron who craved to attract his attention. Modest he was not. But his singing, and sometime loving partner, Passionista had noticed the subtle signs that betrayed his interest and she would not stand idly by and allow herself to be made a fool of yet again with some passing holiday romantic.

Passionista had picked up the two beautiful British blondes on her finely tuned 'babe alert' radar, from the first moment they walked into the restaurant. Julianne and Kira Mae always made an impact on entry. Tonight they were especially show stopping. Dressed in a simple, white shift dress that showed off her traffic-stopping figure with full breasts, curvy hips and a narrow waist, Kira Mae boasted the same measurements as Marilyn Monroe 37-25-37. She wore her long, golden blonde hair loose and it shone with good health and constant grooming. Her glowing skin had been toasted a light shade of coffee by the St. Tropez tan she had salon sprayed before leaving London.

Mother and daughter had been on the VIP guest list for a spa day, a top to toe beauty day at the Red Carpet, a luxurious de Angeles spa in the five star Park Lane Hotel. A sanctuary of peace and calm in the heart of London's West End, Maria de Angeles competed ferociously to make her spa, and the original green tea and ginseng products, the most exclusive in the capital. Kira Mae did not consider herself high maintenance but she certainly enjoyed accompanying her mother on her 'working trips'. Julianne had for so long been employed to check out competitors and evaluate standards of all de Angeles products and services, that she considered herself a connoisseur of fine beauty treatments.

Accessorising her heat-reflecting white outfit, Kira Mae wore bold gold jewellery – so large and eye catching it could be mistaken for costume jewellery – though it was all the real deal, made of hallmarked 18-carat gold and borrowed from mum. Julianne told herself that although she had heard that women shouldn't have to buy their own jewellery, she did and took pride in the fact that she was answerable to no man. Completing the outfit, dangling from her ears, Kira Mae wore leopard striped chandelier earrings. A gift from her designer friend from St. Martin's who was already making a name for himself and had been set up by a patron in a trendy jewellery shop in Chelsea. Tonight the difference between mother and daughter was particularly pronounced. In contrast to Kira Mae's white ensemble, Julianne wore seductive black – a fitted Chanel shift with silver jewellery and silver strappy Jimmy Choo mules.

Reflecting each other, they looked like night and day. Opposite mirror images. The sun and the moon. The purity of youth and the mystery of maturity. The evening was magical and as they thanked Pepe and took their leave, they promised they would return.

'A place in my heart is already reserved for you both – and the best table in the house,' he charmed them, as he kissed their hands and bade them goodnight.

Yet with the best intentions in the world, time passed and soon they had been at the villa for over a month without returning to the restaurant.

chapter fifteen

'Leave her to heaven,
And to those thorns that in her bosom lodge,
To prick and sting her.'
Shakepeare's *Hamlet*

A sacred time of healing was top of the agenda. They had an unspoken agreement not to mention the trauma of what had taken place in London, yet sadly that did not stop Julianne suffering after effects.

Fortunately Julianne knew where she could get the help and support she needed. Though she had not actively participated for many years, Julianne knew she would be understood and listened to at the rape crisis centre. She made a phone call and was again connected to understanding women who knew exactly what she was going through.

'I am not a victim, I am a survivor,' she affirmed. Finding herself again on the emotional roller coaster of terror to shame and from rage to misery she promised herself that she would again recover and reclaim her dignity and strength and power. 'Recovery is a lifetime process,' she remembered.

Already she was using the tools and techniques she had learned all those years ago when she first crawled through their doors, broken and defeated by her traumas and was loved back to health by a community of brave and committed survivors.

Julianne made the phone call and reached out for help. Waking from nightmares in the early hours of the morning, Julianne would be drenched in sweat, paralysed with fear. During the day, without warning, she would be overcome with anxiety and on the verge of tears. No longer suffering alone and receiving the support she needed, she was able to hide much of her distress from Kira Mae who did not appear much different from her usual moody, difficult teenage self. However, Julianne was not fooled by her daughter's show of bravado and she knew she was also hurting.

Every evening at 6 p.m., Julianne insisted on a 'healing hour' reminiscent of the time she had shared with her own mother all those years ago. Out by the pool they lit scented candles, played inspirational music and meditated. Both were grateful for a much-needed period of rest and recuperation and neither was in a hurry to be tempted away from the comfort zone of the pool by day and home cooked food at night.

To keep up to date with events back in England, Julianne listened to the Radio 4 news broadcasts. One in particular caught her attention. 'An extensive investigation has opened into the suspected abuse of boys at a public school in Cambridgeshire. Detectives are following up accusations that back in the 1960s a paedophile ring operated at the exclusive school.'

As they repeated the name of the school, Julianne sat transfixed. In the 1960s, before marrying her mother and moving to Devon, her father had taught at that school. In a flash of clarity, she had a shocking and sudden understanding;

her father was a member of that paedophile ring. A leopard did not change his spots. A man who would abuse his own daughter after his wife died of cancer was without doubt a manipulative sexual predator.

Finally, she had a way to expose her father's crimes to the authorities and hopefully make him pay. Anonymously from the safety of her home in Spain, Julianne called the police headquarters in Cambridge and asked to be put through to the detective unit dealing with the public school paedophile investigation. Evidence was still being collected and the police were interested in receiving names and details of members of staff who might become persons of interest in their investigations. The female detective she spoke to assured Julianne that at this stage, especially with crimes that had been committed many years before, all information was welcome as it helped the police to fit together the pieces of the jigsaw puzzle.

Admitting that she had no direct evidence of his involvement at Cambridge, Julianne responded to the question of why she would suspect her own father, by admitting, 'Because he is a child molester. After my mother died, he sexually abused me from the age of thirteen and made me pregnant at sixteen.'

Declining to leave a contact number, Julianne at least felt vindicated that she had put her father's name in the frame – though she did not wish to be there when the detectives knocked on the door. She prayed that the long arm of the law would finally catch up with him and force him to pay for his crimes against her – and maybe many more children. She would follow developments on the news bulletins.

A deep sense of justice settled down on Julianne, she had

at last reported her father's abuse to the police – and she prayed he would go to jail for his crimes. Whatever the outcome, Julianne knew that with that one act of revelation, she had won her own redemption. The bitterness was washed from her heart and hatred was forgotten. For the first time in her life, Julianne felt completely at peace. The chains fell from her mind and soul – she was free to love and be loved.

★ ★ ★

Since their arrival at the villa, Maria had taken care of mother and daughter's every need. She had given them a tour of the local market and showed them where to buy the best fresh fruit, salads, vegetables and locally caught fish: tuna, salmon, sardines and shellfish, crabs, calamari, octopus, scallops and prawns.

Julianne was not surprised to learn that Spain consumed more fish and shellfish than any other European country. They also bought the locally produced *buey* (beef), *cordero* (lamb), *pollo* (chicken) and *pavo* (turkey).

Each evening Maria conscientiously prepared food for the two English guests. Annabelle had instructed her to look after them and make sure that her special friend and her daughter felt at home. It was Maria who had reminded them of their promise to Annabelle to patronise Pepe's restaurant.

'Tonight would be the perfect time,' Maria assured them. 'Tonight you can hear one of the best flamenco guitarists in the area and see traditional flamenco dancing.'

Julianne and Kira Mae smiled at each other, they needed no second urging to revisit the restaurant and although neither said a word, they were already thinking of the sultry Spanish guitarist.

Pepe greeted them like long-lost friends and welcomed them to his establishment. Tonight Pepe's wife was smiling; she looked a picture of good living, good eating and good loving encircled as she was by her three small children and two tail-wagging dogs. A picture of domestic bliss, they enveloped their customers and welcomed them to the restaurant as if inviting them into their private home.

'You are my guests,' Pepe assured them. 'You shall have anything you want. I will make this night memorable for you.'

The food was superb, Pepe again insisted on choosing for them and he was determined that they would sample all the delights the menu had to offer. For appetisers they had grilled sardines followed by several of the bite-sized tapas dishes and he insisted on sabotaging their diets by flamboyantly presenting a flambéed cream dessert, a speciality of the house – a confection of rich to-die-for pastry with cream and fruit and meringue. They drank sweet white dessert wine and completed the meal with the chocolate liqueur for Kira Mae and a flaming sambuca for Juliana.

Ensconced at their favourite front of house table, savouring their liqueurs, Julianne and Kira Mae were enthused by the warm glow of superb dining, first class wine, pleasant company and the best was yet to come – the evening's entertainment was about to begin.

An electrifying buzz of anticipation swept through the restaurant and it was as if a spark from a flame had ignited the atmosphere of the small, dark wooden bar with its shiny brass and original paintings of an idealised medieval Spain. Julianne and Kira Mae exchanged excited, anticipatory smiles as the lights dimmed and a single spotlight focused on the evening's star turn. Romero sat on a high stool, still, silent, his guitar cradled lovingly in his arms as if it were a woman. He stroked the neck and fingered the strings – building the tension. The white light illuminated his perfect features – exotic, mysterious, challenging. Breathtakingly handsome. Dressed all in black he wore his matador jacket, black tight trousers, and boots of black leather with studded heels.

Suddenly he struck one long, anguished chord and hit the body of the guitar with his hand. His dark eyes flashed and demanded the attention of everyone in the room. His eyes were fixed on a distant point, thousands of years in the past, transfixed by the sights and sounds of the sacred call of the flamenco.

Highly charged emotional tales of love, betrayal, loss and pain poured forth – his voice was strong and angry in one moment, softly, hauntingly seductive the next. Julianne and Kira Mae were mesmerised. They revelled in his every move, his every gesture; they devoured him with their eyes. All the time refusing to look at each other for fear their eyes would betray their longing. For fear the spell would be broken.

Striking without mercy into the depth of their being, each heard the words in their hearts – deep in their soul. Julianne experienced all the pain of her past released and honoured, Kira Mae heard the call of the future, of unending love and destiny. Never before had either experienced this depth of delicious, dangerous passion. Romero seduced them with his music, with his presence, with his complete disregard for their discomfiture, with disdain for the physical longing he provoked. He knew only too well that he could reduce any woman to a state of helplessness with his ungodly siren call. The ancient spell he weaved and manipulated was as powerful as any drug. He had perfected his own brand of wizardry, looking straight into their souls with a knowing gaze, and that slow, seductive smile tantalisingly close to the surface. Promising – not yet delivering. Resistance was impossible. And for what, why would any woman deny herself this chance to be adored, devoured, and owned?

Julianne and Kira Mae had already received more than they had dared to hope for, how were they to know that they had just been seduced by a master? Targeted and played as expertly as if he were playing his instrument. A virtuoso in the art of seduction. A heartless predator. Neither dared acknowledge to the other that they had fallen. Neither wanted to share the sublime experience. It was a secret to savour and treasure and take out and polish like a jewel when they were alone. The secret tryst between eyes and minds and souls was brought to a sudden end by the intervention of another female.

Materialising in the room with a clash of castanets, a flash of frilled fan and the arrogant swirling of layers of black net petticoats and flouncing flame floor-length skirts, Romero's partner, Passionista made her dramatic entrance. Accompanying the centuries' old music in a commanding but plaintive voice, she wailed and cajoled, all the time standing with head held high declaring her stoicism, whilst maintaining her stature and dignity as she sang of loves lost and battles fought. Ancient songs told of the history, the pain and the beauty of the Spanish land.

Romero's playing wove through the tapestry of tales and triumphed in musical duels where love and enemies were confronted, challenged, and conquered. Through music and song and inspired by the spellbound audience, the duo dared to embrace a challenging roller-coaster of emotion, fervour and passion, shrieking to a crescendo as they sang of love but were defeated by the inevitability of death that would part them forever.

Julianne and Kira Mae were transfixed. Hardly daring to breathe, living in their mind's eye the triumphs and tears of love invoked by the handsome gypsy boy who, did they but know it, had already stolen their hearts. Silently, stealthily, with a practised touch, he had parted them from their most precious possessions.

Leaving the stage to roars of enthusiastic and heartfelt applause from the wildly appreciative audience, Romero paused. Plucking a blood red rose from the centrepiece on the table to the side of the stage, Romero walked towards Julianne and Kira Mae seated at their ringside table. With a knowing half smile, he placed the fiery rose on the table – between them. Then he turned and walked purposefully away.

A question left hanging in the air – unasked.

Dear Pepe, ever the watchful proprietor, acted swiftly to avert embarrassment. Rushing forward with a second rose he thanked the ladies for coming and with entreaties for them to, 'come again soon,' waved them off into the night.

In the night-time mountain air, there was a sharp chill and tiny silver slivers of a new moon shone brightly and hopefully in the night sky. And the question hung tantalisingly in the air.

To whom did Romero give his rose?

Before the question was answered, a trio of hearts would be broken.

chapter sixteen

'Whoever loved that loved not at first sight?'
Shakespeare's *As You Like It*

Sitting on the sun-filled terrace the next morning, enjoying a light breakfast of freshly squeezed orange juice and tree ripened figs, Julianne reached out her hand to pick a flower from the beautiful white hibiscus growing so profusely along the hand-made trellis. She contemplated its fate. Blooms whether single or double, lived for just one day – then to be replaced by new flowers. Impulsively she made a decision.

'It's time to put Mummy Mitchell's money to good use,' she declared. 'Also my housemate made a substantial offer to buy me out of my apartment – we're in a really strong market, properties on the river are selling at vastly inflated prices now. It's not safe for us to go back to London; I think we should stay here and buy our own villa.'

The possibility that she had been exploring previously now assumed urgency. Inspired and enthusiastic, with no thought of the consequences, mother and daughter began to consider the options for them settling permanently in the Mediterranean paradise.

Both loved the relaxed lifestyle and the new culture they

had begun to discover. The sights and sounds and smells of Spain had worked their magic on this pair who so loved colour and drama and tradition.

Now they embraced the opportunity for this entrancing country to become their home. Julianne had already made enquiries about the feasibility and legal ramifications of opening a small boutique that would cater primarily to the discerning female residents and tourists who desired exclusive and original designer clothes. A life completely devoid of work and responsibility was not her intention. Instead, Julianne dreamed of nurturing her young daughter's artistic talent and encouraging her to produce her own elite designs to an exclusive clientele of international fashionistas.

Julianne would run the business and administrative side of the company, allowing Kira Mae to concentrate on developing her fledgling fashion flair and creativity. Circumstances had forced the abandonment of her degree course at the St. Martin's College of Art and Design, but already Julianne had tracked down information about an exciting course at the Centre of Design Studies in Malaga. Over seven semesters the foundation course combined fashion design with photography and the learning of Spanish. Perhaps they would apply for Kira Mae to complete her studies. In the meantime, the dream was to find a property where they could combine a retail space, workshop and living accommodation.

'I'll go into town today to check out the real estate agent and also call on the lawyer to ensure that the necessary legal procedures are put in place.'

Julianne was quick to read the look of reluctance that crossed Kira Mae's features. Reacting quickly to the situation, she said, 'Don't worry, you don't need to come. If and when I find something of interest, we'll go and see it together. In the meantime, you don't need to bother your pretty little head with business negotiations.'

Kira Mae rewarded her mother with a grateful smile. 'You're the businesswoman,' she told her. 'I trust your judgement. I'll go along with anything that means we can go on living here.'

Julianne was joyful. 'It will be wonderful. The sooner we can get set up in our own property the better. Annabelle has been very generous but if we are to relocate here, we need our own home.'

After she had waved off Julianne, Kira Mae settled down for a day by the pool. Purposefully she gathered a large stack of fashion magazines, *Vogue, Harpers and Queens* and *Vanity Fair,* as well as their European counterparts, *International Vogue, Top Sante* and *Spanish Elle.*

Within easy reach, on a small white wrought iron table strategically positioned alongside her blue striped sun-lounger, Kira Mae availed herself of all the essentials she would need for a day of indulgence. Carefully applying sun tan lotion, factor 15, to her body and putting moisturiser on her face and neck, she applied a conditioner to her hair and wrapped it in a towelling turban. Kira Mae wore a teeny string bikini in a startling shade of neon blue. She shielded her eyes from the bright sunlight with a pair of Dior white sunglasses and on her head an outsize floppy brimmed straw hat covered the turban. On the table by her side, the silver ice bucket was filled with several small bottles of sparkling mineral water and beside that a couple of brightly coloured picnic glasses. Confident that she would not need to move for hours, she turned her attention to the reading matter she had gathered for research purposes. Fashion magazines were the source material to be used for inspiration, and close to hand a large sketch pad and a set of coloured markers waited. Expecting brilliant creative designs to manifest themselves, she wanted to be prepared. In this land of unashamed sunshine and cloudless indigo blue skies with the renowned Mediterranean luminosity casting a picture postcard effect over the surroundings, the desire to capture the beauty of the landscape in painting, drawing and design was always at the forefront of her mind.

'A perfect day for some *me* time,' she said aloud, though she knew there was no one to hear.

In the sizzling noonday sun she languidly drifted off to sleep. Then there came a rude awakening.

Someone was knocking loudly on the front door. Someone was demanding entry and who that person could be, Kira Mae could not begin to imagine. Maria the maid never knocked and no one else came visiting. Kira Mae was reluctant to make her way through the house and find out who was at the villa door. She considered ignoring it and hoping they would go away, but that did not seem like a reasonable choice.

Dark thoughts filled her mind. What if her mother had had an accident? What if Maria had sent an important message? Could Annabelle be making an unscheduled visit? The terrifying thought came to her in that moment – maybe their father had found them.

Kira Mae conceded reluctantly that she needed to answer the door. She wished her mum was here to tell her what to do. Grabbing a sarong to cover her too revealing bikini and slipping her feet into a pair of jewelled flip flops, she headed for the front door.

'Who is it?' she called through the closed door. There was

a small rusty security chain that obviously was never used, but she now forced it into place.

She opened the door a few inches and peered out cautiously.

It took her several eye adjustments, first from the bright sunlight of the pool area to the shuttered cool darkness of the inside of the house and back to the sunlight that was visible through the partially open front door. Silhouetted in the doorframe she saw, to her amazement, that the unexpected visitor was none other than Romero.

He made no apology or explanation for calling uninvited on foreign visitors, to whom he had not even been introduced. Instead, he smiled, a devastating smile, slow, sensual and full of confidence.

'Can I come in?' he asked.

Kira Mae could not have refused if her life depended on it. Her mouth was dry and her head was a swirling mass of confusion.

She nodded, almost imperceptibly, indicated for him to wait as she closed the door, removed the sticking security chain and held the door open wide.

'We are neighbours,' he finally offered by way of explanation, as he stepped into the cool, still house. 'I need to ask you something very important.'

Kira Mae waited for the question and was not surprised when Romero asked, 'May I kiss you?'

Not knowing whether to laugh or slap his face, Kira Mae did neither instead she stood perfectly still, hardly daring to breathe. I must be dreaming, she thought to herself, this cannot be happening.

As she struggled to compose herself, Romero acted.

Without warning, he stepped forward into her personal space and, putting his hand in the small of her back, he tenderly pulled her into his body and pressed his lips on hers.

As suddenly as he had started to kiss her, he stopped.

'I am overcome with desire for you,' he told her in a quiet serious voice, his heavily accented delivery giving the words gravitas. The expression in his eyes was direct and sincere. He made his declaration almost sadly, as if expecting at any moment to be denied.

'You have captured my heart,' he said with a shrug, as if it was somehow inevitable. 'Forgive me, I do not mean to disrespect you, I know you are a fine young English lady.'

Out of control, as if watching herself in a slow motion film, her perception was that everything was out of focus.

Romero's presence, his smile, the passion of his kiss had caught her completely unawares. In a dreamlike state she murmured to herself, 'Please don't let the scene end.'

Common sense prevailed but it still took a monumental effort of will not to throw herself back into his arms and replay the first passionate embrace. Her lips were already longing to be locked back onto his lips, to be pressed once more against his lovely firm mouth. Her body longed to be held captive in his manly embrace.

To prevent a repeat of the kiss and regain her decorum, Kira Mae turned her back on the object of her desire and walked back through the house towards the open patio doors leading to the pool.

Whatever am I thinking, she admonished herself. I don't know him. I don't know anything about him. This is madness. It's dangerous even for him to be here in the house with me. I need to think of something. I need to get him out of here.

Finely tuned through his basic animal instincts, as if reading her thoughts, Romero became contrite and apologetic. 'Senorita,' he said formally, 'I will embarrass you no more. I was simply overcome by the sight of your beauty. Do not blame me for that, I am merely a man.'

Taking a deep breath, as if to steady himself and draw a line under the incident, Romero continued.

'Please allow me to explain the true nature of my visit today.'

Kira Mae was fascinated. His English was perfect but somehow stylised, spoken like someone who had learned the language from watching old Hollywood movies. Was this guy for real? she wondered.

The boys she had known previously at school and university were much more casual in their approach to romance. Even complimenting a girl was considered uncool, old-fashioned. In this new world order, women demanded equality. For this, they were prepared to sacrifice the quaint romantic notions of wooing and courtship.

'I promise to control myself,' said Romero, faintly mocking himself. Now he was standing by the side of the pool. 'You wish to know the real reason for my visit.' It was a statement – not a question.

'Pepe sent me. He asks that you two ladies be his guests tonight at the restaurant. It is a fiesta, the *Nit de Sant Joan,* one of our patron saints.

'The whole village will turn out to celebrate and he did not wish to be rude and overlook the new guests in our midst. Ten o'clock at the restaurant for a celebration dinner and then there will be a procession to the beach.'

Maria had told them earlier that day about the feast day –

a midsummer feast close to Kira Mae's own birthday – and she had explained that there would be fireworks and a bonfire on the beach, where papier-mâché statues of well-known people – politicians, film stars and local celebrities – would be burned. All in honour of Saint Joan – whose statue would be paraded through the town on a flower-strewn carriage.

'The children especially love it,' Maria had said. 'And when the firemen come to put out the blaze – they turn the hoses on the children. Some of the townsfolk also go down to the beach and on the stroke of midnight they rush into the water.'

Romero did not take the time to go into further detail when Kira Mae admitted she did have some knowledge of the fiesta.

'Fiestas – we have many in Spain,' he shrugged. Abruptly, having delivered his message, Romero seemed to remember a previous engagement and without delay he turned and made his way back to leave the way he had come in.

Not wishing to be shown out, he was gone as suddenly as he had appeared. Kira Mae was dazed and elated by what had happened. She hugged the memory of his embrace close to her. If it was true that he thought of her, she certainly had been consumed with thoughts of him since his spectacular performance at the restaurant the night before. She thought it was fate, destiny, love.

To cool off and give herself thinking time, leaving her hat and sarong on the poolside, she dived into the inviting water of the pool. Yet no amount of ice-cold water could extinguish the fire raging in her heart and mind.

As Kira Mae emerged from the pool, she heard her mother's car pull up outside. Already Kira Mae knew that the story she would tell her mother of this afternoon's steamy encounter, would be heavily edited. She buried deep inside herself the overwhelming joy of her unexpected interlude. Evening time could not come quickly enough for her.

Dodging past her mother in the hallway, still damp from the pool, Kira Mae delivered the invitation in as casual a tone as she could muster.

'Pepe wants us to go for dinner at the restaurant tonight. He sent a neighbour with the message; it's a fiesta or festival or something.'

With that she excused herself to go upstairs and take a shower and a siesta. Halfway up the stairs she stopped and called to her mother, 'We can talk about what you have been up to at dinner.' And, as an afterthought, she added, 'Unless of course you are too tired to go out this evening. I could go by myself. It's only down the road. I think Maria will be there. It's religious, I think. A saint's day. You might not want to go.'

Walking slowly into the main living area and kicking off her shoes on the smooth tiled floor, Julianne answered cheerfully, 'I'm not tired at all. I wouldn't miss out on the feast day celebrations for the world.'

Julianne smiled to herself. Her beloved daughter, the two shared so many similarities but also many differences. She tried to remember back to how she had been at that age. She was already pregnant with a child conceived in inhumane circumstances. Her teenage years were filled with anguish, abuse and isolation. If she had a regret it was that she wished she could have protected Kira Mae from the knowledge of her hateful family secret.

We are doing our best, Julianne assured herself. Get over it. Move on.

Whatever the circumstances, she knew that she loved her

daughter unconditionally and her daughter loved her. Even though the two displayed such different personality traits, different values, different fears and insecurities, while looking like two peas in a pod. Julianne had already made her promise to Romero that she would be at the restaurant to celebrate the *Nit de Sant Joan*.

She hugged the secret to herself.

★ ★ ★

Driving to the town of Alicante, just twenty minutes from the international airport and some half an hour away from the bustling resort of Benidorm earlier in the day, down the steep, curved road through the olive groves, Julianne had been filled with anticipation and excitement.

Meeting up with the local estate agent and viewing properties would confirm the decision she had taken straight after the traumatic experience with her father back in London. It was obviously not safe for her to live in London. At any time of the day or night he could appear without warning and visit his rage upon Julianne and her daughter. Julianne had been determined to leave the past behind her, now, driving in the warm spring Mediterranean sunshine, the dreadful events that had led to her need to move countries seemed like a bad film she had seen in another lifetime.

Instead of all the negative aspects of her situation, Julianne was happy to concentrate on the positive. Driving into the city centre beach town, that despite attracting many overseas tourists managed to retain a traditional Spanish charm, and slowing down to check her bearings, Julianne admitted to herself that she had indeed fallen in love – with Spain.

Alicante's beach promenade overlooked the sparkling waters of the Med in the centre of the town. Crammed between its red, cream and blue tiled walkway and the wide palm tree lined boulevards, were a maze of tiny streets, teeming with tapas bars, restaurants and traditional shops.

Art and culture were revered in Alicante and the Museo Arqueologico offered a superb collection of Iberian art and artefacts. Museo de la Asegurada displayed works of art by Picasso, Dali and Miro. The sixteenth century Castillo de Santa Barbara, which was at the highest point in the city, offered not only panoramic views of the city but a world renowned contemporary Spanish sculpture collection – and a lift down to the beach.

Delightfully juxtaposed in this noble centre of culture and art and religious icons, on market days there were often more donkeys and carts than cars in the charming town square. Towering palm trees shaded the square, still a centre of community life, and in the early evening filled with promenading families, and in this picture perfect people-watching setting between the beach and the port were cafés, restaurants and an outdoor entertainment area. Traditional and modern co-existed side by side and old men still played pétanque and old women still made lace – while each talked about the other.

Knowing that the real estate agent's office was close to the town square, after parking her car, Julianne consulted her map and directions.

'Perhaps I can be of assistance,' said a voice from behind, startled, she turned quickly and found herself staring into a familiar pair of deep velvet brown eyes that had already hypnotised her and burned their way into her consciousness.

The strong, sensual smell of Romero invading her personal space had forced Julianne to step back a couple of paces and regain her equilibrium.

'Why, hello,' she said, a little too enthusiastically. However still feeling puzzled and caught strangely off guard, she quickly decided to take full advantage of the situation. Inside her head a phrase repeated itself – *carpe diem*: seize the day.

Well, today was the start of a whole new chapter in her life, so she chose to be reckless about grabbing this unexpected appointment with destiny.

'What a lovely surprise. I didn't expect to see you here.' Then more boldly, because she had been secretly hoping that after the incident with the rose, there might be a follow up, 'Thank you for the offer of help, I certainly could do with some. I don't speak Spanish so I'm having trouble navigating my way around the street names.'

This was a lie. Julianne was perfectly capable of finding her way in this or any other small town. She'd had plenty of experience doing reconnaissance for photographic shoots in her fashion career. However, she was not about to miss the opportunity of being escorted to her estate agent's office by this most gorgeous of male creatures. When the occasion demanded, Julianne could play the role of damsel in distress as well as any female – and besides she craved some tender loving care – someone to look after her – albeit for just a passing moment of courtesy.

Romero stood smiling broadly at her and waited for her to show the piece of paper on which she had written the address where she was expected for a mid-morning appointment.

She passed the small piece of paper torn from a notebook

to him and almost jumped back at the force of the electric charge which seemed to pass between them when their hands touched.

Romero did not act overtly, but his eyes held the same amused almost mocking gaze that she had already begun to fall in love with.

'Come,' he said, 'follow me,' and leaving Julianne standing in the road, he headed off walking at a brisk pace.

Julianne tried to keep up, but was handicapped by the high heeled shoes she wore, her best Manolo Blahniks in a subtle shade of gun metal grey with a small diamante brooch directing attention to her foot cleavage. She was further restricted by the straight figure-hugging skirt in black and white checks and a wide black patent belt. Having observed that despite the heat, business people still wore formal dress, Julianne had chosen her outfit to reflect that she meant business. To offset the monochrome effect of the skirt, Julianne was wearing a pale apricot tailored jacket, unbuttoned to just the point where the slightest hint of *décolletage* was visible.

Romero by contrast was casually dressed in plain black trousers with a simple, elegant round necked black sweater. On his wrist, he wore an expensive Rolex watch and around his neck a gold chain with a diamond clasp. On his feet he wore tan moccasins. Effortlessly elegant, his whole demeanour was one of confidence, self-assurance and an unmistakable animal magnetism. He moved gracefully, at ease with his body and surroundings. Even in this country of good looking, dark haired, golden skinned, handsome men, Romero still attracted attention.

Anxious not to appear too eager, Julianne tried to speed up

her movements to keep up with him. Politely Romero noticed her discomfiture and offered his hand to guide her.

As if it were the most natural thing in the world, they walked hand in hand, barely saying a word. Julianne walked on air and silently made a wish that the meeting place for her appointment would not be too close by.

Cupid had certainly shot an arrow into her heart as this was the first time she could ever recall having felt this devastating form of spontaneous attraction to a man. Womanly feelings surged through her body and hitherto denied sexual stirrings forced themselves into her consciousness. The glorious realisation came to her – I have the right to love and be loved.

Romero knew every street, avenue and alley of the town. Deeper and deeper into the interior of the town they walked. In contrast to the wide boulevards, the residential streets were narrow and brightly painted with flower covered buildings claustrophobically close together. Above her head Julianne marvelled at the profusion of colourful foliage spilling from the windows and balconies and competing with the brightly painted shutters and doorways. Carnations, almost a national flower, were much in evidence as were terracotta pots of geraniums in every shade from spotless white through to palest pink to brightest red.

Walking close together along the narrow pavements past entryways protected from casual passers-by with ironwork gates, Romero and Julianne were joined hand in hand.

Just when Julianne was beginning to wonder if he really did know where he was headed, Romero tugged on her hand and urged her to follow him inside one of the iron gates. Beside the gate a small brass plaque gave the name of the real estate lawyer that Julianne had made an appointment to meet. It read: Sanchez Valdez, attorney at law, real estate, business and residential.

Climbing a couple of steps and reaching a small platform, Romero stopped suddenly, pulled Julianne into his arms and kissed her passionately. Julianne did not resist. In truth, she would have been disappointed had he not reacted to the undeniable sexual chemistry that was almost visible between them.

Breathless and devouring each other, they stayed locked in this amorous embrace for what seemed like an eternity, springing apart only when a doorway opened further up the stairway and, fearing discovery, reluctantly prising themselves apart. They exchanged a conspiratorial smile and both knew that there was to be an inevitable next stage to this highly charged emotional interlude.

Like a will o' the wisp, as suddenly as he had appeared in the town square, Romero disappeared. He motioned for Julianne to go up one more flight of steps and there she would find the offices of Señor Valdez.

Sanchez Valdez was middle aged, smartly dressed and business like. He welcomed Julianne warmly and formally, asking with genuine concern if she had had any difficulty in finding his offices.

Shaking her head, Julianne smiled and said, 'No thank you. I had no problem.'

The formality of the meeting in his cosy, unconventional office did not last long. Sanchez left his place behind a large highly polished desk covered in papers; some piled a perilous foot high and threatening to topple over at any moment, to sit comfortably beside Julianne on the office's chocolate brown leather settee.

On instruction from her solicitor in London, papers had already been prepared for Julianne to sign, legal requirements before a foreign national could buy property in Spain. Julianne signed and Sanchez countersigned, explaining that she was now validated to be shown property with a view to buying.

Owing to other business commitments, Señor Valdez apologised, he would not be available to accompany Julianne to the properties that had been preselected according to her instructions. However, he had arranged for a colleague to escort her. Passing over a sheaf of papers with photographs and details of potential properties, Sanchez told Julianne that his colleague would meet her downstairs and show her to his car, in which they would drive to the inspections.

Downstairs Romero awaited her.

'Your chauffeur awaits,' he told her with a mischievous grin. 'I am to be your guide today.'

Julianne's surprise at this sudden turn of events was more than offset by the wonderful prospect of spending a day in his company. She made a note to ask him later how this happy state of affairs had come to pass.

Romero was certainly a man of mystery and she presumed he had business connections in the town. Exactly why and how he came to be escorting Julianne as she looked for a house in the sun, she did not intend to spoil her day by trying to puzzle out.

In a gentlemanly fashion, Romero suggested that he drive and she leave her car in town. Julianne gladly accepted. The good offices of Señor Sanchez Valdez had arranged three properties for Julianne, their prosperous British client, to view.

Just twenty miles from the town, the first property was a small farmhouse with an attached shop, previously used to sell farm produce.

Number two was an altogether more glamorous white painted villa style property, which had on the ground floor a self-contained suite with a floor to ceiling window overlooking the small village street and a delightful courtyard entrance. The oversized window, unusual in a country that, as a matter of principle, sought to close and bar their buildings against the rays of the sun, would provide a perfect showcase to display Kira Mae's designs and the small living room could serve as fitting area and workshop. Upstairs the newly decorated and modern, furnished accommodation was surprisingly spacious. Three bedrooms and a shower room with a small kitchenette. Julianne decided that she would definitely bring Kira Mae to check out this property, it had distinct possibilities. On the business front, the fact that so many fashionable Madrid visitors made the town their summer home gave her confidence that those smart dressers would make appreciative patrons for her proposed designer boutique.

Before they went on to view the third property, Romero suggested lunch. During the course of their delicious meal in a small family run pavement café, Romero flirted outrageously with Julianne. Seductive behaviour and loving gestures, more than anything he said, left her in no doubt that he wanted to pursue a relationship with her. Attention from this highly desirable male was exhilarating and a warm glow had spread over Julianne. She felt alive and excited and aroused with sexual expectancy for the first time.

Relationships had always been problematic and Julianne had never even had a proper boyfriend. Fearing that she was sexually broken, forever unfixable, Julianne had reconciled herself to a life devoid of physical relations. Judging herself unable to form a union that would not leave her feeling violated and shamed, she had taken a vow to avoid relationships that might raise the expectation of sex. Until now, when her whole body screamed out with longing for his touch.

Romero had inflamed a place deep in her soul; she felt that he already knew her pain. Now she felt ready to be released, she craved salvation and a profound desire to know love, carnal love and a need to share herself completely with another human being. Casting caution to the wind, Julianne granted herself permission to feel wanted, indulged and flattered.

By the time they had finished lunch, Julianne knew that she had crossed a line. She had answered 'Yes', even though she did not yet know the question.

Romero apologised for the fact that he could not stay and view the third property of the day with Julianne. Marking the paper supplied by the estate agent, he had given her explicit directions and confirmed that she knew which road to take to drive to the aptly named Villajoyosa (Happy Town), home to the Valor Museum of Chocolate. On the way, he had allowed her to drive him back to town where she could pick up her own vehicle. They parted with a brief kiss and Julianne promised to meet him later that evening.

Head reeling with the smell and essence of him, she had driven to the third property, a small *casita* in the exquisitely pretty village. However, even the prospect of living and working in Happy Town, in one of the brightly painted houses that cascaded down to the shoreline, had failed to gain Julianne's enthusiasm, especially now that she had lost her guide.

Besides, she hadn't been convinced that the widows of the

town, encased in black, or the shorts-wearing European tourists – too many of them English for her liking – would make good customers for her brand of haute couture. It was time to call it a day and head back to the villa.

Arriving home, after an excitement filled day, Julianne was determined to conceal from Kira Mae the real reason for her new found exhilaration. Instead she would share the wonderful news that she thought she had found the perfect property for their joint business venture. Seemingly reluctant to engage in conversation, Kira Mae almost knocked over her mother as she rushed past her upstairs and indeed seemed actively to be avoiding her as they began to get ready for an evening out.

Lost in a world of her own, when Julianne tried to talk to her, Kira Mae asked only one question, 'Do we have to move from this area?'

chapter seventeen

'And since you know, you cannot see yourself. So well as by reflection.'
Shakespeare's *Julius Caesar*

Mother and daughter were already cocooned in their own secret world of intrigue, mystery and expectancy. Both took special care with their appearance, as they dressed to go to the restaurant and the festival celebration. One could be forgiven for thinking that they were competing, each one determined to outdo the other. Neither knew the other was on a date.

Julianne wore a tight fitting black and red silk dress, demure and high necked at the front, plunging at the back to reveal a tanned and firm body. She piled her golden blonde hair up high on her head and looked every inch the fashion model that she used to be. Kira Mae had chosen to wear a short puff ball dress with diamante straps and a matching diamante edged wrap. They drove in silence the short distance to the restaurant, each lost in their own thoughts. And dreams.

Romero's top of the range Italian sports car was already parked outside the restaurant. The top was down.

The warm summer breeze ruffled the dresses and hair of mother and daughter as they walked across the gravel car park towards the restaurant.

Graciously accepting a glass of complimentary champagne served by Pepe's wife on a silver platter, they entered the dining room. Decorated with flower garlands in honour of the Feast Day, the atmosphere promised a glamorous evening in the elegant restaurant. The air was filled with the perfume of summer, evening jasmine and the sound of crickets was complimented by the light wind rustling in the trees, as drinks were served on the tiled outdoor terrace beside a small water fountain.

Pepe was enjoying himself tonight, playing host to the town's dignitaries, all dressed in their finery and ostentatious ceremonial robes. He brought a succession of individuals to the table to meet Julianne and Kira Mae. Each one was introduced as his 'very, best most special friend'.

Breaking into their reverie once again, he gestured towards the beautiful young maiden at his side and said, 'Allow me to introduce a most special, special friend.'

With a flourish and what could be interpreted as a small bow he declared, 'The Festival Queen, La Reina. Señorita Michella de Jesus Santa Castellana.'

Michella treated them to a dazzling smile and dropped a small curtsey, holding up ever so slightly the skirt of her shimmering black lace off-the-shoulder ball gown. Her skin resembled porcelain, and her face was small boned and exquisitely beautiful. She looked like a real life version of one of the holy statues of the Blessed Virgin that on special feast days were paraded through the town. Her teeth were even and pearl like, against full bodied red lips that offset her glowing amber eyes. At her throat flashed a row of diamonds. Flicking back the mane of jet black hair, held in place with a small mantilla comb, she held out her hand in greeting.

Michella was drop dead gorgeous – and she knew it.

As she held out her hand, mother and daughter could not fail to be impressed by the large square cut solitaire diamond, sparking fire in the candlelight. She wore the ring on the third finger of her right hand, as was the custom for engagement rings in Spain. Julianne and Kira stood up to greet her.

'Michella is the future wife of our star musician, Romero,' said Pepe proudly. 'The pair are to be married here in the village later this month.'

Julianne gasped visibly as she heard the words and she took in the unfolding scenario. Kira Mae seemed to lose her balance and, as she swayed slightly, a couple of drops of champagne from the glass she held in her hand flicked onto the newcomer's dress.

'Excuse me,' she stammered, before putting her glass down on the nearest table and making a fast exit to the ladies' powder room.

By the time Julianne had followed her to ask if she was alright, Kira Mae had composed herself.

'Yes, of course,' she reassured her mother. 'I just lost my footing on the tiled floor. I blame these new shoes, they're very slippery.' To deflect any further questions she bent down and took off her high heeled shoe and pushed the offending footwear into her mother's hand. 'Feel it,' she said, 'if you don't believe me.'

Julianne stared at her daughter and though of course she did not believe her – she had no intention of making a scene. Besides she herself was feeling decidedly off balance. Struggling against a sick feeling in her stomach and a horrible taste in her mouth, she felt apprehensive and terminally disappointed.

'We'll make a quick exit, as soon as is humanly possible,'

she promised her daughter, knowing full well that it was she who needed to make her escape.

However early they were able to make their exit, it was still going to be a very long night.

Julianne and Kira Mae returned from the ladies to the restaurant. Pepe led them back to their table – one of the best in the house – and began to titillate them with tales of that evening's celebration dinner.

Neither mother nor daughter had any appetite for food, but they were strangely fascinated to see how this scene was going to play out. They were compelled to stay in the frame of the action and see what developed.

They silently asked themselves the same question; does Romero know that Pepe had introduced his fiancée to the two Englishwomen? What will he do about it?

Julianne and Kira Mae fixed all their attention on the small area of dance floor. Romero's guitar was on a stand by his chair – Romero was nowhere to be seen.

They waited for him to appear.

All the culinary skills of Pepe and his famous celebration dinner menu could not give them back their appetites. The two women made polite noises of appreciation and pushed the food around on their plates. Neither had any interest in food or conversation. They longed for Romero. Julianne eventually invented a headache – though it was not altogether a lie – when it became obvious that there was to be no appearance from Romero. Perhaps, she thought, at least not while she was in the restaurant. Kira Mae made no attempt to stay at the restaurant and again the women, usually so verbal and happy to share their observations, could find no conversation during the return journey to the villa.

Each thankfully made their way to their own private quarters. Behind closed doors they could stop the pretence of taking part in a normal mother and daughter evening out.

Julianne wept silent tears of humiliation and thwarted passion, as she removed her makeup, brushed her hair and slipped into a cream silk nightgown. As she lay in bed, tense, wide awake and struggling to find an explanation, her mobile phone rang. She slipped out of bed and walked over to the small vanity table where she had left it plugged in to recharge.

She held the phone to her ear and a deep, throaty male voice said softly, 'I want to make love to you. Please say yes.'

Turmoil swirled in her head. How dare he? What was he playing at? Who did he think she was? How could he treat her like this? But her heart overruled her head.

'Yes, Romero, yes,' said Julianne, refusing to hear the voice inside her that cried out no.

She had to know what this all meant. She had to see him. She longed for him to hold her and wipe away the tears of pain and turn them into tears of joy.

Eagerly, she answered, 'Yes, yes, yes.'

In the small stillness of her rational mind, she mocked herself; Fool, thy name is woman. After waiting so long to feel awakened, she had promised herself that if it ever happened she would only give herself to a man who would treat her with respect and dignity. With abandon she threw self-respect and all caution to the wind, denying all her instincts and overriding all misgivings. Recriminations could come later; tonight she wanted him to make love to her. She was on fire.

He offered no apology. No explanation. The urgency in his voice and the passion in his demands overwhelmed

Julianne. 'Can I come to see you now?' asked Romero. 'I can't bear to be away from you one more minute. I need you.'

Julianne had no intention of refusing him. 'Expect me in half an hour,' he said.

Rushing to the bathroom, Julianne put on lipstick and perfume and changed out of her cream silk nightgown into a shiny black negligee. So excited was she by the clandestine nature of the midnight visit that Julianne never concerned herself with asking Romero where he was when he called. Without being told, she had already figured that here was a man who would answer to no one – especially not a woman.

In her wildest dreams or worst nightmares, she could not have imagined the truth. She would have been devastated to know that he was already in her home, having just left the bed of her beloved daughter.

As she slipped downstairs to let him in, Julianne thought only of the glorious night of love ahead. Dreams do come true, she told herself. Having already passed the point of no return, there was to be no going back. Julianne was already crazily, hopelessly, helplessly in love with the shadow of an intoxicating man. Blinded by dreams of romance, she dared to imagine that there could be a happy ever after. No matter that the object of her desires was already promised to another, the roadblocks of denial descended, she saw only what she wanted to see.

chapter eighteen

'Men's vows are women's traitors!'
Shakespeare's *Cymbeline*

Kira Mae stretched languorously and on her lips played the satisfied smile of the cat that got the cream. She was in no hurry to rise from her luxuriously soft love-bed in the chic, feminine, mellow-yellow bedroom on the opposite side of the villa to her mother's sleeping quarters.

Hugging herself with delight, Kira Mae relived the passion she had shared with her new lover. She felt alive. The smell of Romero was still on her, his masculine odour, his French cigarettes, and his cologne.

Lovingly she stroked the small indent in the snowy white down filled pillow where he had laid his head as she stroked his dark, curly hair and traced the lines of his lips and eyes with her fingertips. Kira Mae thrilled to the memory of how he had run his firm hands over every inch of her body and caressed her gently until the fire came and she cried out for him to take her.

He had held her in a passionate embrace as he whispered in her ear, 'If you don't want this to happen you have only to say no. I will not force myself on you.'

She had wanted to cry out, 'Yes, force me, take me.'

Instead she had responded softly, 'I'm yours. Oh, how I want you. The answer is yes.' With deep inhalations she had joined herself to him through the sacred breath and his beloved name, 'Romero, Romero.'

Romero had gently lifted Kira Mae's barely-there hint-of-pink nightdress over her head. He had run his fingers over her full breasts and bent tenderly to kiss the erect, rosy nipples.

Kira Mae, who had previously known only boys, had revelled in the touch of a real man. He was assured, demanding, in charge, he made her feel like a woman, no longer a girl. He had cradled her face between his hands and gazed adoringly into her eyes.

'This is how you make love,' he had told her, as he guided her young naked body under his muscle bound maleness.

Romero had taken her masterfully, pacing their strokes and holding her tightly. He had sensed her need for gentleness; intuitively knowing that he would scare her away if he tried to overpower her. He had played her like a ballad – tenderly with feeling. Apart from his music, Romero loved few things; his tastes were simple: adventure, sex and fast cars.

At the height of their love-making, Romero had locked his eyes on Kira Mae's. He had read every sign, anticipated every move, breathed with her. Skilful as he was, there had been nothing too complicated about this conquest. Kira Mae had offered herself up – she had craved passion and the one great romance.

Guiding her towards their powerful crescendo, accomplished, masterful, a virtuoso, striving, stretching, melting, conjoined. Unable to bear the exquisite pain, at the moment of *la petite mort*, the blessed little death, Kira Mae had screamed out in ecstasy. From deep in her soul, the anguish had flowed. Released. Free at last of the desperate uncertainty. Answering the primordial desire for a sensation that would transcend the ordinary and compel her to believe in love.

To believe that she was lovable.

How was this teenage girl, in her naively limited experience of sexual relationships, to know that her new lover was as accomplished at playing women as he was experienced in musicianship?

With a deep, dark cunning and unerring instinct for getting what he wanted, Romero had orchestrated every beat. He stroked and strummed and plucked and snapped at the heartstrings until women sang to his tune. Then he snapped shut the trap.

Post coital, as their passion had erupted and peace settled, Romero had taken Kira Mae's hand, held it to his lips and kissed the tips of her fingers.

'Trust me,' he had said earnestly. 'There are things you need to know but not yet. I promise myself to you. You will know the truth soon enough. Do not question me. Trust me.'

With his entreaty ringing in her ears, he had left her. Slipping from between the sheets in haste he had dressed, walked purposefully towards the door, exiting her bed chamber, mission accomplished. Romero had pulled his cell phone from his hip pocket, switched on the lighted display and began to dial.

At the door he had stopped, blown a kiss and disappeared into the night.

★ ★ ★

Julianne was waiting for him. He had told her only that he was close by. 'So close I can almost hear your heartbeat,' he teased. 'Wait for me, *amore mio*.'

Silently, barefoot, she crept to the back door to allow him entry. Romero took hold of Julianne in a fierce embrace and pulled her outside.

'Under the stars,' he whispered. 'The gypsy way. We make love and seal our fate.' She offered no resistance.

Romero encircled her in his manly arms and she boldly responded with her arms around his waist. He held her close and she felt his heartbeat as it pulsed against her breast. He pressed his cheek next to hers and whispered words of love in a low seductive voice.

'*Cariño mi amore*,' he repeated over and over like a mantra. The hypnotic effects of the words and the controlled passion of his strong embrace lulled Julianne into a place of safety as she realised he had no intention of rushing her.

Tenderly he reached down for her hand and led her towards a poolside lounger. He laid her down and sat beside her. Stroking her hair and face, it seemed more like a child he caressed than a grown woman. In her ecstasy at the nearness of him, Julianne failed to recognise the practised art of the sexual manipulator.

'Close your eyes,' he murmured, 'trust me to take you on a journey to heaven – up in the stars. You will see and feel delights you have envisaged only in your wildest dreams.' Julianne thrilled to the sensation of reverence, a holy coming together of two people still tentatively exploring each other. Neither demanding nor threatening. She succumbed gladly.

She sighed and let go of all her inhibitions, after the decision that she would allow him to have his way with her. Slipping down the straps of her flimsy negligee he exposed her breasts and smiled as he saw them in their full voluptuous glory.

'Beautiful,' he murmured as he reached out to squeeze and stroke first one then the other. The nipples hardened under his expert touch. With the fingers of his right hand, he rubbed the nipples and then ever so gently licked his finger, before resuming the rhythmic movement of fingers on nipple.

Julianne opened her eyes as he licked his lips, before bending down to kiss the breasts. Emitting a sharp intake of breath, she was surprised at how good it felt as he sucked and allowed his teeth to gently nibble her nipples. The sensation was exquisite and served to distract Julianne from his other hand which was finding its way inside her flowing night gown and pushing the silky material aside to allow him access to her secret places.

All thoughts of protest were silenced as he covered her mouth with his and delivered passionate, breath-stopping kisses while working his tongue into her mouth.

His hand had reached its goal and he stroked her clitoris, gradually increasing the pressure until Julianne squirmed under his masterful caress and without suggestion or coercion, reached down to press her own hand against his erect manhood. Fear and fervour fought within her as she realised that she had reached an orgasm through his sustained stimulation and she became aware of the wetness between her own legs. He raised his finger to his lips and gently licked it.

'Are you ready for the real thing?' Romero asked.

Julianne nodded, but she was far from convinced.

Feel the fear and do it anyway, she told herself. At the moment of penetration she held her breath and prepared to avert the pain, but there was no need. Romero held himself above her, balanced on his strong arms, he entered her and began to move rhythmically, feeling his way into her inch by inch.

He kissed her gently and constantly checked, 'Do you enjoy my lovemaking? Tell me what you like. Does it feel good? Tell me, cariño. Tell me.' As he increased his speed and the pressure inside her, he continued to murmur endearments and cover her lips, her cheeks and eyelids with kisses, which landed softly like being stroked with butterfly wings.

His protective arms securely held her as he clasped her buttocks and raised her body to meet his for one last time. Triumphantly, he expelled his sexual energy in a final powerful thrust as he moaned, 'Come, come, come.'

Joined in the aftermath of sexual satisfaction, the couple lay on the sun lounger in the emerging moonlight holding each other. Julianne smiled at the man who had bewitched her and made her feel for the first time in her life like a well-loved woman. Instinctively he had treated her gently, with consideration and respect even without knowing the reasons for an inbuilt wariness on her part.

'It almost feels like I got myself a virgin,' he told her teasingly. 'You seemed so scared and reluctant. Right up to the end I thought you were going to refuse me.'

Unaccustomed as she was to sexual bantering, Julianne smiled, 'Well, you certainly have a knack for deflowering maidens,' she told him with a saucy laugh.

Romero declared that it was time for him to leave, but he promised to be in touch soon. 'Trust me,' he implored. 'Don't believe everything you hear about me from the village gossips.'

★ ★ ★

The next morning, sunshine filtered through the louvered

blinds of Julianne's first floor bedroom. The jasmine tree outside the window was reflected on the bedroom wall in shadow and the heady smell of vibrant purple passion flowers scented the room. Through the open window wafted the sweet smell of yellow jasmine and her heart leapt in response to the joyful sound of church bells ringing in the village.

Julianne had awoken from her dreamlike state. All her senses alert and entranced. She stretched luxuriously in her snow-white bed and reached her arms high up to grasp the smooth brass railing.

It felt good to be alive – and in love.

After all the pain and unhappiness she had suffered, Julianne convinced herself that she deserved happiness. Even if she had to grab it at the expense of another woman, Romero's fiancée. Love had been denied to Julianne for so much of her life, she now refused to see that the situation could only inflict more pain on her already damaged self.

It's not an affair, she told herself dramatically. It's a *love* affair.

On the other side of the house, Kira Mae was already up and dressed. She had woken at first light and taken an early morning swim. After showering and slipping into a white denim mini-skirt and cropped baby pink top, she had walked down the narrow, unpaved roadway to the village store.

Most of the villagers observed the Holy Day and Kira Mae felt unusually underdressed in her casual, figure-revealing outfit.

Behind the counter, Madame Oberato, a middle-aged widow, was formally dressed in a smart, navy dress. Her hair was in a tight bun and she wore only a small gold cross at her neck and a thin gold chain link bracelet. Beside the counter, waiting patiently for their weekly church appearance, a straw hat with a small corsage on one side and a navy blue handbag – this to match Madame's Sunday best navy blue court shoes. A woman of unflinching devotion and propriety, even the opening of her shop on Sunday was done for a pious reason.

'The villagers are thankful for the convenience of the shop to buy little gifts for the priest on their way to church,' she would offer by way of explanation to anyone who seemed to question her Sunday trading practice. A fine bottle of wine, sweet pastries and country cheeses were all appreciated by Monsignor Pordon and most villagers would arrive at Sunday service bearing a small donation.

Kira Mae was not a regular churchgoer but she and her mother often visited the small village church and lit candles or joined the congregation if a wedding or christening was taking place.

Madame Oberato greeted Kira Mae politely but with no warmth. 'The purpose of your visit, Señorita?' she asked. It sounded like an interrogation.

Kira Mae handed over the armful of provisions she had already collected. Half a dozen croissants, some soft cheese, a small jar of home bottled peach preserve, a carton of fresh milk and a small bar of black chocolate.

'Just these items, thank you, Señora,' she answered, wishing now that she had gone the extra few miles into the local supermarket where tourist dress was not frowned upon. Problem was, she had no transport of her own and avoiding her mother had been enough reason for leaving the house so early and alone.

Madame Oberato scribbled the prices and total of the items on a brown paper bag and made a small, neat package of the cheese and preserve, wrapping them in strong brown paper and tying them with string.

As she handed the package and change to Kira Mae, Madame Oberato gave a sly smile. 'Romero's most favourite,' she said.

Kira Mae was nonplussed.

'I'm sorry,' she stammered. 'Excuse me?'

'The peach preserve,' explained the storekeeper. 'Romero is most partial to it.'

Kira Mae was feeling decidedly uncomfortable and had no intention of waiting to ask any questions or receive any answers. All she wanted to do was get out of there.

'*Gracias*,' she managed to mumble as she walked quickly towards the door. '*Adios*,' she added, exiting.

'Romero's favourite.' Kira Mae repeated the words over and over to herself, as she climbed the small unmade road back to the villa.

Despite her misgivings, the thought that she had chosen Romero's favourite gave her a small glow inside. Knowing only that she was competing with one drop dead gorgeous fiancée, Kira Mae had no idea that there was another rival for the *numero uno* spot in Romero's heart. In fact did she but realise, Romero's conquests of girlfriends, mistresses and other men's wives was legendary.

'Romero's favourite,' she laughed out loud. 'I certainly hope so.'

Had Kira Mae the slightest inkling of the extent of the competition, her mood would have not been quite so cheerful.

Not paying attention to the few villagers climbing the hill to the small church dressed in their Sunday best, Kira Mae almost collided with a woman who looked a little familiar. Stripped of her extravagant scarlet flamenco dress, in sombre church-going clothes, the singer Passionista, looked less intimidating. It was a false image.

As Kira Mae passed, the woman grabbed her arms, stared directly into her eyes and hissed, 'You will not escape the gypsy curse.'

Shocked and scared, Kira Mae broke free, but not before the spiteful woman spat out her venom on the dusty, unmade road at her feet and ground the bile with her well shod foot.

The threatening gesture left Kira Mae in no doubt as to its meaning. She hurried to the safety of the villa, shaken and unsettled. Arriving home, Kira Mae was greeted by Julianne who had set up a breakfast table by the pool.

Mother and daughter sat in the sunshine, drinking hot chocolate out of goldfish bowl sized white china breakfast cups and eating fresh buttered croissants with peach preserve.

Neither said much. The silence seemed companionable, but in reality each was deeply lost in their own thoughts to the exclusion of the other. The ringing of the telephone startled them. Generally no one used the landline, not unless they were calling to speak to the villa owners. The only other people who did sometimes call to issue invitations were Brian and Marleen, a British couple who lived in the nearby town of Altea. Friends of Annabelle, she had suggested them as good sources of information and amusing dinner companions. Julianne and Kira Mae had visited a couple of times and availed themselves of their local knowledge and hospitality.

After a moment's hesitation, Julianne made her way into the house to interrupt the phone call before the answer phone was activated.

Kira Mae could hear snatches of the conversation.

'How lovely. We'd be delighted to see you. Of course it's

no trouble. You come out whenever you are ready. You'll find everything perfectly in order.'

Annabelle was coming over for a visit. She warned Julianne that she also had some news to share with her. It would wait until she arrived.

Trying to work out, in advance of an announcement, the nature of the news, Julianne and Kira Mae speculated that the villa was to be sold.

'Time for us to move on,' said Julianne, reaching into the covered basket to take out another warm croissant. 'Buy that place of our own and set up shop.'

The last thing she had anticipated was Kira Mae's angry outburst. 'I'm not moving from this village,' she said defiantly. 'I won't be forced out. You can go. I'll find myself somewhere to live here on my own if you try to make me leave.'

Julianne stared at her daughter. Whatever had got into her? She was acting distinctly strangely these days. Well, more strangely than usual. As a mother, she knew that there were various ways to handle the situation. Now she weighed up her options. She could provoke further confrontation by demanding that she would have the final decision in choosing a place for the pair to live. Or, she could compromise.

'Okay, we'll review the situation when Annabelle arrives and tells us exactly what the position is here. In the meantime,' she added reasonably, 'you can come with me to view the property I have found for us. You may be pleasantly surprised.'

Thankful to have averted a row, Julianne and Kira Mae turned their attention to plans for the rest of the day. Both agreed that this was a good day to take up a long-standing invitation to Sunday lunch with Brian and Marleen at the yacht club in Altea. At least they would not be forced to make conversation with each other all day. Adding other people to the mix seemed a good idea.

As they drove the twenty miles to the coast and the upmarket resort of Altea, whose pebbled beaches had saved it from the developers' cranes and over-population of Benidorm from which it was separated by only a slice of the Sierra Helada mountains, the two talked fondly about the expat friends they were to visit.

Marleen and Brian Toker were colourful characters who had lived on the Costa Blanca for over twenty years. They made it their business to get to know the new arrivals in the area and were a mine of information for newcomers – not all of it accurate, but most of it well meaning. Running bars in Spain's hottest holiday spots gave them a unique insight to the British abroad. The couple were great storytellers and amusing companions. Julianne and Kira Mae had been treated to their generous hospitality on several occasions. Marleen and Brian knew how to gather a full table of interesting lunch companions. Sunday lunch at the Altea Yacht Club was guaranteed to be a jolly affair.

Julianne and Kira Mae looked forward to being introduced to some new people and so avoid the prospect of being left to amuse each other all day. Marleen and Brian welcomed mother and daughter, their first guests, warmly and when all were settled on the terrace with drinks and spicy nuts and savoury nibbles, they began to regale Julianne and Kira Mae with all the latest gossip. The midday sun was a little too fierce and the quartet sat under a light blue umbrella on the outside terrace overlooking the ocean. Chilled drinks in hand, they relaxed and enjoyed the company. Brian held court and told a humorous story of the night he and a group of British holidaymakers got stranded on a glass bottomed boat. Search and rescue helicopters had been called out, but had failed to find the boat. They had no flares and no lifeboats – and little in the way of supplies. Only as dawn broke had the brave adventurers been spotted, washed up on a sandbar not a mile from the coast. They could have swum ashore or, in the shallow waters, just walked into land.

'Fortunately we did have several bottles of Spanish brandy to keep the cold night at bay. Badly needed as the entire boatload of customers and crew, some dozen people, were dressed only in swimwear and shorts. A one hour pleasure trip had turned into sixteen hours lost at sea.'

As Brian finished his story and enjoyed the laugher it elicited from his small audience, he waved to a couple who had arrived below in the marina. Expertly they tied up their small pleasure craft and he gestured for them to come and join the lunch party.

'Drink?' he called, bending his elbow.

'You will enjoy meeting this couple – he's the local newspaperman,' explained Brian. 'Knows everything that's going on in the area. If he doesn't know about it it's not worth knowing.'

Brian and Marleen greeted their friends. Antone, a handsome grey-haired Spaniard and his beautiful blonde wife, Josephine, were dressed casually in boating wear but they still managed to look elegant – and rich.

'What's new?' asked Brian heartily, as the pair accepted a glass of champagne from the bottle in the silver cooler by the side of the table.

Antone shook his head sadly. 'Hot off the press. I've just got back. A terrible tragedy. A fatal crash on the mountain road. A young girl died. Seems she lost control of her car and crashed down the mountainside. No other vehicles were involved; the rescue crews winched her vehicle up and took her body to the morgue.'

He shook his head to get rid of the image of the poor dead girl lying on a mortuary slab.

'Of course there will be a post mortem to see if she had been drinking or taking drugs. No matter, it is still a terrible loss of a young life. Her family have not yet been informed.'

Josephine interrupted. 'That road is a death trap. This is the third fatal crash this year. Something needs to be done.'

Before any criticism could be levelled at him, Antone explained, 'My newspaper has been very active – we have campaigned for warning signs, but you'll never stop young people driving too fast on dangerous roads – especially if they are drunk.'

Everyone at the table fell silent for a moment as they contemplated the senseless loss of a young life. They thought sadly about the devastation of a family who were about to learn of the death of a daughter.

Antone had more information to relay. 'The police told me that she was driving her fiancée's sports car. Apparently, he is quite well known in these parts. A musician, he's a member of a flamenco act that plays in the local restaurants.'

Julianne and Kira were shocked rigid.

'Do you know his name?' asked Julianne in a quiet voice. 'Perhaps we know him.'

Antone checked the notebook he had taken from his shirt pocket. 'Romero Santo Rosario,' he read.

Julianne and Kira were rendered speechless. Neither could find the words to elaborate when Antone asked casually.

'Sound familiar?'

Julianne's voice was little above a whisper. 'Not

personally,' she lied, 'but he sings at the restaurant in our village. As you say, he is quite well known locally.'

Determined not to give away any more information than necessary, Julianne waited for an opportune moment to excuse herself and Kira Mae. Her daughter had sat silently through the whole conversation.

'Don't take the mountain road,' warned Antone. 'It is probably still blocked while investigations go on to discover the cause of the accident. I doubt they will open it again today.'

Helpfully he added, 'Take the coast road, it's a beautiful journey at this time of day – you can watch the sun setting over the ocean. You can also see the sun fade from sight below the King's Window, the piece of rock cut out of the mountain.'

'Thank you, we know the story,' said Julianne a little too sharply, cutting him off before he could tell the fairy tale.

'Drive carefully,' their friends cautioned as Julianne and Kira Mae descended the stairs towards their convertible.

Neither mother nor daughter dared express their emotions on the drive back to the villa. This was no time to reveal the true reason for the shock they experienced. There were no words to say. Each was suffering their own personal nightmare of doubts, fears and unanswered questions. The short journey that they had so enjoyed a few hours earlier seemed to take forever.

Both claimed to need a siesta and hastened to their own quarters as soon as they arrived back home.

Neither noticed the unmarked police car parked just out of view on the opposite side of the narrow road. Nor if they had, would they have known the significance of the constant observation. Waiting, waiting.

chapter nineteen

'For aught that I could ever read, could ever hear by tale or history,
The course of true love never did run smooth.'
Shakespeare's *A Midsummer Night's Dream*

Julianne paced around her bedroom. The four walls now felt like a cage. For the hundredth time she checked her phone. No messages. In an attempt to get some order into her befuddled head, she decided to rearrange the clothes in her double-mirrored wardrobe. She had to do something. Anything. First she sorted all the skirts, colour coding them from light to dark, even though they had already been in order when she started, now she refined the process more and more, culling clothes as she went. I must ask Maria if there is a charity shop where I can pass on these clothes, she told herself.

In London she had always recycled her clothes, there were some excellent vintage designer shops in the Kensington area, and it made her feel virtuous that even if she would not wear last year's fashion some other customer would get pleasure from her extravagant designer cast offs.

Examining necks and cuffs, she checked for missing buttons, signs of wear or spots or marks. Each item was assigned a padded hanger, also colour coded. She tried to implement the two inch rule inspired by the designer, Giorgio Armani, whereby all clothes on rails had to have two inches breathing space between them. No piece of clothing must touch its partner.

Each was to claim its own space following a flow line of ascending colour – from light to dark – summer to winter – day to evening – inner wear to outer. Julianne sorted and organised – drilling her wardrobe like a military parade. Sleeveless T-shirts, long-sleeved blouses, skirts, trousers, cardigans, jackets and coats. On a higher shelf, hats, handbags, beachwear.

The ordering calmed her mind temporarily. Next, she counted. Sleeveless T-shirts – fourteen – ranging in colour from snowy white to blackest black with pastel shades of blue, pink and citrus in between.

Next, long sleeved T-shirts and blouses – a dozen, mostly white with the occasional beige and of course, the ubiquitous black. Next on the carefully measured hangers – skirts. Six of these – two white, two beige, one navy, one black. Slacks – six also in the same colour ways as the skirts.

Even Julianne was impressed at how disciplined were her buying habits that every separate item in her wardrobe was in the correct colouring to co-ordinate with the corresponding items. No impulse purchase for her – no wild coloured prints – no loud checks. Julianne continued to sort and colour co-ordinate her wardrobe. This was one area of her life over which she had control. One area in which she could delight in a propensity to obsessive compulsive disorder.

She checked her phone again. Still no message. And why would he phone? Just how large did she figure in his life? Did she figure in his life at all?

Dresses on padded hangers were separated into day and evening wear. Jackets too were classified into casual daytime wear and more formal evening wear.

Bringing up the rear – just one coat – the beige Burberry trench coat that Julianne had worn so often in London. Now it made an occasional appearance at times of the characteristic Spanish sudden light downpour that disappeared as quickly as it had come.

The inside of the wardrobe now having passed inspection, Julianne opened a high cupboard to the side, intending to organise her shoes. Even she could find nothing to sort. Her shoes, all thirty pairs of them, were neatly stored in see-through plastic boxes with a Polaroid photo stapled to the outside of the box showing the shoes inside the box. Row upon row of sandals, court shoes and strappy evening shoes, none had dared to get out of order.

Even in her demented state, Julianne could laugh at herself as she surveyed the boxes and assured herself, 'All shoes present and correct.' She prided herself on the daily checking of her shoes for any needed repairs and cleaning them after each wear. Once a fashionista, always a fashionista. Satisfied at last with her wardrobe duties, Julianne sat down on the edge of the bed.

She stared listlessly around the room, this comfortable bed chamber that had been such a haven of peace, relaxation and intimacy, just a few short hours ago, now brought her no solace. Its smallness made it feel like a prison. The lowered louvered blinds half open at the windows resembled bars and the white, fresh painted four walls formed a cell. What had been a statement in simplicity, now felt barren and bleak, like a life stripped bare. No personal photos, no ladylike clutter, just clean, straight lines, white furniture and a white cotton duvet cover and pillowcases.

The purity of the whiteness was now stained with blood – the blood of a young girl. Julianne now imagined she was in a hospital room, a stark, white clinical environment. A single plain white, light – nothing hidden. The reality of her anguish laid bare.

Julianne felt trapped. She felt sick. Her mind raced with unanswered questions.

Why didn't he call? Could she risk calling him? What to say? Remember me? You made love to me last night under the stars a few hours before your fiancée hurtled towards her death in your car.

Although she couldn't fully understand the reason for it, Julianne knew beyond doubt that she had played some part in that young woman's untimely death. Guilt gnawed at her insides though she tried to deny it. His place was with her – not here with you, the voice of conscience would give her no peace. She had to get out – get some fresh air. Clear her head – think of what was the right course of action to take.

Fearful of bumping into her daughter and determined to shield her from the uncertainty of the unfolding story, Julianne tiptoed downstairs silently – just as she had done the night before. Deceit seemed to come easier to her than she would previously have imagined, having always prided herself on maintaining high standards of personal integrity. As quietly as possible, she made her way out of the back gate and into the lane.

For the first time since hearing the tragic news, Julianne felt herself able to breathe. Then she saw the police car. Panic gripped her and her throat was dry, but her eyes filled with tears of fear and frustration. Desperate not to be seen, she turned and walked quickly back to the house.

Pulling open the gate, she heard Kira Mae's voice. 'Mother, come quickly. You're wanted on the phone.'

Julianne responded immediately. Her head was reeling and it was impossible to slow her body down. She ran up the last few steps into the house and grabbed the receiver from Kira Mae.

'Hello, hello,' she said urgently. 'Who is it?'

The voice of her friend Annabelle took her by surprise. Julianne had been expecting someone completely different. She couldn't keep the irritation out of her voice.

'Yes, Annabelle,' she said almost rudely. 'What can I do for you?'

Julianne listened as Annabelle apologetically explained that her plans had changed at the last minute. Instead of flying out to Spain as she had intended, she had travelled to Italy on urgent business. Not only was she not able to come to her own villa – she needed a big favour.

'She has an emergency,' Julianne explained to Kira Mae after concluding the conversation with her jet-setting friend. 'She needs someone to fly out and meet her in Rome. There are important documents here in the house that she needs to have delivered for a business negotiation.'

Julianne knew even as she hung up the phone that she had no intention of leaving Spain. Her mind raced furiously as she searched for a plausible explanation that would persuade Kira Mae to undertake the journey. Unaware as she was of the real reasons why Julianne would not make the trip herself, Kira Mae accepted her mother's request and was thereby coerced into making the trip. Assured that she would be there and back in three days, Kira Mae agreed.

But there was a condition. She would only act as courier if she was allowed to drive rather than fly. The two argued for a long time. Kira had passed her test only the year before on quiet Scottish roads having had many lessons on a closed circuit. She had minimal experience driving on busy London streets. Now she wanted to drive half way across Europe. Kira insisted. Julianne denied her request. As the impasse continued, Julianne felt her resistance being worn down.

'Do what you want,' she said. Kira Mae's ability to get her own way was at times endearing, but also in stark contrast to Julianne who had always found it difficult to be too demanding.

She classified herself as a people pleaser. Kira Mae was more a 'please herself' kind of girl. Julianne had reluctantly agreed, knowing she was closing her eyes to the fact that in normal circumstances she would have come up with a whole raft of reasons why her daughter should not be driving alone on the continent. But Julianne was beyond thinking rationally. She cared only about her own desperate need to stay at the villa, in the village, near to Romero. Now she had found him, she would not be separated from the love of her life. Even if in the process she gave her daughter up to a mission of mercy from which she might never return.

Without delay, they drove to town to hire a sturdy SUV from the local dealer. Julianne ensured that Kira Mae was equipped with road maps and supplies, including a hands free mobile phone that she could use to make calls while driving. The journey should take some twenty hours to travel up to northern Spain, across France and south into Italy.

Truth was that under any other circumstances, Julianne would have been excited to take such a road trip with her daughter. Now she was simply relieved to be rid of Kira Mae for a few days. It would give her space and time to discover what was going on with Romero.

chapter twenty

'How sharper than a serpent's tooth it is. To have a thankless child!'
Shakespeare's *King Lear*

Before retiring to bed that evening, Julianne busied herself in the kitchen making hot, milky chocolate drinks and oven fresh biscuits. Together, she and Kira Mae sat in the kitchen contentedly sipping the chocolate and eating the biscuits. It had been a long and distressing day and both looked forward to a good night's sleep.

It was at times like this that Julianne felt most close to her daughter. They had always prided themselves that they were more like best friends than mother and daughter, but since Mummy Mitchell's death and everything that followed, their relationship had been strained with both pulling away from each other in their pain and fear.

Julianne promised herself that one day, in the not too distant future, she would make it a priority to strengthen and develop the relationship with her only daughter. All it required was understanding – and time.

Julianne kissed Kira Mae and climbed the stairs. There was just one last job to do. She had to locate the attaché case that was to be delivered to Annabelle.

The instructions she had been given were that it was in a safe place, the small attic space in the roof above the study. Pulling down the brass ring on the overhead door revealed a small ladder attached to the underside. Julianne secured it and climbed up into the loft. Inside it was surprisingly well arranged, though a small space, everything was neatly stacked and the area was clean and dry. Julianne quickly located the small black lacquer beauty case that Annabelle had described – and alongside it a businesslike Louis Vuitton attaché case.

Her brief had simply been to find and then deliver the cases, it did not occur to her to open them or check the contents. Not that she would have known what she was looking for. As she was to tell the police later, she did not think it was any of her business.

Julianne turned off the light, climbed back down the small wooden ladder carrying the two cases, closed up the attic door and went to bed.

Just one last time she checked her mobile phone. No messages.

Julianne slept fitfully and was reluctant to get up when she heard her daughter moving about downstairs early the next morning.

Still wearing her dressing gown, she walked into the kitchen carrying the beauty case and briefcase. Kira Mae was already dressed and ready to set off on her journey.

'These are the cases you will deliver to Annabelle,' she told Kira Mae. 'Take good care of them, she says they are very important.'

Annabelle had given precise instructions for when and where she expected to meet up with Kira Mae. She was staying at The InterContinental De La Ville Roma, a seventeenth century landmark in historic Rome. Annabelle explained that the luxurious hotel offered an authentic Eternal City experience, located at the top of the Spanish Steps and being the ideal base for shopping, sightseeing and attending cultural events. It was within just a short walking distance from the Trevi Fountain, the Coliseum, Via Condotti, Piazza di Spagna and the Borghese Gallery and Museum. She would book Kira Mae a deluxe room.

'We can do some tourist things together,' said a grateful Annabelle.

Julianne called and told her Kira Mae would arrive in just over twenty-four hours, bringing with her the urgent documents.

'I can't thank you enough,' said her friend. 'You've saved my life.'

Julianne had no inkling that she was being told the literal truth.

After breakfast she set about confirming that Kira Mae had everything she needed. They drove together into town to collect the hired silver Jeep Cherokee with black leather seats and a state of the art satellite navigation system. Kira Mae was looking forward to her adventure and told her mother: 'It's like a rite of passage for me do this journey. Perhaps then you will realise that I am not a child – and stop treating me like one. You don't need to worry about me, I'm responsible and you can trust me.'

As an afterthought she added, 'Did you get me some sweets for the journey?'

Seeing her mother about to laugh, Kira Mae quickly corrected herself, 'Travel sweets, I mean. The air conditioning in the car can make your mouth dry.'

'Yes, dear,' said Julianne, keeping a straight face.

Guilt at having delegated this vital mission to her daughter had made Julianne extra generous.

She stopped by the ATM in town and drew out £1000 in Euros – and even gave Kira Mae her cash card in case she needed emergency funds. The motoring service office was helpful and supplied toll free numbers in case of a vehicle breakdown.

The kind man behind the desk, enjoying being of assistance to two such beautiful English ladies, went out of his way to be helpful. The journey from Alicante to Rome would take approximately twenty hours and he recommended a couple of easy access places on the motorway to stop overnight. Approximately half way through the journey – some five hundred miles – there were a cluster of Service Areas – *Aire de Narbonne-Vinassan, Aire de Montpellier-Fabrègues* and *Aire d'Ambrussum* – all available before entering the toll portion of the A54 motorway.

Kira Mae sounded confident and cheerful as she kissed her mother goodbye and assured her that she would be in constant communication on the mobile phone. For the hundredth time she reassured Julianne that she had Annabelle's mobile phone number and also the telephone number of the hotel. The beauty case and attaché case were safely stowed in the trunk of the Jeep, along with Kira Mae's overnight case.

Anxious to be on her way, she jumped into the Jeep, waved her mother goodbye one more time and set off on her adventure. Julianne watched her go – and suddenly was filled with an overpowering feeling of foreboding.

Not for the first time, she asked herself, do you know what you are doing? What kind of mother are you?'

There was no easy answer. For an hour she wandered

around the small town aimlessly, before stopping for a latte coffee and some thinking time. She would go to the office of the solicitor and make an offer to lease the shop and apartment premises she had viewed days earlier.

The situation called for affirmative action and it seemed a good time to be leaving the village. The new dwelling was less than an hour's drive – and she could continue her romance with Romero, away from the prying eyes of the village.

chapter twenty-one

'O, then, what graces in my love do dwell, that he hath turn'd
A heaven unto a hell!'
Shakespeare's *A Midsummer Night's Dream*

Julianne laughed at herself, despite the despair that clouded her mind and made her feel nauseous. The refrain rang in her head, Romero, Romero, wherefore art thou Romero? Surely he would phone today.

True, even in a mildly deluded state brought on by the intoxication of a heady romantic encounter, albeit brief, Julianne did not fool herself that she occupied a major place in his life, especially after the tragic event that had just passed, but a phone call was all she asked. A reassurance that the passion they had shared was real.

Only huge reserves of willpower and a modicum of pride prevented Julianne from checking her phone yet again – she had to content herself with the knowledge that the instrument would emit a bleep if a message was received.

'No,' she lectured herself sternly. 'You need to reserve all your energy for the important business ahead of you today. Kira Mae will have a lovely surprise when she returns – a new home and the business she had already dreamed of – a boutique of her own.'

Julianne felt momentarily elated, the black cloud that had hovered over her head since the devastating news delivered at the yacht club, cleared. Everything was going to work out fine – she was in control – she was taking charge of her life. The battles of all the past years had honed her survival skills and generated a demonic fighting spirit.

Oblivious to her mother's pain – and more importantly the reason for it – Kira Mae was enjoying her drive through the French countryside en route to Rome. The weather was beautiful; she played soulful love songs on the car sound system and dreamed of her new love.

Romero's handsome face had imprinted itself on her memory. She longed to see him, to hold him, to assure him of her loyalty.

Fate had intervened. No longer was Romero an engaged man about to be married to his childhood sweetheart – now he was free. Destiny had made the choice for him. Romero and Kira Mae, their initials entwined, on an invitation, on a wedding cake, in her heart.

Kira Mae had taken the precaution of leaving a detailed message telling Romero where she was going and how he could contact her. Oh, how she prayed he would contact her.

As she reached her journey's end, having driven through France and crossed the border into Italy, Kira Mae was feeling decidedly pleased with herself. Despite all the best advice, she had chosen not to stop overnight – instead she had kept herself awake en route with steaming cups of espresso coffee and a natural herb supplement called Energy Bombs – a sweet honey-based combination of ginseng and guarana.

She navigated her way through the crazy Roman traffic and gratefully pulled up outside the palatial eight storied sandstone washed villa, with its silver grey shutters and fluttering international flags above the grand neoclassical marbled entryway.

Kira Mae was impressed and enchanted by the elegance and glamour of the fashionable InterContinental De La Ville Roma and she made a mental note to share some of the stories she heard about the hotel with her mother. It was a favourite hotel of Sophia Loren and the composer Leonard Bernstein used to live there, she would boast. Kira Mae felt invigorated and excited and experienced a powerful rush of anticipation.

If only Romero could be here to share the beauty of the Eternal City with her. Kira Mae knew what she was going to wish for when she threw her three coins in the famous Trevi Fountain. One that Romero would respond to the message she had left and follow her to Rome. Two that he would declare his undying love for her. Three that he would propose.

Even if they did have to keep it secret for a while, in view of the recent tragedy with his last fiancée. Kira Mae believed in love at first sight and though to others it might all seem a little too rushed, she was convinced that her brief romantic encounter with Romero had been the start of a long and happy relationship.

The hotel was awesome and a recent renovation had lovingly preserved the original Empire style décor in its marbled floors, Murano glass chandeliers, gold encased mirrors and opulent ceiling-high sumptuous drapery and matching upholstery. Annabelle was obviously a lady of taste and discernment – not to mention the vulgar subject of money. She had chosen well.

Reception was ornate and opulent, with polished wooden

desks and impeccable service. Kira Mae checked in and was shown to her deluxe room overlooking a courtyard by a handsome and attentive valet. Kira Mae laughed off his gentle flirting and promised she would ask for him at reception if she needed a guided tour of Rome.

After showing Kira Mae around her tastefully and ornately furnished suite, with its warm toned cream and gold décor and delicate china blue scroll patterned silk bed coverings with matching drapery, the valet took time to walk her out through the glass doors onto the sun filled terracotta tiled balcony, ostensibly to show her the view.

Once outside, with the magnificent backdrop of ancient Rome to endow him with boldness, he cheekily observed, 'Rome is no place for a beautiful young lady without her lover.'

Annabelle had left a message saying she would meet Kira Mae for dinner in the world famous Rotunda Restaurant at 9 p.m. – Italians loved to eat late. Becoming aware that the journey had tired her and it being just 6 p.m., Kira Mae decided to take the opportunity for a well-earned rest before she dressed for dinner.

Kicking off her shoes, she lay down on top of the bed but as soon as she closed her eyes, the telephone rang. Although she knew it was foolish, her heart skipped a beat. Too early for Annabelle, she dared to hope that it might be Romero.

No, she might have guessed, it was her mother; seeking reassurance that her darling daughter had arrived safe and sound. After a brief conversation, Kira Mae hung up and tried to resume her nap.

When the phone rang again almost immediately Kira Mae angrily snatched up the receiver, expecting it to be her mother again.

In a petulant tone, Kira Mae asked, 'Yes, what did you forget?'

'What did I forget, my beautiful lady?' asked Romero. 'What can I tell you? Except I miss you and wanted to hear your deliciously sexy English voice.'

Giggling childishly, Kira Mae explained that she had mistaken his call for that of her mother. 'You know what the older generation are like,' she said. 'Always fussing.'

'How are you enjoying the City of Love?' Romero asked seductively. 'Would you not enjoy it more if you were indeed with a lover?'

Kira Mae loved being teased and it did not occur to her to question how unlike a grieving fiancé Romero sounded. A small voice of conscience tried to force its way into her consciousness but she pushed it away. Fate had conspired to bring her and Romero together and she was not going to be the one to question the morality of the situation – or do anything that would push him away.

'My huge king size bed is desperately in need of someone to take up some space,' she teased him back. 'I shall need to imagine you here, holding me – and,' turning suddenly shy she added, 'and, other things.'

Romero teased her with more words of love before he revealed, 'I too am in Rome, I followed you here. I only need a command from you and I can be at your side.'

Kira Mae was reeling. Wow – and she hadn't even thrown her coins in the fountain yet. This was what she had dreamed of; she knew he would follow her. She was breathless with excitement.

Stopping the moment before she succumbed and said, 'Yes, come this minute,' Kira Mae cautioned herself. First she had to complete the mission for which she had come to Rome. The case had to be delivered to Annabelle.

Besides, apart from her sense of responsibility, the real reason was that she needed time to prepare herself. What self-respecting young woman would want to meet her lover when she was still hot and dishevelled from a long journey?

Without explaining to Romero the reason for the delay, Kira Mae insisted that they turn their assignation into a romantic game.

'Midnight,' she said mysteriously. 'You must come to me at midnight. I will meet you in the InterContinental Hotel. I shall tell the reception desk I am expecting a guest. Be here – wait for me.'

Romero sounded puzzled but did not argue. 'Okay, after dinner,' he said gently. 'I'll be there. Just please one thing.'

Kira Mae agreed quickly, 'Anything, tell me.'

'Just promise me,' said Romero earnestly, 'that you are not meeting a man for dinner.'

Enchanted by the implied jealously in his question, Kira Mae assured him, 'No, no, not a man. A friend of my mother's. I need to complete a favour for my mother, an urgent delivery and then I am all yours. All yours.'

'*Adios cariño*, until later,' he whispered and with the sweet murmurings of love in her ears and the expectation of what was promised, Kira Mae fell asleep.

★ ★ ★

At 9 p.m. the concierge called to say that Madame Annabelle Anstruther was waiting in the foyer. Kira Mae was already dressed and ready to go. She checked her reflection in the mirror. Her long blonde hair shone like gold, she wore a short beaded white mini skirt and a silky white camisole. As a contrast, her handbag and shoes were black. The Jimmy Choo cross strapped sandals were in soft black suede with a small rhinestone buckle. The matching evening bag was just large enough to hold credit cards, keys and lipstick. The image she had cultivated was simple, classy, and elegant to emulate the Italian ladies. Youth was on her side, so she really did not need to try too hard. Her beauty turned heads in every language.

Preparing to leave the bedroom, having checked that she had her key card, Kira Mae satisfied herself that everything was ready for her anticipated assignation later that evening.

The luxurious king size bed with rich silk coverings had already been turned down by the evening maid and a small chocolate flower on a glass tray placed by the bedside.

Kira Mae sprayed the room with her favourite perfume – *Star* by Thierry Mugler with its yummy chocolate base notes. Rose petals had been spread across the bed, courtesy of room service. She turned the radio to a station playing soft music. The scene was set, the sound, sight and smell were all designed for a sensuous night of love.

Picking up the Louis Vuitton attaché case and black lacquered beauty case from beside the door, Kira Mae held her head high as she walked quickly down the corridor to the elevator.

Descending the five floors to the lobby, she checked her watch, mentally calculating yet again that there was ample time for dinner before she needed to be back for her midnight rendezvous. One call to reception had informed them she was expecting a guest who would be staying the night in her suite.

She could have added that she planned to have a permanent 'Do Not Disturb' sign on the door.

Hardly able to contain her excitement, Kira Mae knew she just had to play the polite guest for a couple hours at dinner with her mother's friend and deliver the bags as arranged. After that, her time was all her own and she made up her mind to ask Annabelle to extend the hotel reservation for the whole weekend. No way was she going to miss the opportunity to spend a romantic weekend in this city of love. Romero was going to be at her side – there was nothing more for which she could ask.

The mirrored elevator doors opened to reveal the bustling foyer – Kira Mae walked across the marble lobby looking for Annabelle.

Annabelle looked businesslike in an expensive beige suit – probably Chanel – with a tailored skirt and mustard silk blouse under a short cut jacket with huge gold buttons. She wore simple beige leather court shoes. Without hesitation Annabelle relieved Kira Mae of the two cases she was carrying. In one smooth movement, she handed them on to a man who was standing behind her.

'Take them straight to the office,' she demanded.

Having despatched the cases, Annabelle turned her attention to Kira Mae, embracing her and kissing continental style on both cheeks, complete with a loud *mwah* airbrushing sound she said, 'You've done me a great favour. I really can't thank you enough.'

Kira Mae felt a little awkward as she had never known her mother's friend well and it was already many years since she had seen her.

'It was my pleasure to help,' she told her host graciously.

'You have been so kind allowing us to stay at the villa. Please think no more of it.'

Annabelle smiled her acceptance, but even as she responded to Kira Mae she did not take her gaze from her companion as he walked out of the hotel carrying the cases.

Kira Mae's eyes followed too. As the man, who had not been introduced, climbed into a car waiting at the hotel entrance, a gentleman already in the driver's seat leaned over to unlock the door.

Kira Mae couldn't believe her eyes. Surely that was Romero? But no, she chided herself, how could that be? She could not make sense of it. What connection would Romero have to Annabelle or the man with the attaché cases?

The street was dark, her line of vision was not clear and having seen him for just one second, the man's face was no longer visible. The car pulled away and Kira Mae was left bemused. Kira Mae composed herself. She had no intention of attracting attention to her planned assignation in this strange and bewitching city. She pushed the doubts and unnamed fears to the back of her mind. Returning her attention to Annabelle, she tried to focus on the question she was being asked.

'The hotel restaurant – that will be okay with you?' Annabelle repeated.

'Oh, yes, certainly,' said Kira Mae quickly. She had no desire to stray too far from the hotel – the scene of her love tryst.

Annabelle steered her towards the courtyard restaurant on the hotel's ground floor. The Rotunda restaurant was one of the best in Rome and its gourmet fare was world class. Classical Greco-Roman murals decorated the walls, the windows were dressed with tasselled damask silk drapes, elaborate swag valances and an imposing Murano glass chandelier illuminated the whole room. Snow-white tablecloths were laid with solid silver cutlery and an array of cut glass wine ware. The centrepiece was a white vanilla candle and an exquisitely arranged bowl of white roses. The whole effect was understated elegance and the food, out of this world.

Kira Mae fancied she could almost be a guest of the Roman glitterati, at one of film star Sophia Loren's legendary birthday parties in the splendour of this exquisite dining room.

Annabelle was an attentive hostess; she helped Kira Mae make her choices and admitted that she frequently dined in the restaurant. She offered to order the food and wine for both of them.

Kira Mae was so glad she had agreed; as each dish was presented she became more and more delighted by her host's choices. Annabelle had chosen a selection of the restaurant's signature dishes. They started with stuffed artichokes, followed by homemade pasta with salmon and organic vegetables and a mint sorbet to clear the palate, before sharing a delicious hot chocolate cake drizzled with amaretto and raspberry coulis. To accompany the meal, Annabelle, who spoke fluent Italian, ordered a rosé wine and to finish off they both had the Emperor Terrace house speciality cocktail, a secret blend of spirits, orange skins and Baloro Chunato.

Service from the white-jacketed waiters was super-efficient but discreetly unobtrusive and Kira Mae was delighted to note, as Annabelle ordered the check and passed over her executive level Black American Express card, that the time was just 11.15 p.m.

The two ladies had engaged in polite but uncontroversial

dinner table talk – their conversation covered the attractions of Rome, the culture, art and fashion of the city and the relative merits of living in a Mediterranean climate. Annabelle encouraged Kira Mae to tell her about plans for the proposed fashion boutique and asked how Kira Mae's mother's property search was progressing. She expressed no desire to return to live in the villa or the village where she had invested so much of her time and resources, prior to making the decision to go back to England. On the contrary, Kira Mae sensed a real desire on the part of her host to distance herself from talk of the villa, the village and her former home in Spain.

At one point she let her guard down and admitted, 'I will never return to live in the villa, there are too many unhappy memories.'

Kira Mae did not think it would be appropriate to ask for an explanation. After all, this was her mother's friend, a woman nearly twenty years older than herself. Also she sensed an unspoken agreement that no personal matters were to be discussed.

Not sure how much her mother had told Annabelle of the reason why they had needed to flee London at such short notice, Kira Mae felt embarrassed and hoped not to be asked to reveal any details. Smiling, but unquestioning, she was quite content to allow Annabelle her own personal reasons for not choosing to stay in the villa. The matter of the attaché case, its accompanying beauty case and the urgent need for their contents was another perceived no go area.

Much as she usually enjoyed fine dining, Kira Mae knew she was just going through the motions. She colluded in keeping the conversation light and was much relieved when the time came to make her escape.

Kira Mae felt distinctly light headed as she left the table and thanked her mother's friend for the hospitality.

Annabelle indicated that she had work to do the next day when Kira Mae expressed a desire to go and see the sights; she was happy to go solo she told a plainly relieved Annabelle.

They ended the evening politely, both thanking the other for a most pleasant dinner and agreeing that they had each other's cell phone numbers if they needed to get in touch.

Kira Mae certainly intended to keep her upcoming rendezvous secret and, depending on how much time Romero had allowed to spend together, her latest plan was to suggest that they take a romantic drive down the scenic Amalfi coast to the picturesque village of Positano perched high on the hilltop and overlooking the ocean. Kira Mae had seen a film where the lovers made this journey and had filed it away in her fertile imagination as one of the 'romantic things I will do at least once in my life'.

Relieved of her duty, Kira Mae breathed a sigh of relief as she walked towards the elevator for the return ride to her room. For one mad moment she even thought of climbing five flights up the hotel's much admired sweeping eighteenth century marble staircase, but thought better of it. She preferred to conserve her energy.

Full of anticipation and filled with expectation at the clandestine delight that lay ahead, she walked purposefully down the gilt framed picture gallery corridor to her room. Once inside she first checked the messages on the hotel answering system and then prepared to ready herself for a night of love.

She slipped out of her elegant white evening clothes and into a short black silk negligee. She brushed her hair, reapplied lipstick and sprayed the room lavishly with her signature *Star* perfume. Then she turned up the volume on the late night Latin station, poured a nightcap and stretched out on the chaise longue, idly flicking through a glossy, Roman fashion and art magazine. Kira Mae waited for her lover to arrive.

The room was seductive and inviting; she adjusted the lights and opened the French doors that led on to the balcony overlooking the stunning night-time city landscape, the dazzling location for so many enduring classic movies; her favourite was Audrey Hepburn and Gregory Peck in *Roman Holiday*.

Son et lumière displays proudly showcased the architectural wonders of ancient Rome and Kira Mae fancifully imagined that she and Romero would go late night sightseeing, throw coins in the Trevi Fountain – just like in the movie *Three Coins in the Fountain* – and paddle in the cool waters as Anita Ekberg had done in the movie *La Dolce Vita*. Kira Mae breathed in the night air and sipped at her night cap. She pretended to enjoy the mellow taste of a fine brandy from the mini bar, when really she would have preferred the creamy taste of a Bailey's liqueur. On the mantelpiece, an ormolu clock struck the witching hour and Kira Mae waited.

As the striking clock reached its ultimate destination, midnight, the phone rang.

'Señorita, you have a visitor,' said the night desk clerk.

'Send him up,' said Kira Mae.

Within moments there was a soft knock at the door and as she eagerly opened it, she caught her breath at the sight of Romero standing there. He had never looked more handsome.

His thick curly hair was slightly damp, as if he had just stepped out of the shower, and his white shirt was open at the neck providing a contrast to his café au lait coloured skin.

Taking Kira Mae's hand in his, he put her fingers to his lips and kissed her hand. '*Encantada*,' he said softly.

Still holding her hand, Romero guided her backwards, closed the door with his foot and walked her to the middle of the room.

Putting down the opened bottle of champagne he was carrying, Romero took Kira Mae in his arms and kissed her deeply. In the spell of his embrace, she felt herself swoon. The lovers stood rapturously kissing in the centre of the room for several minutes before Romero took her firmly by the hand and led her towards the bed.

'Let me undress you,' said Romero, already doing so with his eyes.

Kira Mae was totally in his sway – even had she wanted to, she could not have refused. He slipped the tiny shoestring straps down over her slender shoulders, all the time pressing barely-there butterfly kisses on to her face and arms.

The negligee slipped silently to the ground and he indicated that she should step out of it. She now stood before him wearing just a flimsy pair of black lace panties decorated with a glittering rhinestone heart and on her feet a pair of black stilettos.

Romero stroked her naked body. He ran his hands tantalisingly over her fulsome breasts and encircled her slim waist with his strong hands. He knelt down in front of her and passed his hands lovingly over her hips, her thighs and between her legs. He covered every inch of her body, right down to and past the knees, calves and to the feet. He lifted her foot and kissed her shoes, stroking the heel and pressing it into the flesh of his thigh.

Kira Mae responded and encouraged every intimate caress.

Without hurry, he backed her onto the bed. Without taking his eyes from her face, he kicked off his Gucci loafers.

'Tonight you will be ravaged,' he promised. 'You are powerless to resist. Give yourself to me. Tonight we will become one.'

As he laid her on the bed, Kira Mae trembled. Stretching out a hand to help him undress, she was refused. 'You naughty girl,' he whispered. 'Do not rush.'

So saying he turned his back to her and unbuttoned his shirt and unzipped his trousers, letting them fall to the floor. He wore no underwear. He turned again to face her, his magnificent manhood already erect and proud.

With a wicked glint in his eyes, he grinned and said, 'Prepare to be ravaged.'

Romero was a man of his word. Their lovemaking was passionate, urgent and intense. They delighted in each other's bodies, exploring, stroking, and kissing.

He was determined to enjoy the foreplay for as long as possible and when she reached down her hand to stimulate him, Romero gently discouraged her. Manoeuvring into position on top of her and between her legs, he declared, 'He is greedy for you.'

The two moved together in a satisfying rhythm, first slowly and then building like waves crashing on the shore.

Romero held tightly to Kira Mae's hair and moved her head in rhythm with his strokes. He choreographed the dance of love, guiding her to move and rest and raise her body upwards to meet him as he thrust himself into her.

Kira Mae gave free rein to her emotions of alternating supreme pleasure and intense pain. For tonight, she had no need to hide her love. She cried out in ecstasy. As she pulled

Romero ever deeper inside her, she gave herself up to him with wild abandon.

When it came, the climax was explosive; they bucked and cried out together. Orgasm, *la petite mort*: the little death. They drowned in the intensity of the satisfying and inevitable conclusion.

Through the night, the pair challenged each other to repeated performances. The night seemed to last forever and their lust knew no bounds. Locked in each other's arms, they made love, they slept, and they woke and made love again.

Kira Mae had never felt so alive. So complete.

She had no reason to believe that Romero was not sincere. How was a naïve young girl to know when she was being used, subjected to the expert charms of an arch manipulator?

Romero knew every trick in the book.

Whatever happened from now on, Romero would have no doubt that she was in his power. She had given herself to him with her body and her soul and every ounce of her being.

The only prayer she had left was that they would be together, forever. But, forever is a long, long time.

Kira Mae had briefly stirred as he got up and went into the bathroom. She heard the shower run as she drifted back to sleep.

When next she opened her eyes, Romero had departed, leaving a note on the bedside table. Written on a sheet of gold embossed hotel notepaper two short sentences: *You looked so beautiful, did not want to wake you. Will call*. This was not what Kira Mae had in mind. She had the whole weekend mapped out, including her plans for a drive to the Amalfi coast. First off she had anticipated a leisurely romantic breakfast together, followed by a stroll to the Baroque Trevi Fountain to throw her coins and make a wish. The haunting melody from the classic song played over and over in her head.

'Three coins in the fountain... which one will the fountain bless?'

Kira Mae was momentarily distracted – were lovers allowed to throw three coins and get granted three wishes – or each to throw one and only one wish would be granted? Three wishes sounded better than one, she told herself, I'll go for the triple.

Then she remembered that she had no idea whether Romero would return in time to accompany her on this romantic mission. Never one to hesitate too long, Kira Mae decided to at least shower and dress. Sad as she was to wash from her body the tangy masculine smell of her lover, it was time to move on. Do the next right thing, Mummy Mitchell used to encourage her. Put one foot in front of the other, breathe deeply and the road ahead will open up.

Kira Mae knew that having been thwarted in her schemes, she was on the verge of frustrated tears and very close to throwing a tantrum – but there was no one there to see it. So instead she chose decisive action.

Angry with Romero for not waiting for her to wake up, she quickly adapted the plan to fit the circumstances and decided to drive to the coast alone. Instead of waiting around here, she told herself, I'll drive down the Amalfi coast, find an idyllic hotel, call Romero and ask him to meet me there.

She certainly did not want to stay and explain to Annabelle about the change of plans – nor did she intend on going home. No, she was determined to hug the warm, wonderful feeling of being loved close to her heart – she refused to explain it to anyone. Most of all her mother. Kira Mae picked up the phone and dialled the villa. At least she needed to pass on the information that she had delivered the cases as instructed to Annabelle.

Thinking on her feet, she also concocted an excuse to counteract any questions her mother may have for her. Julianne would have to agree, this was the perfect opportunity to make a reconnaissance of designer boutiques in Italy. Remembering a snippet of news about one of her mother's favourite designers, Giorgio Armani, Kira Mae enthused about the new boutique he had opened in the fabulously fashionable resort of Positano.

'I am going to drive down there and check it out. Expect a lovely gift,' she told her mother, hoping to deflect her ever present radar and naturally suspicious mind.

Kira Mae felt guilty about lying to her mother but consoled herself with the thought that she did not want to worry her. Her mother had been through so much, Kira Mae's best intentions were to protect her, but her actions often looked more like wilful rebellion.

She dialled the home number again. 'Mummy, I love you,' she said when her mother answered. 'I'll be home soon. Honestly, you don't need to worry about me. I'm a big girl now. Love you loads. Oh by the way, I've got a great story to tell you about Sophia Loren and Leonard Bernstein.'

She giggled as her mother expressed surprise. 'No, not the two of them together. I'll tell you all about it when I get home.'

As she packed, Kira Mae turned up the music system and tried to drown out the sound of her own head. Although she did not know the words to the songs that were playing, she understood the emotions they charted. Love, loss, pain. Without warning, tears sprang into her eyes and ran down her cheeks. How had her life suddenly become so chaotic? Full of lies and subterfuge. How could she have been so stupid as to fall for someone who was so obviously totally unavailable?

In the cold light of day, she could see clearly. The village lothario, a breaker of women's hearts, an emotional bandit. A crazy mix of emotions threatened her thin veneer of happiness. She cried tears of pain and pity for herself.

So loud was the music that Kira Mae did not hear the phone ringing. By the time she heard the signal the caller had left a message. When she listened to the message, her tears turned to rage.

Kira Mae had never reacted well to being denied, like many young ladies used to being spoiled and indulged, she wanted what she wanted, when she wanted it – 'no' was not an option. Romero, how dare he! She listened to the message again.

'Beautiful lady, thank you for a wonderful night. We will be together again soon. But not today and maybe not till we get back to Spain. I have business to take care of, please understand.' Now it was his turn to sound frustrated. 'I know you are there so answer the phone. I need to talk to you. Please do not turn away from me. I love you. Let me explain. Please, call me straight away. I await your call.'

Kira Mae melted at the sound of his voice, of course she wanted to hear his explanation, but pride prevented her calling back straight away. Kira Mae completed her showering and hair-washing routine, dressed in casual clothes, straight leg Levi jeans with a white T-shirt and slipped on a pair of comfortable Nike trainers.

Once she had finished packing, she made a final check of the room and slipped a pad of fancy notepaper into her handbag. Too impatient to wait for a valet to come and collect her luggage, she wheeled her case down the corridor and into the ornate lift. Exiting the lift, she made her way to the reception desk and asked for the bill. Annabelle had arranged for the bill to be forwarded to her company. Kira signed to confirm the amounts and reminded herself to call her mother's friend later to say thank you and goodbye.

Rising from a comfortably upholstered chair in the grand marble lobby, a detective watched Kira Mae step from the lift and he signalled to a colleague, identifying the retreating figure as the English lady that Italian police wanted to question. Miss Kira Mae Gordon.

chapter twenty-two

'Action is eloquence.'
Shakespeare's *Coriolanus*

'Action is the magic word.' Julianne repeated one of her favourite mantras and ordered another café au lait, as she sat in the warm sunshine at an outdoor restaurant on the colourful tree-lined Alicante Boulevard close to her solicitor's office.

Fishing in her handbag for her small silver-backed notebook, she began to tick off items on the list of bullet points. Julianne mentally complimented herself on how much she had accomplished in a few short days.

Take over lease on premises, *Tick*. Transfer funds from England, *Tick*. Register name of new business, *Tick*. Contact suppliers, *Tick*.

After waving goodbye to Kira Mae in the town square, Julianne had gone straight to the lawyer's office and instructed them to negotiate a one-year lease on the premises she had viewed with Romero.

Having made her decision she was adamant that she would delay no longer. Her mind was calm and she brushed aside doubts that she was being reckless.

This is *not* about Romero, she endeavoured to convince herself. It is a sound business proposition.

Moving out of the villa and out of the village as soon as possible was the right thing to do. Now was the time to pursue her dream of opening the designer boutique.

On a mission to gather information, Julianne had been directed to the world's first beach library located in Playa de Levante and Playa de Poniente in Benidorm. There she had found newspapers, magazines and books in seven different languages. Researching the town where her new premises would be located, Julianne had become ever more convinced that she had made an inspired choice. According to the guide books, her San Juan location was renowned as a playground for rich Madrileños.

Just north of Alicante, the beach resort was second home territory for the rich of Madrid and during the summer the wealthy and fashionable residents of Alicante also decamped to San Juan to be part of the restaurant, nightclub and yacht scene.

By September, the crowds departed and San Juan returned to village pace. Julianne had identified this as being a perfect scenario for the clientele she needed to attract to her designer boutique. Wealthy, fashion-conscious and eager to be titillated with new designers and original creations. Also a seasonal trade was good, giving her and Kira Mae time to work on developing designs, networking for suppliers and enjoying a slower pace of life out of season.

In her mind's eye she surveyed her perfect premises. High on the hill in the village of San Juan, the white-washed stone building covered in purple and white wisteria, with the showroom window and a darling apartment where she and Kira Mae would live above the shop. Idyllic.

Climbing the stairs to the lawyer's office, Julianne felt a frisson of excitement as she recalled the first time she had visited the office and her fateful encounter with Romero. Her body shuddered and she felt suddenly faint with desire as she stood for a moment on the steps and relived their passionate embrace. Could it really have been just a few short weeks ago when she had been awakened to the excruciating bliss of love and longing?

Romero, Romero, oh, where... Julianne stopped herself; she had ceased to be amused by the irony of the declaration. Romero was nowhere to be found. Not a call, not a message, nothing. It was as if he had vanished off the face of the earth.

Romero had not been in touch since the day of his fiancée's accident. What else could you expect? Julianne admonished herself. Through her pain, Julianne allowed herself a wry smile. It shows respect.

How ridiculous it all is, she told herself. You, a grown woman, behaving like a love-sick adolescent. Just remember, your name is Julianne, not Juliet.

Engrossed in the strict talking to she was delivering to herself, Julianne jumped when the door of the lawyer's inner office opened, even as she stood outside with her hand on the brass door knob.

'Can I help you, Madame?' asked the receptionist, gazing admiringly at Julianne's eye catching ensemble.

Dressed head to toe in Chanel she was effortlessly casual and ultra-chic. Her white tailored cigarette pants contrasted with a black chiffon blouse, dominated by a large floppy bow. On top of this she wore a striking red blazer with gold buttons and high heeled white sandals, detailed with gold medallions.

Her shiny blonde locks flowed freely and she hid her eyes

behind large, round white polished Jackie O sunglasses. To complete the ensemble, a large multi-pocketed white Chanel bag, with a gold padlock and the CC logo entwined on a gold disc on the zipper.

Having explained the reason for her visit, the lawyer came out and assured her that he had drawn up the lease according to her instructions and completing the formalities would be a simple process. Julianne agreed the terms of the lease that had been explained to her by Romero on her first visit to the premises. Handing over a cheque for the deposit of three months' rent in advance, Julianne waited while the young assistant to the lawyer was dispatched to collect the keys from the owner.

Accepting the offer of a small cup of espresso coffee, Julianne, trying to make her enquiries sound like mere polite small talk, seized the opportunity to quiz the lawyer about Romero.

The shutters came down. 'I have no news of him,' the lawyer told her, before abruptly excusing himself, walking back into his office and closing the door firmly.

Julianne felt herself blush involuntarily as the receptionist gave her a small, embarrassed smile. To cover the tension in the room the eager to please receptionist made small talk. She asked whether Julianne and her daughter were enjoying their stay in Spain.

Politely she also enquired about, 'The other English lady.'

Julianne was puzzled and then realised that the lady referred to was her own friend and landlady, Annabelle.

Of course, Annabelle had been the one who had recommended the law office in the first place. It now seemed a lifetime ago since she had first come to Spain.

'Miss Anstruther? She is fine,' said Julianne. 'Thank you for asking.'

Looking perplexed, the receptionist struggled to make herself clear. 'Annabelle, yes, but it is not Miss Anstruther. It is Mrs Rosario. She and Mr Romero were married before she returned to England.'

Julianne felt her blood run cold – she froze. A million thoughts and questions tumbled over each other. She was embarrassed to notice that a tremble in her hands was making the coffee cup rattle against the saucer.

Annabelle and Romero. This couldn't be right. Please don't let it be true. Julianne felt like she was drowning. Her mouth was dry, her head was spinning. Bursting into tears or fainting seemed distinct possibilities. Julianne took a deep breath.

'Mrs Romero Rosario?' she asked, after what felt like an eternity. She tried hard to keep the panic out of her voice.

Smiling, the receptionist elaborated. 'Yes, they make a lovely couple. We were all so sad to hear the news when Mrs Rosario's father was taken seriously ill in England. She of course had to return to take care of him. Her new husband had to stay on here in Spain – for business reasons.

'Such a lovely couple,' she repeated. 'So sad they should be apart.'

Julianne's head pounded; she had heard more than she could bear. The return of the messenger with the keys brought the conversation to an end and she almost ran from the office.

Tears blinded her eyes as she walked swiftly towards her car and she was thankful for the large sunglasses behind which she could hide. Jumping in, she slammed the car into gear and screeched down the highway out of town. Driving like a woman possessed, she headed for San Juan.

Incapable of rational thought, her mind raced out of control. Nothing made sense. The information she had been given was a bolt from the blue – but what did it mean?

All Julianne knew at that moment was that she had been deceived and cruelly misled. Getting out of the village immediately was a top priority. She could not stay there in the villa, in the village another day.

Fear gnawed at her insides and the humiliation she had suffered made her feel nauseous. The intimacies she had allowed embarrassed her and the arousal of her sexual nature felt like a betrayal. Bring down the curtain, she told herself; let me not feel, let me not breathe. Her hands on the steering wheel felt clammy and her head began to throb.

None of it made any sense. If Annabelle was married to Romero, who was the fiancée who had been killed? Why had Annabelle not told her she was married? Oh, please God, she prayed, let me find a way out of this mess. She could find no answers. Even identifying the questions was a struggle.

Julianne suddenly felt alone and frightened in a strange land. Then as if hit by a lightning bolt, she remembered.

Kira Mae. Kira Mae was with Annabelle. What does she want with her? What was in the attaché case? What have I done? I've sent Kira Mae into the lion's den and I don't even know how or why.

Julianne could not escape the chilling realisation that she had put her own wants and needs ahead of those of her daughter. Now she knew she would pay for her selfishness. She had been concerned only to get Kira Mae out of the way for a few days. Now she was in the middle of an emotional maelstrom and she could not protect her own daughter.

There was no one to turn to, no one to ask for an explanation. If only Kira Mae were here with her now, at least they would be together. Knowing that she would not be able to tell her all that was going on, even just having her daughter by her side would have relieved the dreadful, terrifying feeling of being all alone.

Pressing speed dial on the phone, even as she drove, Julianne needed to speak to Kira Mae without delay.

Voicemail. 'Call me straight away,' Julianne almost shouted into the receiver. 'I love you.'

Julianne arrived in San Juan at the new accommodation feeling like a woman possessed. Parking her car at the rear of the building, she opened up and surveyed the property.

It was in good shape. The last tenants had not long since vacated the premises. Desperate to keep herself occupied, Julianne found a willow broom in the small back kitchenette area and started to sweep out the premises. She threw open the shutters and breathed deeply of the wholesome air. The shop was immediately filled with air and light and sunshine.

There was not a moment to lose. Julianne used her mobile phone and a scruffy old copy of the local telephone directory to call local craftsmen. The sign writer and the shop fitter agreed to get to work straight away. They knew the premises; it was not a big job and besides the summer was always a quiet time for construction work.

Most locals would wait till the weather turned cooler and the summer visitors departed before starting renovation projects. A new customer was always worth cultivating even in a culture where *mañana* was a way of life.

That afternoon she showed the workmen around the small shop. Tomas, the sign writer preened visibly as he discussed colours and concepts and costs with the beautiful and elegant blonde English lady. Responding to the urgency in her voice, he even agreed to set aside his busy work schedule and start the sign the following day. The carpenter, skilled at fitting out retail premises, was reluctant to be excluded and so also agreed to start work immediately.

Taking inventory, Julianne observed that the shelves in the shop would do to be going on with and on the phone she ordered a half dozen garment racks from a supplier known to her in London.

Getting the business up and running as soon as possible was her intention. Certainly she and Kira Mae would be moving into the apartment at once.

Kira Mae. She still hadn't heard from the girl. The last conversation was when her daughter had informed her she would be spending a few more days in Italy driving down to the coast and gathering research on designer boutiques.

By the end of the day, Julianne was exhausted, physically and mentally. She had surprised even herself with how much she had achieved – working at a frantic pace was designed to keep her mind off the gathering storm.

She had left numerous voice messages for Kira Mae and was now desperate to try to work out what should be her next move. Should she call Annabelle? Yes, she should call Annabelle, but she couldn't bring herself to do it. Should she make arrangements to drive to Amalfi? But she didn't know where Kira was staying. It would be a wild goose chase. Should she call the police?

Julianne got back into her car and even before switching on the engine she laid her head on the sun-warmed steering wheel and sobbed. What a mess. I'm a lousy mother, she told herself over and over again. In anger and frustration she beat herself with her fists, her arms, her legs, and her stomach. Unaware that she was being watched by one of the villagers, she continued to inflict punishment until she felt some sense of relief. The villager hurried away to impart this piece of juicy gossip about the loco tourist lady.

Now for the trip Julianne had been dreading. She could not avoid returning to the villa to collect her own and her daughter's belongings. She was adamant that she would be packed up and out of the house the next morning.

In this respect, Julianne was grateful that Kira Mae would not return home until after the weekend. But she was still beside herself with worry.

Julianne tried to analyse the conversations in which Kira Mae had told her about meeting up with Annabelle. There had been nothing to arouse suspicions or suggest that anything was untoward. Feedback was that the pair had enjoyed a wonderful meal together, the cases had been delivered, mission accomplished.

However, Julianne was aware that now the genie was out of the bottle, the story was not finished. Another chapter was already being written and she had no idea what would become of them.

'Damn, you, Kira Mae, why don't you pick up your messages?' she said aloud to no one but herself.

Driving on the right-hand side of the road, instead of her UK default setting on the left, Julianne was not properly concentrating. Loud hooting from several angry drivers told her that she was about to turn the wrong way out of an intersection. A common mistake with visiting drivers who were used to manoeuvring on the other side of the divide. She had even heard of one tourist recently who had died because of just such a lapse of judgement. Calm down, concentrate, she admonished herself.

★ ★ ★

Arriving at the villa Julianne was grateful to be in the relative safety of what had been first her refuge and now was her prison. Even the betrayal she had been subjected to from Annabelle – how could she be married to Romero? – could not completely obliterate the sense of safety and sanctuary that had so restored herself and Kira Mae after they were forced to flee from London.

Unexpectedly she caught sight of herself in the hallway mirror and was startled. She looked like a shadow of her usual self. Hair dishevelled, eyes red, makeup rubbed off. Even her clothes were grubby – what was she thinking of doing all that dirty work in white trousers? Her beautiful bright red polished nails, her pride and joy, were ingrained with dirt. She had worked like a demon at the new premises, concerned only with her maniacal desire to open her boutique as quickly as was humanly possible – and establish a new home for herself and her daughter. Julianne had been a woman possessed and she felt seriously that she was on the verge of a breakdown. Two of her lacquered scarlet nails were broken. That was the straw that broke the camel's back. Sinking into a welcoming deep cushioned, bright yellow, fabric armchair in the familiar living room that she had come to think of as home, Julianne wept bitter tears.

Dear God have mercy on my soul, she prayed. Take away the hurt and pain. Grant me peace and send my daughter home safe and sound.

Julianne lost track of time as she sat, miserable and dejected, in the armchair. Thinking herself barely able to move she still sprang out of the chair and rushed across the room at the first ring of the telephone.

Romero's first words were of contrition. 'Please forgive me. I wanted to call. It was difficult. Can we meet?'

Weak with relief that he had not abandoned her, Julianne was powerless to refuse. Tearing off her grubby work clothes, she raced upstairs and stepped into the warm healing waters of the shower.

I'll see him just once more to tell him what I think of him, she mused. His behaviour has been unforgivable, but he deserves a chance to explain himself. I need to know the truth about his relationship with Annabelle. I'll see him again – just this once.

Anger at him was dissipating by the minute, as Julianne relished the thought of seeing Romero again. Even if it was to be just one last time. Julianne could not deny the excitement in her stomach, the longing in her heart. She settled on a plan. Following through her intention to move out of the villa, she would pack a couple of suitcases and what was left, she would return for the next day.

Hardly knowing why it was so important, but also knowing that Kira Mae considered the painting from her grandmother's house her prized possession, Julianne wrapped the pastoral scene in a large fluffy towel. She planned on laying it on top of the cases on the back seat of the car.

When Romero next called to finalise plans to meet up, she would suggest he drive over to the new shop. To meet at the villa was certainly no longer an option.

Taking the initiative, Julianne dialled Romero's number. His teasing tone cajoled Julianne into losing all sense except the deep desire to see him. Willingly he agreed to come to her new home. Wickedly he even reminded her of their first visit there.

'No wonder it held such wonderful memories for you,' he said in a deep sexy voice. 'Perhaps we can make some more memories. Yes?'

Julianne was already lost in her own memories. 'Yes,' she agreed. The visit had been even before the two had made love, but their passion and desire for each other had sparked and ignited the very air all around.

They had very nearly overstepped the bounds of decency and social acceptability in the master bedroom of the simply furnished apartment.

'We should try out the bed to see if it is comfortable,' Romero had joked. Innate good manners had prevented Julianne from taking up his suggestion.

Having showered away all the dust and grime of her hard day's labour at the shop, Julianne chose carefully the outfit she would wear when Romeo came to visit that evening. A classic, Grecian style white silk jersey dress with a halter neckline, studded with white pearls and a long deep V-neck opening which covered but did not conceal her breasts. The dress clung provocatively to her hips and skimmed her knees. She chose white gladiator sandals with silver straps. It had been several days since she had set eyes on Romero and Julianne was determined to impress him by looking drop dead gorgeous. She blow dried her silky hair, parted it to the side and brushed it into place to enticingly frame her face.

'No man could resist you,' he had told her the first time they made love. 'You certainly know how to turn on the glamour.'

Tonight she would turn up the volume. Even though she knew there were awkward questions to be asked, Julianne was determined not to deprive herself of the opportunity to get Romero into bed.

Happy with her own reflection in the mirror, Julianne turned her attention to packing suitcases. Having packed her clothes and toiletries, Julianne returned to her wardrobe and removed the *piece de resistance*. The secret weapon to entice rich female clients into her new boutique. Lovingly she fingered the exquisite couture, scarlet evening gown that had been her parting gift when she left the high class Italian fashion house where she had worked so happily for many years.

The to-die-for full length shimmering scarlet gown was an exclusive Roberto Cavalli design styled in his signature shiny satin with net insets on the lower skirt. The heart-shaped bodice resembling a jewelled tutu was delicately boned and defied gravity, plunging between the breasts to the waist – the waist was cinched and the skirt of the dress hugged the thighs down to the knee where it fanned out in a breath-taking fish tail of red ostrich feathers. A super skinny rhinestone belt encircled the waist and was replicated by the spaghetti straps studded with matching flashing rhinestones. In a corset crunching size zero, the dress had the power to transform any woman into a goddess. And any man into a slave.

Marvelling at the dress and caressing it tenderly in her arms filled Julianne with a sense that fashion was power. It was a work of art, the colour rich as a rare Pompeian red, the feathers outrageous, and the glamour majestic. She held it up to her own reflection in the mirror.

Visualising the window of her new boutique, Julianne had

known instinctively that the dress had to be the centrepiece. The boutique was to be named in honour of the dress: *La Dama Escalata*. The Scarlet Lady.

Lovingly holding the scarlet creation and her own suitcase, Julianne carried both downstairs and laid them carefully on the back seat of her car. She returned for Kira Mae's belongings and the painting.

At the villa, she checked all windows and doors were locked and walked quickly to her car. There was no time to lose, she had an important date.

Kira Mae had said she would be staying in Italy for the weekend and then it would take her a couple of days to make the return journey to Spain. By that time Julianne planned to have completed the move of the last of their belongings from the villa to the new premises. Julianne could hardly wait to experience her daughter's excitement when she was informed that their dream of owning their own designer boutique was now a reality.

Well used to changing perception and even altering reality to match her own world view, Julianne was adamant that any reservations her daughter had expressed about moving from the villa would be overcome by her excitement at the opportunity to run her own fashion emporium and create her own designs.

Our lives are about to change forever, she told herself optimistically.

Driving down the hill away from the villa, Julianne allowed herself a backward glance. She did not want to deny the affection she had once held for the village that had been a safe haven. And brought her to Romero. A place where she had been introduced to the joys of love, passion and life in all its mysteries.

For a fleeting moment she remembered that Annabelle too had been a member of the village community. Maybe one day she would know how the jigsaw fitted together. How her friend had become Mrs Rosario and why she did not live with her husband here in Spain. This village held the key to the mystery.

Mr Romero Santo Rosario had a lot of explaining to do.

Romero would arrive under cover of darkness. Julianne had dictated the time and place in her phone call.

'I'm leaving the villa now,' she had told him, 'and apart from collecting my remaining belongings, I shall not return.'

Before he could question her further, she hurriedly continued, 'Meet me at the boutique this evening. I'll be arriving about nine o'clock – I'll cook dinner for us.'

The villa would always hold bitter sweet memories. If she hadn't been staying here, she would not have met Romero, and despite all the complications, her clandestine romance was still a source of great excitement. She felt exhilaratingly alive for possibly the first time in her life. The profound psychic change in her felt like a victory – a vindication of her true value and her ability to give herself lovingly to a man. Romero had ignited a fire of passion inside her and she would not deny the joy he had brought her.

★ ★ ★

Triumphantly unpacking the gorgeous scarlet dress, she impulsively decided to put it immediately on display in the store window. In the absence of a mannequin, Julianne draped the dress over a brushed gold velvet armchair that she had carried down from the furnished apartment above the shop.

To add perspective to the tableau, she positioned Kira

Mae's beloved painting above the red armchair. Its old-fashioned impressionist pastoral scene of a courtly young man and young lady out walking in the countryside added the finishing romantic touch. The window was dressed to perfection.

Beside the chair she lovingly placed a pair of Manolo Blahnik classic stilettos in ripe red velvet – with huge floppy bows on the front. Completing the display, an elegant marble topped console table – previously a piece of bathroom furniture – was positioned to hold a small red evening bag with rhinestone strap and clasp.

Proudly reviewing her window display, Julianne spoke to her image in the glass.

'Meet *La Dama Escalata*,' she declared dramatically. 'Unafraid, free, and fabulous.'

Little did Julianne know that at that moment free was not a description that could be applied to her beloved daughter, the one for whom she had undertaken this extravagant business venture.

chapter twenty-three

'When sorrows come, they come not single spies but in battalions.'
Shakespeare's *Hamlet*

Kira Mae had not even started her journey from the hotel in Rome to Positano. She was too deeply entangled in trying to convince the Italian police of why she was in Rome in the first place.

Unfortunately Italian police procedure had not stretched to the regulation one phone call that she would have been allowed in the British justice system. Therefore Kira Mae had no way of letting her mother know of the nightmare she was currently enduring. One person who could have imparted the news, Romero, had other things on his mind when he had come calling on her mother. Julianne had promised herself that she would demand answers from Romero before she allowed herself to be seduced or enticed by him.

All good intentions flew out of the window as she held the door invitingly open for him to enter. He swept her into his arms and held her so tight she could hardly breathe.

'*Mi amor,*' he whispered, 'it feels so good to be with you again. I have dreamt of this moment so many times during the dark days and lonely nights. Don't deny me,' he pleaded.

Allowing herself to be led up the narrow staircase, Julianne offered no resistance, as Romero laid her gently on the bed. His lips, his hands, his very breath, seduced and entranced her – this was no time to be demanding explanations.

Romero did not wait for permission to undress her. Instead, he tore hungrily at her clothes and even ripped the fastening of her halter neck in his desperate desire to free her breasts.

He helped her get naked – and she returned the favour. Unlike their first time together, this time Romero took her with an assurance that required Julianne to revise her previous languorous response to his lovemaking.

Romero covered her body in dreamy kisses starting at her lips, working his way down her throat, to her breasts and onwards to her stomach and beyond. As his delicious lips, sensuous fingers and demanding tongue explored her mound of Venus and prepared to enter the deeper sacred places; Romero rose to his knees and parted her legs.

He grasped her tight buttocks firmly and buried his exquisite tongue deep inside her. Shocked and aroused as never before, Julianne wound her fingers through his dark, curly hair and forced him deeper and deeper. She moaned with pleasure and cried out in ecstasy as his expert tongue taught her the divine delights of clitoral stimulation.

When he judged that his indulgences had left her weak and ready to explode with sexual appreciation, he stopped and kneeling up between her legs invited her to stimulate him. Sensing her reluctance and inexperience he patiently showed her how to use her hand to stroke him firmly, not exerting too much pressure or too little.

'Slowly,' he ordered, 'slow down, grasp me tighter. Don't

stop. Don't stop. It feels so good. That's my girl. Hold me tight. Make it happen.'

He controlled her movements and when he was ready, covered her hand with his and encouraged her to guide his throbbing penis into the ripe place he had already prepared between her legs. 'God, you're beautiful,' he said. 'You're driving me crazy. I can't hold off any longer. Let me take you to ecstasy, come with me, come with me.' Their writhing entangled the silky double sheet and he pressed the large bolster pillow into action to raise her hips up ever closer to his thrusting body.

They came together in a powerful explosion of pent up passion and sexual desires. Overwhelmed, powerless, Julianne gave herself up to Romero and shared blissfully in the joint demands of their sexual gratification.

Falling asleep in each other's arms, they stayed that way for hours. Through the night, pressed close to him and feeling his breath mingle with hers, Julianne thanked God for allowing her this glorious fantasy, an all consuming dangerous romance with a handsome stranger. Now she knew what they – whoever they are – meant when they said, better to have loved and lost than never to have loved at all. As the light of dawn illuminated the scene of their lovemaking, Julianne opened her eyes and remembered the meal she had prepared but never served to her red hot Latin lover.

We were hungry only for each other, she reminded herself. Every fibre in her being had cried out for him. Julianne had never felt emotions like these. She vowed that she would sacrifice everything to go on having him inflame and control her.

Of course, she had already realised that no one must know

of their frantic desire-driven relationship. Julianne did not dare to contemplate where the relationship was going or how it would end. All she knew, without a doubt, was that if it were to end, she would die.

For today she knew she would deny Romero nothing. He had her under his spell and even though he did not demand her silence, she knew that there was no way their affair could be allowed to become public. Her new neighbours would already have plenty of questions about the owner of *La Dama Escalata;* she did not intend to provide answers.

Julianne crept out of the bedroom, leaving Romero asleep. She soaked herself in the warm fragrant waters of the bright red, claw-footed tub in the unmodernised bathroom. Applying makeup, she strained to see her reflection in the small shabby chic antique wall mirror that cried out for re-silvering. She dressed in a simple ivory shift with cream leather strappy sandals which showed off her scarlet painted toenails before descending the small metal spiral staircase down to the shop – and the first day of her new life.

When Romero awoke a couple of hours later, Julianne took him a cup of coffee in bed, resisting the temptation and his entreaties to join him and gently encouraged him to come down and see the shop window of which she was so proud.

Away from the prying eyes of Romero's own village, she felt liberated. Romero praised the way she had already started to work magic and transform the boutique into a place of style and high fashion. The window alone, which cleverly concealed the fact that there was not yet any other merchandise inside the shop, was a triumph of smoke and mirrors. Window dressing at its best.

However, he calmly warned her. 'You are inviting trouble

with the name of the shop. You are not in England now. Traditional values still apply and you will *become* the scarlet woman.'

And as if the thought had just occurred to him, he added, 'Is that what you wanted? To be thought scandalous?'

Julianne brushed off his concerns and promised to model the dress for him one day. 'My own lady in red,' he smiled. 'I know the song that your Chris de Burgh sings. The English tourists play it on the karaoke machines in bars in town.'

Reluctant to spoil the mood of romance, Julianne wished she could avoid the subject of Annabelle and also Michella, his fiancée. But she knew she could not put it off forever.

Urging Romero to sit at the white-washed table on the small flower-filled outdoor terrace, Julianne quietly asked for an explanation,

'It has been devastating for me,' she told him honestly, 'to find out first that you had a fiancée and then to learn that she had been killed in a car crash. But even more soul destroying was the revelation that you are married to Annabelle.'

Romero looked solemn for a moment. 'Michella, yes, that was a terrible shock,' he admitted. 'She was a beautiful girl, my childhood sweetheart. Our parents have been planning for many years that we should marry. I am reluctant to call it an arranged marriage but in our society often the parents do get together to make a good match for their children.

'Michella would have made me a good wife. An honourable mother for my children. Our families would have been happy to join their resources and properties and to continue the cultural traditions of our gypsy heritage.

'Her death was a great blow to me. I will go to my grave with the knowledge that our families' hearts are broken. All their plans and dreams for the future have died with Michella. We will never forget her.'

Julianne felt tears in her eyes; she was moved by his eloquent speech and by his noble willingness to follow the traditions of his culture. She felt no jealousy for Michella, just a deep respect for the relationship that had been forged in the bonds of childhood and should have brought such joy to the now grieving families.

Julianne knew that Romero would have made Michella a good husband – even if his idea of love and fidelity was different from the old values of the family. But just maybe it was acceptable in a Latin society where the idea of an official mistress for married men had long since coexisted beside married life. She believed too when he told her that the love he felt for her was different, was special, was impossible to deny.

'From the moment I saw you, I knew that we would be lovers,' he said with conviction. 'Do not compare the love I have for you, to the arrangement between families that I would have shared with Michella.'

Julianne was so scared of doing anything to drive Romero away, that following the declaration of his love for her she was reluctant even to challenge him about Annabelle, but challenge him she must.

Standing up and turning her back to him so that she did not have to look into his eyes, Julianne spoke the name loudly. Gathering all her courage, she took a deep breath and asked, 'What about *Mrs* Rosario?'.

There was silence. Romero did not answer and Julianne could not resist the temptation to turn around and look at him. Shaking his head, a smile spread over his face.

'*Mrs* Rosario?' he repeated, as if he had not quite heard correctly.

Julianne waited.

'Annabelle, your friend Annabelle?' he jousted with her.

'Yes,' Julianne nodded, 'my supposed friend.'

'She didn't tell you?'

'Tell me what?'

'That we married so she could gain Spanish residency. It made the bureaucracy so much easier if she was married to a Spaniard. It was simply a marriage of convenience. I did her a favour – and saved her taxes. As soon as she had been granted residency – we were to have the marriage dissolved. We would already have set the divorce in action if she had not needed to return to England.'

Gathering speed with his explanation, he went on. 'Her father was dying and she had to return suddenly. Our arrangement was left as unfinished business and I did not want to pressure her until such time as she would return and complete the process to end the marriage. We planned to apply for an annulment, having never consummated the marriage.

'You will understand that with the family situation involving my darling Michella, the fewer people who knew of the marriage the better. It was a civil marriage not religious.'

Julianne listened and couldn't help questioning whether she was indeed hearing the truth, the whole truth and nothing but the truth. Surely divorce, even a civil one, was not so easy to obtain in a Catholic country?

Romero certainly had all his arguments laid out – he assured her by insisting that she check out the story with Annabelle when they next met.

'She will confirm everything I have said,' he declared

earnestly, 'but do me one favour – do not discuss the matter on the telephone. Of course what we did is illegal, so better to leave it as a private matter and discuss it with her in person.'

Julianne accepted his version of events. She refused not to.

'Now, my lovely,' said Romero, standing up and moving swiftly towards the front door, 'I must leave you. I have business to take care of in town. Give me a kiss goodbye and until I see you again, remember, you hold a special place in my heart. In the midst of sadness, you have made me a very happy man.'

Julianne was eager to believe Romero as he looked deep into her eyes. A small voice of dissention tried to make itself heard but she made the decision to ignore it. Closing down her critical emotional responses was a device she had applied all her life. Denial and delusion were comfort zones for her.

'Everything will work out for the best,' she asserted to him and herself. 'You'll find me waiting here when you return.'

Julianne did not know that she would be forced to wait a lifetime.

★ ★ ★

There was no news from Romero for the whole weekend. More worryingly, there was no news from Kira Mae. Julianne had swallowed her pride and called Annabelle several times. No one had answered her phone in England and there was no response to messages left on her international mobile phone. All calls remained unanswered to Kira Mae and Julianne drew a blank. Julianne was frantic.

chapter twenty-four

'Oh, thou foul thief!
Where hast thou stowed my daughter?
Damned as though art, thou hast enchanted her.'
Shakespeare's *Othello*

Kira Mae paced up and down the claustrophobic prison cell. There were no windows in the eight foot by six foot room. The walls were painted in a sickly dark green colour and the ceiling was chocolate brown. Or was that nicotine brown?

The few sparse pieces of furniture were all screwed down. A small pull down bunk bed was attached to the walls with chains – a metal chair was affixed to the walls, as was a small metal wash basin. There was a metal jug for washing and a small galvanised steel bucket covered with a wooden board served as a toilet.

Determined to use neither the bed nor the toilet, Kira Mae occasionally stopped pacing long enough to walk to the wash basin and splash her face with water. As an added respite from pacing, Kira Mae perched on the edge of the uncomfortable chair – hanging on tightly to the seat, as if to stop herself from falling. She had no way of knowing how long she had been in the cell. At a guess, she would say more than a dozen hours.

Her light summer clothing felt impossibly grubby and she was cold and frightened. After her arrest by the two policemen in the hotel lobby, she had been brought straight here. Her treatment had been perfunctory rather than cruel.

Kira Mae had no idea what crime she was supposed to have committed, her limited ability to understand Italian meant that even when a policeman had tried to explain, she still did not understand. Playing the universal policeman's game of good cop/bad cop, one of the policemen, a kindly older man, had tried to reassure the young foreign girl that an interpreter would be brought for her. The other, young and self important, had been surly and refused to answer any questions.

Now Kira Mae longed to hear the sound of the key turning in the locked door of the cell. Surely someone would come soon to explain to her what this was all about. Although she was reluctant to admit even to herself that she knew why she had been arrested, one nagging thought kept forcing its way into her consciousness.

What were the Louis Vuitton attaché case and black beauty box doing in the back of the police car? Could it be the same ones she had transported from Spain? Surely it was too much of a coincidence to hope that there were another two. And, the more important question, what did the bags contain?

Standing in the middle of the cell feeling helpless, hopeless and alone, Kira Mae allowed herself to cry.

Without making any effort to hold back the tears, she enjoyed the relief of letting go. She deserved this outburst. Huge soulful sobs shook her body and she cried like a baby. In the middle of all this loss of control, Kira Mae was startled by the bad timing of the long awaited sound of a key unlocking the heavy iron door.

A pint sized, unsmiling Italian policewoman stood at the door and gestured for Kira Mae to follow her. Down a long, bare corridor past three more cells and up a short flight of concrete steps to a small interrogation room. In the middle of the featureless room, there was a battered wooden table and three chairs. The walls of the room had at one time been painted a sickly chartreuse colour – now they reflected the years of decay and neglect as dirt, perspiration and an unhealthy humidity made a thin film of moisture trickle down the paintwork and gather in dirty pools around the scuffed and blackened skirting boards. The floor had no covering, the original charcoal grey concrete tiles were chipped and uneven. No redeeming feature had been allowed to add hope to the forlorn decor of the depressing and cheerless interview cum interrogation room. The archetypal single naked light bulb was relieved only by a matt dark green metal lamp shade.

Kira Mae shuddered, her body chilled with the damp and hostile atmosphere.

'Sit,' said the young, dark haired policewoman in a brusque voice, as if she was giving instruction to a dog, 'I will bring you coffee. They will come to speak to you soon. Stay here.'

Kira Mae couldn't see any possibility to go anywhere else so she did as she was told, sit and stay. The 'they' turned out to be the two arresting officers and a third gentleman. To her relief, Kira Mae discovered that the third person was a lawyer who spoke English.

'Whenever a foreign national is arrested,' he explained, 'the police are obliged to contact the embassy of the person's country of origin.

'The British Embassy in Rome was informed of your arrest and they called me to come and assist you.'

'Thank God for the British,' said Kira Mae, finally managing a smile.

Paolo Grazia was the lawyer and Kira Mae judged him to be probably in his late thirties or possibly even forties. He was the whole package. Confident, handsome and immaculately dressed, a silver fox, a middle-aged man comfortable in his own skin, who could still attract girls decades younger than himself. An obvious gentleman, in any language, he exuded confidence and gave the impression of being eager to help a damsel in distress. Especially such a beautiful one.

Under any other circumstances, Kira Mae would have been tempted to flirt with the charming Italian lawyer, but the uncertainty of her situation had made her scared and unsure of herself. Also she was acutely aware that after her long hours in the cell, she was looking far from her glamorous best. Her handbag containing makeup and hairbrush had been taken from her when they were signing her in. Still she managed to flash a friendly smile of gratitude at Paolo. It was good to have someone on her side.

Paolo questioned the policemen as Kira Mae sat looking forlornly from one to the other, trying to get a sense of their discourse. Writing rapidly in a yellow legal notebook, Paolo wrote down their answers and from time to time nodded reassuringly at Kira Mae.

When he felt confident that he understood the full situation, Paolo courteously turned to the policemen and dismissed them.

'I wish to speak to my client in private,' he said in English. 'I will call you when I am ready.'

The policemen nodded politely and left the room.

When client and lawyer were alone together in the barren

interview room, Paolo nodded reassuringly at Kira Mae. Studying his notebook he read in silence for a while as if deciding how best to translate to his anxious client the accusations that the policemen had revealed.

When he spoke, Kira Mae was totally engaged and ready to listen to his every word. She leaned towards him and concentrated, alert and hopeful.

'You are in a lot of trouble, young lady,' was his opening statement. Kira Mae felt her lower lip start to tremble.

'What do they say I did wrong?' she asked, hoping against hope that it was something as simple as a traffic violation, a misunderstanding. A case of mistaken identity.

Paolo again consulted his notebook and then cleared his throat. 'If they have their way, you will be facing a charge of murder,' he said quietly.

It came as such a shock that Kira Mae almost laughed at the absurdity of the accusation.

'Murder? Murder, me? You cannot be serious – there is some mistake. I don't know what this is all about. It can't be true!' Stammering and stuttering Kira Mae tried desperately to make him see how ridiculous the whole situation was.

'Let me start at the beginning,' said Paolo patiently. 'We may be in a position to establish some of the facts. We'll take it slowly. There is no rush. Number one: do you know a man called Jesus Floris?'

Kira Mae was relieved to be able to honestly answer that no, she did not. So that proved it was all a mistake. Can I go now? she asked silently.

'No, never heard of him,' she said adamantly.

Paolo looked at her sadly. 'You must tell me the truth,' he admonished her. 'I can't help you if I don't know the real situation. This man visited you at your hotel last night.'

The pain of realisation made her feel as if she had been hit in the stomach. 'Jesus? No, only Romero visited me,' she stated, desperate to confirm her own alibi even if she would have preferred to avoid the obvious implication. A man with a name she did not know visiting her in the middle of the night. Not a good look, she admitted.

'Romero was with me,' and, pausing for effect so that there could be no doubt about the exact nature of the revelation, she emphasised, '*all* night. I met no other man in Rome.'

Paolo took her at her word and set to quoting from his notes and filling in additional background that he had elicited from the police officers.

To ensure that Kira Mae was up to speed on all developments he gave her a detailed report relaying what he had been informed were the circumstances surrounding her arrest.

'The English lady was first put under surveillance when she handed over two attaché cases in the lobby of the InterContinental Hotel to an accomplice of Jesus Floris. Jesus was observed to be sitting in a silver Fiat – a rental car – outside the hotel though the two did not meet at that time. He had made a phone call to the hotel earlier in the evening and the receptionist put the call through to the room of Miss Kira Mae Gordon.'

Keen to show off their great detective skills, the older policeman had responded to Paolo's questioning look during his interrogation.

'We have been monitoring his phone calls for months,' the policeman admitted. 'A tracking device was installed by our department onto his cell though the range is limited and he has been changing his devices frequently. Right now we have no signal.'

'Last night Jesus was followed by police officers from the InterContinental Hotel, as he drove off to a previously identified apartment block in the city. This man is no fool – he checks for tails and always uses different routes even on regular journeys.

'He dropped his passenger and stayed but a short time before returning to the city and driving to various addresses, some of which are identified by us as the haunts of drug dealers and low life criminals.'

Law enforcement officers had been on duty outside the apartment of the accomplice all night.

The young officer had been keen to take up the story. 'At dawn he came out and got into his own car which was parked in the underground garage. Looking around he must have decided that he was not being watched though he is no stranger to arrests or dawn raids. His poor wife and young children have been put through that indignity many times. It is an occupational hazard for career crooks. This particular small time criminal is actually a nice enough guy. He acts as a courier for Jesus – and an informant for us.

'Often we leave him on the street even when we know he is up to no good because he is valuable in picking up information. But this morning we stepped in and slapped the cuffs on him as he dug a deep hole in the woods to bury the cases he had collected on his trip to the hotel with Jesus last night, the same ones that your young English mule handed over.'

At the use of the word 'mule' in connection with his client, Paolo politely asked the young cop to refrain from using that name at this early stage. 'We shall see what she has to say in her statement,' he informed him.

So far, the little fish were trapped in the net, big fish like Jesus had evaded the clutches of the law.

Kira Mae's mind was racing. Too much information. Her tired brain was having trouble processing it all. Some of what she had heard she knew to be true, other aspects of the situation she was being confronted with for the first time. Immediately after she had handed the case to Annabelle, for a fleeting moment she did indeed think she had seen Romero in a car outside the hotel. She had dismissed the idea, there being nothing to suggest that Romero was even in the vicinity, though he had promised to visit her at midnight.

Now came the startling revelation that it had indeed been him. But where did Annabelle fit into the picture? She was the one who had asked Kira Mae to deliver the cases from her villa in Spain and rendezvous with her in Rome. Paolo was about to enlighten her.

'Jesus Floris has a long record of convictions for drug running, arms trafficking and money laundering. So too has his wife, Annabelle Anstruther, also known as Mrs Jesus Floris.'

Kira Mae could not believe what she was hearing – but there was worse to come.

'The attaché case you delivered to this individual at the InterContinental Hotel contained a gun which had been used in a recent murder.

'You also were the courier of a large consignment of cocaine and a huge amount of cash. Tools of the trade of an international drug runner,' explained Paolo seriously. 'You were already under surveillance when you handed over the contraband to the English lady, Annabelle after your arrival in Rome.'

Paolo was not enjoying this interview at all. The room was airless, stuffy and growing ominously dark with the fading light from the tiny barred window up where the wall met the ceiling. A cranky propeller fan may have once delivered a change of air and some relief but now it hung limply from the low roof, two paddles broken. He would not waste his time reporting its dilapidated state to the authorities. Who cared, they classed all the suspects here as criminals – there were no innocents.

By the law of ratios and his personal experience over the years in this room and others like it, Paolo, public defender had to agree with their reasoning. But that was no excuse for refusing even hardened criminals breathing rights.

Generally on official lawyer visits, Paolo kept his time strictly rationed but he felt sorry for the young girl sitting opposite him across the bare wooden table. As the messenger, he felt partially responsible for the fear and demoralisation he saw in her eyes and her deflated demeanour as she listened to wave after wave of bad news. It wouldn't be the first time that he was blamed as the bearer of bad tidings. Don't shoot the messenger he wanted to tell her, I am here to help.

She looked at him accusingly and then surprised him by smiling suddenly. 'And now for the good news?' she said with a laugh that must have taken her final reserves of good humour. He busied himself, seeming to organise items in his briefcase which he had lifted from the floor beside his chair and opened on the table in from of him. Paolo attempted to avoid Kira Mae's gaze as he steeled himself to deliver even further devastating news.

'Jesus and Madame Annabelle are cold-blooded killers. They have evaded the hangman's noose many times, in many countries and they are on the run again. They have the money and resources to avoid capture and are probably already back in their adopted homeland of Columbia. It is they who should be in the dock, of that I'm sure but as co-conspirators, you are to be charged with murder along with the other accomplice.

'If it is any consolation,' he smiled wryly, 'he too is a small fish, like you – the real criminals will continue to evade capture. Arrests, convictions and acquittals are a way of life for them. We cannot guarantee to keep them locked up even if we do convict. They escape or buy their way out and go to ground, often changing their names, identities and not unusually their faces. When they judge it to be safe, they surface again to continue their murderous and highly profitable trade.'

Kira Mae was having trouble breathing, she gasped for air and Paolo handed her a glass of water. Her voice sounded strange as she asked, 'Who did they murder?'

Not sure yet how the murder fitted into the ever more confusing labyrinth, Paolo was able to impart the information he had received from the two detectives. He had done his job well in collecting information about the fascinating case that was unfolding. Paolo was a traditional lawyer, one who prided himself on doing a thorough job – he was honourable and professional. Relaying what he knew, he informed Kira Mae that the victim was a young Spanish girl – he had only her first name, Michella.

'At first it was thought that her death was as a result of a road accident, her car had crashed off a mountain road in a small village in Spain. However, the fire that engulfed the vehicle failed to completely destroy the body and a post mortem examination discovered that she had been shot. She may have double crossed a gang member or been the victim of an inter-gang revenge killing. Human life holds no value for the drug barons. Murder is the currency they deal in – a life for a life. It goes on constantly and mercilessly. No person is safe who gets involved with these devils.

'Forensic tests have established that she was already dead when her body was put in the driver's seat. The car was then pushed from the mountain road onto the cliffs below to make it look like an accident and cover up the true cause of death.'

Tears sprang to Kira Mae's eyes. 'Poor, Michella,' she said. 'She didn't deserve to die like that.'

'You knew her?' asked Paolo in surprise.

'Yes,' admitted Kira Mae. 'She was the fiancée of my lover Romero. Or should that be Jesus?'

The scheduled end to his visit was long overdue but Paolo promised to call Kira Mae's mother and let her know of the terrible events that had befallen her daughter. Kira Mae was returned to her holding cell and the next day made her first court appearance to answer the trumped up charges.

Kira Mae stood in the dock shaking. 'Yes, sir,' she answered to the establishing questions about her name and address and status. She was not yet formally charged so not required to swear an oath but the judge lectured her on the seriousness of the pending charges. Her lawyer had already indicated that if found guilty her sentence could be up to twenty years. Paolo accepted that he had a monumental task on his hands. Even he was having trouble believing that she was a complete innocent duped and left to face the consequences.

Paolo held out just the faintest hope that he would be able to plea bargain with the prosecution – if Kira Mae turned collaborator and gave evidence against the real criminals.

In return for information leading to the arrest of Jesus and Annabelle, Paolo would endeavour to negotiate a remission on any sentence that was imposed. There was already too much evidence for him to believe she would not be convicted.

The Italian justice system moves notoriously slowly and Paolo warned Kira Mae's that it could be up to a year before her case came to trial. The prospect of spending any more time in the dehumanising and overcrowded prison system was a torture. Kira Mae would have been even more distressed had she known that she would also be awaiting another important event.

chapter twenty-five

'Now does my project gather to a head,
My charms crack not, my spirits obey.'
Shakespeare's *The Tempest*

Shutting up shop after a hectic day in which she had prepared the premises to open when her first order of stock arrived from London, the proprietor of *La Dama Escalata* was feeling decidedly pleased with herself.

The spectacular window display had attracted lots of attention and many of the most chic and fashionable womenfolk of the area had visited the shop and wished her well with the new venture. Julianne was already making judgements about the ladies and beginning to assess which designers and accessories would be most popular.

Such designer names as Dolce & Gabbana, Armani and Versace were always top of the must-haves for well-dressed international ladies – and Italian couture buyers were unfailingly loyal to the Latin designers.

Several of the new clientele had also expressed an interest in one off designs. Kira Mae's unfinished but still impressive graduate portfolio, in which she had developed her flair for producing exquisite evening wear, was prominently displayed and had attracted a great deal of attention. *La Dama Escalata* was showing early promise to be the latest trend-setting boutique for the local fashionistas.

'*Buenas noches, adios* madam,' said Julianne with well-practised cheer, as she bid a warm farewell to the last visitor of the day. Julianne closed the door and reached for the '*Lo siento, cerrado*' sign. An auspicious start to the new life she envisioned for her and her beloved daughter.

Julianne admonished herself for the fact that already in a few short weeks they had lost much of the closeness that they had enjoyed back in London. Then, through necessity and fear, they had clung to each other. Sharing long and emotionally charged conversations about their dreams of a sunshine lifestyle, they had inspired and encouraged each other. But, inexplicably, almost as soon as they had arrived in Spain, a gulf had opened up between them. Julianne already accepted the blame. She had become so obsessed with Romero and frightened that her secret romance would be discovered.

'Mummy will make it up to you, darling,' Julianne said out loud. If talking to yourself was a sign of madness, she calculated she was well on the way.

'Nothing and no one will come between us,' she said forcefully. 'We've come through so much – I am determined to get back the unbreakable bond that gave us our strength.'

Unfortunately, as Julianne was forced to observe wryly, she could not even begin to put her good intentions into effect until she had heard from Kira Mae.

All phone calls had gone unanswered. She knew of course that Kira Mae could hold a sulk for days, but usually she would have called, if only to engage in further argument. Julianne had expressed her disapproval of Kira Mae's intentions to extend her trip and told her to come straight home – Kira Mae had refused.

Trying hard not to see it as an immediate cause for concern, Julianne nevertheless was beginning to worry for the safety of her only daughter. In an effort to assuage some of her guilt, she promised herself that if Romero suggested coming to pay a call this evening, she would refuse his advances.

An expression of Mummy Mitchell's came to mind, 'Cutting off your nose to spite your face', but Julianne felt she was justified in trying to make bargains with the Gods. 'I'll be a good girl, if you just make everything all right.'

Strange as it seemed, Julianne realised that she had never discussed Romero with her daughter or her daughter with Romero – she had been obsessively single minded about keeping the two in separate compartments.

Now, Kira Mae had to come first. Mother and daughter, together, forever. Blood is thicker than water, Julianne reminded herself.

Overcome with sadness, Julianne realised that she had become desperate to hear her daughter's voice.

'Please, please, phone,' she silently begged.

When the phone did ring, Julianne rushed to answer her mobile. Her life had degenerated into waiting for phone calls, first Romero, now Kira Mae.

'Kira Mae, is that you?' she asked breathlessly.

'No, it is not your daughter,' said a strange male voice, 'but I do have news of her.'

'News of her?' intoned Julianne. It sounded ominous. 'What do you mean?' she asked, feeling the panic rise in her throat and sound in her voice.

Paolo Grazia, the Italian lawyer, introduced himself and as gently as possible, explained the circumstances in which he had met Kira.

Tears flowed down Julianne's face and she wiped them away with the back of her hand – the other hand gripped the cell phone until her knuckles turned white.

'Tell me where she is, I will come immediately,' said Julianne urgently.

'You will not be able to see her at this stage,' said Paolo gently, 'but I will arrange it as soon as I can. I do not wish to unnecessarily alarm you, however, the situation is serious and we are doing all we can to find solutions or compromises. Your daughter has got herself mixed up with a group of very dangerous and manipulative criminals. We cannot yet establish the extent of her involvement; she denies all knowledge of any wrongdoing. We are undertaking preliminary investigations and appealing to the authorities to not press charges until we confirm whether she was an accomplice to the crimes or an unwitting victim.'

Julianne was beside herself, her voice almost at a screech, she demanded answers. 'Who are these people? Have they hurt my daughter? What is she supposed to have done? She's a child, not a criminal.'

Paolo asked patiently, 'Do you or your daughter know a man called Jesus Floris?'

'No, definitely not.' Julianne breathed a sigh of relief. 'This is a case of mistaken identity. It should not be difficult for you to prove it and get her released.'

'I will keep you informed of all developments,' he said in reply.

★ ★ ★

That hour before dawn, the darkest one, engulfed Julianne all night. Rigid and sleepless she lay in her bed, the only activity her constantly racing mind.

Since the phone call from Paolo, who said he was acting under instructions from the British Embassy, Julianne had been tormenting herself. Armed with a few sketchy details about her daughter's arrest in Rome, Julianne knew that she was somehow to blame.

Paolo had persuaded her to wait until morning before starting her journey, which would give him time to make the necessary arrangements.

'Late at night in your emotional state the drive will be dangerous – and unnecessary,' said Paolo solicitously. 'Try to get some sleep and take a flight out here in the morning. I will make an appointment to take you to visit your daughter. I will update you with all the details when you arrive.'

Paolo had invited Julianne to meet him at his office at the British Embassy, which was situated just yards from the Porta Pia gate in the centre of Rome.

'We will go to the prison together,' he had reassured her.

Julianne wept bitter tears of frustration and fear after the phone call from Rome, her peace of mind completely shattered.

The excitement of her first day in the new shop and plans to fix up the apartment, which was comfortable but not luxurious, for Kira Mae's return had consumed her thoughts. Even her unease at not having heard from Kira Mae had been put on the back burner in the frantic activity of her preparations.

Tossing and turning, unable to get any rest, Julianne

endured a dark night of the soul. There was no peace to be had and she tormented herself with questions about why, where, how? She was reluctant to take anything to help her sleep as she knew there were many long days ahead – and she had to be up early in the morning. She put on the small bedside lamp again – and again checked the time. Not an hour since the last time she had checked.

Now a deep well of panic and dread threatened to overwhelm her, as she confronted the reality of her beloved daughter all alone and living a nightmare of uncertainty in an Italian prison cell. How would her baby survive the tough correctional regime that she had heard about – in any prison, let alone a foreign one?

Julianne berated herself for instigating the situation that had forced Kira Mae to take the attaché case to Annabelle in Rome. She was also forced to admit that she would not have been so anxious to be alone in the villa had there not been the prospect of Romero coming to call.

There was no consoling her – nor was there anyone to do so had she wanted it – Julianne knew without a doubt that she had failed her daughter.

Ostensibly she had brought her to Spain to keep her safe and away from the man who was father to both of them. Instead she had allowed her own vanity and desperation for love and affection to overshadow her responsibilities to her vulnerable daughter.

She swore to herself that whatever it took, she would fight to make sure that her only child was given all the legal expertise she needed to free her as soon as possible. Paolo, in one brief conversation, had managed to convince her that he was the man for the job.

Paolo had reassured her that once she arrived in Rome they would formulate a plan of action and do everything in their power to alleviate Kira Mae's plight.

Julianne was already aware that this could be an expensive legal business and she mentally gave thanks to dear, departed Mummy Mitchell for leaving them a legacy that ensured she could at least cover the lawyer's costs. Also the contracts were about to be signed on the sale of her London home, so she would soon have the necessary funds in the bank.

Furnishings in the bedroom which she had only moved into twenty-four hours earlier were minimal and her mind had worked overtime on redecoration plans. The big double bed in which she had already lain with Romero was dressed rustic style in a colourful bedspread with plump soft feather pillows. All she had needed last night was the bed and that was fortunate, as there was the minimum of furniture in the room. A small white wood dresser and a basket weave chair. The windows were curtain-less and the overhead light had a single white canvas lampshade. Julianne daydreamed about how she would turn this bedroom into a palace full of sensuous delight with rich jewel-coloured fabrics, vibrant sky blue Mediterranean painted walls and the seductive aroma of scented candles.

Now in the glow of early morning sunlight, Julianne glanced around the featureless room and wondered when she would next sleep here. She had not even properly unpacked the bag she had brought from the villa the day before.

Twenty-four hours or a lifetime ago? Now she repacked, she would require clothes to cover all eventualities. Mostly she chose casual clothes but she might also need to dress to impress the British Embassy officials, judges and Italian lawyers. She also planned to pack some clothes for Kira Mae. Putting herself first, as she was now beginning to realise she did more than she would have chosen to admit, Julianne cursed herself for leaving so many of her daughter's clothes and personal items at the villa.

She knew Kira Mae so well; not having her favourite Vidal Sassoon shampoo and conditioner would easily become as big a problem as facing criminal charges that could keep her in jail for decades. Julianne had to make quick decisions, not even sure whether Kira Mae had a change of clothes with her. Kira Mae would be furious, but most of what she was able to rustle up were London clothes that Julianne had thrown into the boot of the car to wear when clearing out the new premises. Long sleeved T-shirts, track suit bottoms and flat shoes. The chill in her own bones convinced Julianne that Kira Mae would need warm clothing. Neither mother nor daughter were normally inclined towards comfort dressing, but on this occasion, Julianne cared little for how she looked, her only concern was to keep herself and her daughter wrapped up, cocooned. Of course she could have gone back to the villa and brought the rest of their clothes but detours were not an option as she wanted to get started on her mission of mercy.

Julianne locked up the shop and taped a hastily scribbled sign to the window: *Lo siento, familia enfermo, no abierto hoy* – Sorry, closed – family illness.

Driving away from her start-up business and the new home that just yesterday had held such promise, Julianne tried to swallow the lump in her throat. She had already packed and now she drove the car to Alicante airport where she would catch a flight to Rome with a transfer in Madrid – all in all the trip would take just over five hours.

★ ★ ★

In a flash of déjà vu, Julianne had a brief memory of the day aged sixteen when she had left Devon with her father for the long journey to Scotland. Pregnant and scared to death. There had been no one to turn to that day and there was no one to turn to now. At the worst moments of her life, she realised, she was alone and had been expected to make decisions about situations of which she had no experience. How can I be expected to act like an adult when I have never had the luxury of being a child? she asked herself.

The sky above her was a cheerful shade of bright blue and even the clouds looked playfully soft and fluffy; the early morning sun was not yet offering any warmth but it did not matter. Julianne knew that once the icy feeling in her heart took hold, she was destined to suffer its chill effects for a long time. There was a way to release it but she angrily pushed all thoughts of self-harm from her mind. There had to be a better way. Cutting herself was part of the problem – not a solution.

Steeling herself not to cry again, she put a large suitcase in the boot and climbed into the driver's seat. Pushing a mellow classical music CD into the compact disc player, she drove off determined not to look back.

chapter twenty-six

'Men at some time are masters of their fates,
The fault, dear Brutus, is not in our stars but in ourselves.'
Shakespeare's *Julius Caesar*

Julianne prayed the whole way through the uneventful flight. Not for herself or her safety but for her darling daughter. Arriving in Rome in the early afternoon, she took a taxi from the airport to the British Embassy where Paolo was to meet her and personally escort her to see Kira Mae.

Striking a balance between being polite and not prepared to divulge the reason for her trip to Rome, Julianne gave little information to the flirty Italian taxi driver who wanted to know, 'Do you want a guided tour of the Eternal City? Are you meeting a lover here? Are you on business?' He drove as if he was on the dodgem cars at a funfair – narrowly avoiding other cars, cutting up drivers and honking his horn; it was obviously a national sport to make a game of the fast-paced journey through Rome's noisy and congested streets. Julianne wished she could take more joy in the passing panorama straight out of a Fellini film; classic architecture, fabulous fashion, stunning marble statues and breathtaking displays of art and culture. Rome perched on its Seven Hills – the City of Love.

Not a moment too soon for her peace of mind, the taxi pulled into the compound of the British Embassy. Julianne guided the driver, who had now cheekily moved on to inviting her on a date, to drive into the courtyard close by Rome's famous Porta Pia. As the smitten taxi driver reluctantly deposited Julianne at the gates of the contemporary marble building she was impressed by the grandeur. And thankful to be British.

Erected on the old site of a former Renaissance villa, Villa Bracciano, home of the Duke of Bracciano, the original building had been destroyed in a terrorist attack in 1946. The new embassy building was designed by the famous British architect, Sir Basil Spence, and opened in 1971.

After giving her name to the gatekeeper, Julianne was waved through and directed to the west side of the enclosed courtyard. She walked around the landscaped courtyard and into the building past a towering bronze sculpture, titled Back to Venice.

The ceremonial entrance boasted an impressive double staircase leading to the upper level of the building with its marble walls and floors and doors of light oak – and visitors using the lifts were confronted by a large picture of the Queen in her Order of the Garter robes. She presented herself at the wood panelled reception desk after a brief visit to the ladies room. She was expected and the receptionist directed her to the office of Paolo Grazia on the second floor.

Paolo was waiting at the lift to greet her; he enquired politely about her journey and walked her to his office.

Now it was Paolo's turn to be impressed. Julianne was even more beautiful than her daughter. She had an air of elegance and confidence that the younger girl had not yet had time to acquire. Julianne accepted the offer of a cup of English tea – the embassy's daily concession to preserving a taste of home.

When they were seated with their earl grey tea, which a secretary had brought in china cups, leaving the tea pot and a hot water refill, Paolo informed Julianne, 'I will not insult your intelligence by trying to minimise the facts. The situation is most serious.

'Though I tried not to unnecessarily alarm you on the telephone, your daughter is charged with crimes that potentially carry life sentences – if she is found guilty.'

'Please tell me everything you know,' said Julianne calmly, despite the fear that gripped her heart. Already she trusted this man and would be guided by his assessment of the situation.

Paolo consulted the notes that he had taken when being briefed on the case and following the conversation with the officers at the police station.

'Your daughter walked into a police trap,' he admitted. 'Surveillance had been going on for months and the people she met in Rome were already under twenty-four hour observation. On the evening in question, your daughter was observed handing over a Louis Vuitton attaché case and a small black vanity case to a known criminal and two of his associates in the foyer of a hotel here in Rome.

'After the arrest of these men, the case was confiscated and found to contain drugs – they will need to be analysed but at this stage we suspect cocaine – a gun and counterfeit money.

'Kira Mae is to be charged as an accomplice to a whole raft of major crimes, including murder, drug running and money laundering.'

Julianne could not believe her ears. 'This is preposterous,' she said indignantly. 'My daughter is completely innocent of all these charges. She's a child. The only thing she is guilty of is delivering cases of which neither of us even knew the contents. It wasn't our business to enquire.'

She couldn't fail to notice Paola's perplexed expression and was grateful he didn't question her further. Julianne knew there was a danger of becoming an accomplice by association in this whole sorry saga. She had been the one to concede to Annabelle's request to have the cases delivered; she had found the cases and given them to Kira Mae. She had even packed them into the car for her.

Julianne was in full flow, 'If anything, I am more guilty as I am the one who asked her to take the case to my friend Annabelle in Rome. It was a favour for someone who had been kind to us.

'Kira Mae is not implicated in any way. She is innocent of all charges and I will prove it. It is all a dreadful misunderstanding.'

Paolo nodded sympathetically. He was mesmerised and enchanted by the lovely English lady and already knew that he would do everything in his power to see that justice was done in this case.

Already he had been briefed at the highest level by his bosses and Interpol about the gang of international criminals. In global operations stretching from South America to Europe and right across Asia, this bunch of desperados were running one of the biggest multi-million pound drug smuggling cartels ever identified. With mafia-like influence, and murder used as a routine enforcer, their activities covered gunrunning, arms trafficking and money laundering.

A ruthless gang of violent criminals, the bad news for the British Embassy was that the operations were being controlled from England and the mastermind had been named as a Londoner. Police authorities in England and Italy were determined to smash the gang and put the ring leaders behind bars.

Paolo had no intention, at this stage, of telling Julianne just how dangerous the gang were into whose clutches her daughter had fallen. However, what he knew for sure was that Romero or Jesus or the Spaniard who was known by a dozen other aliases, might not be Mr Big, Numero Uno but he was pretty high up the food chain.

Instead of alarming revelations that could only scare the living daylights out of her, Paolo said kindly to Julianne, 'Come, let us go and see your daughter. She needs you.'

Walking down the grand staircase of the British Embassy building, Paolo put his hand on Julianne's arm.

'The embassy and my legal department will do all we can to help you and your daughter,' he promised. Without going into detail, he revealed, 'The British authorities and Interpol are taking a special interest in this case. You will be legally represented and have access to a support system. Do not worry – you are not on your own. This case will be conducted by the British authorities; it is not a civil case.'

The two walked and talked as they made their way to the car park, through the well-tended lawns, past the sweet-smelling rose bushes and tree-lined courtyards.

Holding the passenger door of his car open for Julianne, Paolo waited for her to be seated and walked around to the driver's seat.

Paolo was a man with immense style and the uninhibited desire to attract attention. As befitted a successful Italian lawyer about town, Paolo's car was a top of the range Italian sports number, the coveted Ferrari Testarossa. He handled the gleaming red convertible like a racing driver, as they zoomed through the streets of Rome on the short drive to the jailhouse.

Enjoying the sight and smell of the gorgeous blonde in the passenger seat next to him, Paolo was almost lulled into forgetting the judicial nature of the business between them. At the headquarters of the carabinieri in Questure Centrale he parked and walked quickly round to let Julianne out. He offered his hand and she accepted. Julianne smiled gratefully at this gallant gentleman who was so attentive to her comfort. She was well aware he could have been treating her with disdain – like the mother of a criminal.

Thank God for an ally in the midst of my nightmare she thought. And thank God for small mercies, like having the time to freshen up and change from my travel clothes in the ladies' restroom at the embassy.

Julianne's heels clicked seductively on the flagstones as she walked with Paolo up the stairs and into the imposing courthouse at the Palace of Justice. Each person they encountered turned to look appreciatively at the beautiful blonde, dressed modestly in a navy blue shift dress and white high heels. Even when she played down her womanly attributes, Julianne was still the centre of attention. In a city of ravishing dark haired, dark eyed, Latin beauties, the cool English blonde's blue-eyed looks were different enough to be coveted by men and women alike.

Paolo escorted her proudly, as if they were on a date rather than visiting her daughter who was in jail for attempted murder. Gloom descended on Julianne as she walked down the dark, dank narrow corridor to the basement where Kira

Mae was being held. Julianne instinctively clutched Paolo's arm tighter. She needed moral support and he was more than happy to oblige. Accompanied by a burly policeman who wore a jangling bunch of cell keys on his belt beside his holstered revolver, Julianne was relieved when the iron key was inserted into the heavy wooden door and the cell door swung open.

Julianne stepped warily through the open door and gasped as she saw the terrible conditions in which her daughter was being held. Certainly she had not expected a room out of *House and Garden* but the foul smell and the airlessness of the small cell caught at her throat and eyes and made her gag.

This is about Kira Mae not about you, she told herself angrily. Don't you dare be sick.

Kira Mae was seated forlornly at a small rickety table with her head held in her hands. She looked up and burst into tears when she realised that the visitor framed in the unlit doorway was her mother.

Julianne rushed forward and put her arms around her daughter. Both stayed locked together for some time, crying, holding on to each other. The guard had gestured that he might make a move to part them – physical contact was discouraged in case they were passing drugs – but a severe look from Paolo ensured that the 'no touching' rule was not enforced.

Have a heart, they are mother and daughter, not big time criminals, Paolo's look said. He hoped he was right.

Paolo did not rush them. He stood silently, watching the sad scene and waiting for them to be ready to sit down at the small functional table and start the business that was the purpose for which a visit had been granted. A legal consultation.

Paolo had been brought up in a household of women, his mother and three sisters with no father to be seen, so he was always very solicitous towards females. His heart was touched and he felt desperately sorry for the two lovely ladies and, although as yet he had no evidence to support his theory, a lawyer's intuition told him that these two were innocent victims of a cruel circumstance.

I won't rest until this situation is resolved, he told himself. More than ever, he was determined to help them prepare the defence that would be necessary to fight the case. Already he had some good news that he was eager to share with both of them.

chapter twenty-seven

'Live loathed and long,
Most smiling, smooth, detested parasites.'
Shakespeare's *Timon of Athens*

In a declaration of solidarity, mother and daughter sat on the same side of the interrogation room's scruffy wooden table. They held hands.

Paolo waited until they had composed themselves before launching into the details of the news he had to impart.

'You will make a further appearance in court tomorrow,' he told Kira Mae. 'A formality at which you will be read the charges and we will enter a plea. Presuming that you intend to plead not guilty, I will then ask the judge to grant bail.

'You will need to surrender your passport and you will not be allowed to leave the country. However, you will certainly be much more comfortable than if you have to await trial in the overcrowded women's prison northeast of the city along the Tiber River.

'A bond will need to be posted but at this stage I do not know how much that will be – in Italy you need to put the money up front, it will of course be returned when you show up for your court appearance.'

Julianne interrupted to quickly explain that money would not be a problem as long as they could get Kira Mae out of there.

Paolo admitted that he was pleased with the progress he had made already. The prosecutor was a friend of his and he had seen him with the judge in his chambers that morning – he felt sure bail would be a formality.

'We still do not know the whereabouts of Mr and Mrs Jesus Floris,' he told the ladies, 'but his accomplice, the man in the car, has already been interrogated and he has not implicated you. In fact in his statement he has confirmed that as far as he knew, you were merely a messenger.'

'As I told you on the phone,' said Julianne smoothly, 'we do not know Mr and Mrs Jesus Floris.'

Kira Mae had been reassured by what she was hearing and with her mother by her side she was feeling altogether more hopeful about the whole situation. Now she was frightened.

'We do know them,' she told her mother in a soft voice. 'Jesus is Romero from the village and his wife is your friend Annabelle.'

Julianne looked as if she had been slapped in the face.

'I was as surprised as you,' said Kira Mae anxiously. 'I knew nothing about the contents of the bag. I handed it over to Annabelle and that was the last I saw of it.'

Relieved to be telling her side of the story, Kira Mae now elaborated. 'No one was more shocked than me to know that Romero was involved in any way. I still feel sure that if I could talk to him there would be an explanation for all this.

'I'm sure he wouldn't have deliberately left me in this nightmare situation,' she finished. Julianne's brow was furrowed. She was desperately trying to make sense of what she had just heard.

'Romero? Romero? What does he have to do with anything?' She couldn't keep the anger out of her voice.

Kira Mae looked embarrassed and bit her lip before admitting to her mother. 'I've only just found out myself, but Annabelle was in Rome with Romero – they are man and wife.

'But, honestly, I didn't know that,' said Kira Mae, starting to cry and trying desperately to convince her mother and lawyer that what she was saying was the truth. 'I swear I didn't even know Romero was going to be here in Rome.'

Turning accusingly on her mother, she added, 'It's not my fault. I only did what you told me to do – bring the bag to Annabelle.'

Knowing that there was indeed more to be revealed, Kira Mae buried her head in her hands and, like a baby who thinks that because it can't see you, you can't see it, she admitted in a small scared voice.

'Oh, God, it's such a mess. I didn't want you to find out. I didn't want you to know that Romero and I are lovers.'

Julianne felt the physical sensation as surely as if she had been kicked in the stomach. The pain was excruciating. Her head started to spin and her tongue felt as if it was stuck to the roof of her mouth. Struggling to make sense of what she was hearing, emotion overtook analysis and she struck out.

In one swift movement she raised her hand and slapped Kira Mae hard across the face. Both women were shocked by the suddenness of the attack and simultaneously they both began to cry. Julianne looked at the crumpled face of her little girl and immediately regretted that for the first time in her life she had raised her hand to her daughter. The trust between them was now truly smashed. Kira Mae seemed to be as much humiliated as hurt, though a slight redness was already apparent on her right cheek where the blow had landed.

Paolo had already left the table and discreetly moved to the other side of his room, with his back to the scene being played out between mother and daughter. He misunderstood Julianne's reaction and thought it was the pain of a mother finding out that her young daughter was not quite as innocent as she had thought. Of course, that was part of the reason but he could not have begun to guess at the complicated set of circumstances surrounding both women's relationship with the same man.

'What did you say?' said Julianne, with a hardness in her voice and anger in her eyes.

'Romero,' said Kira Mae softly, 'and I are lovers. We have been since we came to Spain. I love him and he loves me.'

Julianne exercised utmost control to stop herself from slapping her daughter again. All her composure gone she pushed the chair back from the table, stood up and turned her back on her daughter. Putting a hand to her temple, Julianne tried to massage away the burning pain that seared through her head and her heart. She did not look at her daughter.

'Paolo,' she said. 'I need to leave. I think I am going to pass out.'

Before leaving the room and while Paolo signalled for the guard to come and unlock the door, she picked up her large white tote bag and, opening the main zipper, tipped the contents out on the table.

'These are for you,' she said pushing towards Kira Mae the two pairs of sweat pants, flat shoes, a couple of pastel coloured long sleeved T-shirts, a bottle of water, a box of tissues, a tin of mints and a pack of fruit containing apples, a pear and some grapes. From a side pocket she took out a small plastic bag holding essential toiletries and a couple of glossy magazines.

Kira Mae stared sullenly and did not bother to say thank you.

Paolo felt his loyalties divided. Officially he was here to represent the interests of Kira Mae, but it was her mother for whom he was feeling most sympathy. Surely she did not deserve to be dragged into such an impossible and dangerous situation by her daughter. Bringing the interview to a swift conclusion, he assured Kira Mae that he and her mother would be there for her in court the following day.

'Let's try to return you to the care and protection of your family,' he said kindly, even though he already knew his benevolent reading of the situation to be ironic in the circumstances.

'It won't be long now.' His tone allowed no argument, as he reassured the frightened girl how determined he was to get her out of the smelly, dark holding cell in the police station. 'Be strong,' he urged. 'It will all be over soon.'

Julianne couldn't leave her daughter alone as a prisoner without at least trying to make up for the horrible turn of events. Trying to put her arms around her daughter and reassure her, she said, 'Mummy will make everything better. I love you. Everything will be okay.' Although Kira Mae's body strained with resistance, she did not actually pull away. Julianne kissed Kira Mae's hair and hugged her.

'See you tomorrow, sweetheart,' she whispered through her tears as she walked out·of the iron door, leaving her trembling child to face another night in a cell.

Julianne was frightened and she clung on to Paolo's arm as they walked out of the jailhouse into the fresh air.

'Please, please promise me,' she pleaded, 'that you will get her out of there.'

Paolo drew his body up ramrod straight and assumed an

air of righteousness, glad to be cast in the role of knight in shining armour. 'The British Embassy will exert its influence,' he confirmed. 'We will see that justice is done.

'We do not like to see our citizens languishing in foreign jails. Especially such beautiful ones,' he added. 'Trust us.'

Julianne liked that he chose the words 'our citizens' even though he was only British on his mother's side and had lived all his life in Italy. But of course his employers were the British Embassy.

In contrast to the dark, hopelessness inside the police station, outside the day was bright and the weather was warm. It was a beautiful summer's day in Rome with the sun shining and a balmy breeze drifting lazily through the city.

Paolo guided Julianne towards his waiting car and opened the passenger door to let her in. 'Where to, Madame?' he said when they were seated, as Julianne suddenly realised she had made no arrangements for a hotel.

'May I offer a suggestion?' said Paolo, when she explained the situation. Relieved to have someone to take care of her, Julianne gratefully agreed. Pleased to be of service, Paolo was eager to tell her of his plans.

'My friend is manager of a hotel and spa on the outskirts of the city. Allow me to call and reserve a room for you there.'

Leaning her head back against the soft black leather headrest, Julianne allowed Paolo to take control of arrangements. All it took was a short phone call conducted in rapid fire Italian and he passed on the message, 'They are expecting you.'

There was nothing else to be done, Julianne settled back into the comfortable leather seat and enjoyed the crazy but confident high speed driving as Paolo raced his way across the city and out into the countryside.

Conversation was almost non-existent. Julianne was grateful, she had nothing left to say and certainly small talk would not have sufficed after all that had gone on so far today. It felt like a pneumatic drill was going off in her head, her heart was breaking and her mind was racing. Julianne needed to lie down in a darkened room – but in the meantime, she was just going along for the ride. The motion of the journey lulled her to sleep and she was startled to find that almost an hour had passed when she awoke and looked at the clock.

Paolo finally slowed down his mean machine and turned onto the gravel of a tree-lined country driveway.

The sign at the stone built gatehouse read Residence L'Andana Gregoriana. Julianne caught her breath. She had not envisioned anything like the magnificent edifice now laid out before her in all its glory.

Residence L'Andana had been built as the summer palace of an Italian Duke in the sixteenth century, but in its new incarnation now excelled as a world renowned hotel and luxury spa. Paolo and Julianne stood together in awe, looking up at the beautiful towers and turrets of the spectacular palace.

At the far end of the courtyard, resplendent in all its grandeur, stood a terrace constructed in marble and limestone typical of the late Baroque style. It was surrounded by wrought iron and gilded bronze Rocco balustrades with a sweeping Imperial staircase descending to the formal gardens and the ornamental lake in the distance.

Stepping over the threshold into the rarefied atmosphere of the beautifully decorated grand residence, gold was the predominant colour, glittering chandeliers, highly polished mirrors and the lavish use of white-veined marble proclaimed the privilege of royalty and the immense wealth of the old aristocracy. The gilded Rococo style, Chinoiserie patterns in Prussian blue and China yellow and heraldic motifs, featured on the pompadour rose and purple blue lapis painted furniture. Stencilled walls contrasted with the exotic black lacquerware. Julianne was overcome with the beauty of the palace and she felt humble that an individual she had only just met, and in such an unorthodox way, had considered her deserving of this height of luxury.

'My friend is waiting to welcome you to L'Andana,' said Paolo, and taking Julianne gently by the hand with supreme charm, he added, 'I told him that you need spoiling.'

Julianne smiled, she had reservations though she was too worn out to argue. 'You are very kind,' she affirmed, 'but what about my luggage? I left it with your secretary at the embassy and what about my daughter? I left her in a police cell.'

'All have been taken care of,' said Paolo confidently. 'I took the liberty of having your bags brought here earlier. As for your daughter, as her lawyer I have done everything I can for today. Tomorrow we will go to court and, as I told you both, I expect her to be given bail.

'As her mother you have also done everything you can for today. Kira Mae would not begrudge you a good night's sleep and a decent place to lay your weary head.' They smiled together at the huge understatement.

Julianne did not even stop to question the cost of staying at such a grand hotel. Her American Express card – though not the Black level of Annabelle's but merely Platinum – would take care of it – fortunately she never left home without it.

'I shall ensure that you are delivered back to Rome in time for the court appearance tomorrow,' Paolo assured her.

Julianne breathed a sigh of relief – he had thought of

everything. Paolo was certainly a real gentleman – and a devilishly handsome one at that.

'Come, your *palazzo* awaits,' he said with authority.

Julianne smiled. 'Might as well enjoy it,' she conceded. 'Who knows what tomorrow might bring.'

Paolo's friend and hotel manager Victor was waiting in the hotel reception to welcome the couple. Previously the ballroom, the wood panelled lobby area was a temple of marble columns and a magnificent frescoed ceiling. The whole atmosphere was serenely elegant.

As befitted a world class hotel, every detail had been considered and the former palace was a sanctuary of luxury, refinement and the highest standard of impeccable taste. Huge oil paintings lined the walls and depicted the ancestors of the archduke and his beautiful wife, the countess. Entering this refined world, Julianne felt like the honoured guest of a member of the Italian aristocracy.

As if reading her thoughts, Victor said, 'You are our guest and we will do everything to make your stay memorable and special. I will escort you to your room. Please follow me.'

Paolo discreetly left Victor to show Julianne to her second floor room via the ornate, gleaming gold and black gated lift. On the short journey Victor, who was dressed in an immaculate black evening suit, entertained her with a brief history of the magnificent building and its illustrious former owners. Victor unlocked the impressive ornamented wooden door to her room with a large brass key and Julianne was starkly reminded of the iron key that had locked her daughter into a prison cell. Standing back after opening the door, Victor ushered Julianne into her suite.

Sumptuous, with a central crystal chandelier that sparkled

and reflected its dazzling light onto heavily embossed golden satin sofas lining the walls, the suite had tiled mosaic flooring and luxurious Italian silk rugs. Julianne was reminded of a trip she had taken to the Palace of Versailles.

A king-size bed, draped in a damask silk bedspread in peacock blue, dominated the room. In a luminesque white vase atop a round mahogany console table, a gigantic bowl of white roses perfumed the air. A bijou seating area alongside the fine bed had an imperial red velvet chaise lounge and a large over-stuffed armchair. On a small crimson lacquered coffee table, copies of *Italian Vogue* and *Architectural Digest* rested.

In contrast to the Baroque style living area the bathroom was ultra-modern. Stark white Italian marble walls with shower and bathroom fittings in polished antique gold.

'I trust you will be comfortable,' said Victor, with a proud sense of the understated.

Julianne flashed him one of her most radiant smiles, 'Thank you,' she said graciously.

Victor turned to go, 'Your bags are in the closet. Would you care for me to have someone come and unpack for you?'

Julianne shook her head, dreading for a moment that any member of the luxury hotel's staff would see the uninspiring set of clothes she had packed for the journey, which had not listed a palatial Italian hotel in its original itinerary.

'Then I will leave you to freshen up. I will join Paolo in the bar; he and I have much catching up to do. We will see you there when you are ready?' he enquired politely.

Julianne walked him to the door, agreeing that she would be down to join them shortly. Why did I not refuse? she asked herself. The last thing she wanted to do was socialise. She had just had the day from hell and being alone to think was what she needed. Too late, she had already said she would join them, but she promised herself she would make her escape at the first possible moment.

Standing alone, surveying the opulence of the room, Julianne wished she had packed more formal clothing. Crossing to the closet she retrieved her case, opened it and considered her limited choices.

No contest. Julianne already knew that she was going to choose the ubiquitous black dress. Modelled on the classic black dress that Givenchy designed for Audrey Hepburn in *Breakfast at Tiffany's*, the style Julianne chose to wear was neither overly severe nor overly risqué. The dress was short with few decorations so that the neck and shoulders stood out. Pulling this favourite item from her suitcase, Julianne reached into the wardrobe and found a large padded hanger.

As a tribute to her Italian hosts, Julianne was pleased that this particular little black number was by Dolce & Gabbana. Tailored and fitted, it was sexy but understated. At the waist, a super slim silver belt defined her model girl measurements. Silver Jimmy Choo sandals and a small silver clutch bag set the seal of class on the outfit. Years of travelling as a fashion ambassador ensured that Julianne retained the ability to make an impact even when her resources were limited. As she never tired of telling her daughter, 'style outlasts fashion'.

Julianne did not want to keep Paolo and Victor waiting any longer than necessary, so she had a speed shower – though she always preferred a bath – changed her clothes, reapplied make-up, brushed her hair, clipping it with a diamante clip at the nape of the neck, all in super-fast time.

Examining her reflection from all angles, Julianne declared herself ready to go and socialise, although in truth it was the last thing she wanted to do.

It would be churlish not to make the effort when the two friends, who had been strangers to her a couple of hours before and still had no need to be so gracious, had chosen to be so kind at her time of need.

Pasting on a smile, Julianne descended the theatrical staircase and went to meet Paolo and Victor in the cocktail bar. Entering the bar, Julianne's spirits sank as she observed that Paolo and Victor were not alone. At the sight of the policeman talking to the pair, Julianne felt like she would burst into tears. Biting her lip to stop the tears, she approached the group.

'Allow me to introduce Madame Julianne Gordon,' said Paolo formally, turning to the uniformed policeman standing at the long polished wooden bar.

'Madame,' he replied, bowing with a small flourish.

Julianne looked enquiringly at Paolo and he acknowledged the unanswered question.

'Officer Valero is here on official business. He has news of the missing fugitives. Jesus Floris has been arrested while trying to leave the country. He was a passenger on a high speed cruiser – we call them cigarette boats – a vessel often used by criminals who attempt to outpace the police launches. It was intercepted at sea by the Italian authorities. He is in custody.' Julianne swayed slightly and put her hand on the seat of a bar stool to steady herself.

'What does the arrest mean for my daughter?' she asked anxiously. 'Is it good or bad for her case?'

Paolo stepped in, took her by the arm and gently guided her to sit down. Patting her hand reassuringly, he endeavoured to answer her question.

'While he was on the run we had to rely on Kira Mae's evidence and the accomplice to corroborate her story. Now we have the mastermind of the crime, it should be easier to prove your daughter's innocence.'

A white-jacketed waiter had been standing discreetly a few yards away from the group and on Paolo's raised hand signal he approached and enquired, 'Would Madame care for a drink?'

Julianne nodded, 'Yes, a brandy, please. Napoleon and make it a large one.'

Sipping her Napoleon brandy, Julianne felt disconnected as she strained to follow the conversation in Italian between the policeman and the lawyer. Victor had already excused himself to go and attend to hotel business.

Coming as not too much of a surprise, it transpired that in Italian law, plea bargaining was the usual way of conducting legal business. Jesus would be offered the opportunity to admit his offences – even some the authorities did not know about – and plead guilty, while allowing his co-conspirators to be released. In turn, he would face reduced charges and look like a hero to his criminal associates.

The prosecutor was in the process of offering Kira Mae, and the other defendant, a legal get out clause.

'Jesus is a very big fish in the drug smuggling world. We want to make sure he goes to jail this time. He has evaded incarceration before. Your daughter could be the key to our removing a dangerous career criminal from the streets.

'This man is a murderer and an arms and drug dealer, as well as running a hugely lucrative international money laundering business. It is no exaggeration to say he has more money than he knows what to do with.'

Paolo's speech was impassioned. 'This is a master criminal who needs to be brought to justice, and we won't let him escape again,' he appealed.

Sitting at the bar drinking brandy, Julianne felt the effects of a long and shocking day overwhelm her. She felt exhausted. Only when she was alone would she be able to give vent to her real feelings and begin to process some of the terrible things she had been forced to face.

'Would you please excuse me?' she asked politely. 'I am very tired.'

Paolo looked disappointed. 'You won't join us for dinner?' he asked. 'The food is superb.'

'No, thank you,' said Julianne firmly. 'I need to get a good night's rest before the trials of tomorrow.'

Reluctant to let her go but accepting that her reasoning was correct, Paolo was solicitous.

'Of course you must get a good night's sleep – it has been a distressing day for you. Let us pray that tomorrow will bring good news.'

Julianne thanked him again for his hospitality and as she prepared to go back upstairs, mentioned that she had not officially checked into the hotel.

'There is no need for formalities,' Paolo informed her with a smile. 'You are a personal guest of the manager – he is like a brother to me – there will be no charge. Order anything you choose from the room service menu and it will be sent up to your suite. You must be hungry.'

Julianne was again overwhelmed by the kindness of this urbane handsome man. She had no idea why she merited such VIP treatment, but was very glad that the British Embassy had chosen to treat one of their citizens so well.

It hardly occurred to her that the good offices of Paolo Grazia, rather than the British Embassy, was the provider of her high level of attention and protection. The embassy motto and mission statement 'situation contained' was certainly being upheld in her case. Beautiful blondes – especially an exciting combination of competing yet complimentary females like mothers and daughters, have a way of exerting influence on impressionable men – young and old. It was ever thus.

Climbing the stairs to her room, Julianne allowed the mask to slip. Entering the room she slammed the door and kicked off her shoes.

chapter twenty-eight

'If you prick us, do we not bleed?
If you tickle us, do we not laugh?
If you poison us, do we not die?
And if you wrong us, shall we not revenge?'
Shakespeare's *Merchant of Venice*

'The bastard!' she yelled, throwing her bag onto the bed. 'I'll kill him. I swear I will.'

Rage coursed through her body and torrents of tears flowed down her face. Filled with rage, she pulled her dress violently over her head and threw it across the room.

Old familiar feelings of anger powered her tantrum and fuelled her fury. 'Filthy, dirty, lying bastard!' she screamed, her voice resonating around the empty room.

Tearing at her black silky balconette bra and not caring that she had broken the delicate clasp, Julianne stood dressed only in her black La Perla lace panties.

Tearfully and sadly she acknowledged what she needed to do. Harm herself.

In those long ago dark, desperate nights of her lost childhood, Julianne had learned how to relieve the inner pain. Now, she knew it was her only solution.

Releasing the demons from where they lay trapped deep inside her, she acknowledged that the only relief from the excruciating torment was to be found in mutilating herself.

Now the new torture inflicted by Romero meant that the wounds were open and aching. She wanted to reach inside herself and rip out her heart, claw her own body to stop the grief, the anger, the shame. The betrayal she had suffered at his hands would torment her forever. How could she have given herself to him? How could she have trusted him? How could he have made love to her and also seduced her daughter? He was a monster, a devil, a dark, malevolent force that had poisoned their lives.

Her tortured mind was like a maelstrom. The brooding thoughts, the recurring sight of his cruel face in her mind, laughing at her. She wanted to tear him limb from limb. Make him suffer like she was suffering – and her daughter too. Locked in a cell. How could she have allowed all this to happen? She would not rest till she had made him pay for what he had done to her family. Jail was too good for him – she wanted him dead. *Morto*.

Fired up with righteous indignation, Julianne walked towards the bathroom, pausing only to pour a large measure of brandy from the heavy glass decanter on the well-stocked drinks trolley, into an exquisitely cut crystal glass. Sipping the drink, she walked purposefully into the bathroom and started to fill the white marble tub with extra hot, steaming water.

Arranging her hair on top of her head, Julianne removed her makeup and cleaned her teeth. She slowed her breathing, outwardly calm, inside she screamed.

'Don't do it, please don't do it,' said the small scared voice inside her head. 'Don't make me bleed. Don't hurt me.'

Julianne knew it was too late. From her toilet bag she took

a new razor blade. Removing the wrapper she laid it on the side of the bath beside her drink.

Defiantly she picked up the drink, took a long hard swallow and drained the glass. Quickly she walked into the lounge to again fill it with the fiery liquid. Fortified with Dutch courage she returned to the bathroom and the almost full bath. Bubbles were an unnecessary distraction, clean clear water allowed her to savour the full effects. Without removing her underwear she stepped into the over hot water.

Lowering herself an inch at a time, Julianne refused to ease the pain by adding cold water. Hurting was good. Lying full length in the bath, she sought comfort in the alcohol.

'Please don't do it,' she heard the scared voice in her head but there was no stopping her. Julianne was determined on her path of self-destruction.

Parting her legs she positioned the right limb on the side of the bath, with the left one under the water, she held the razor firmly and, gritting her teeth, made the first cut on the upper thigh.

Deep enough only to scratch the surface, she made sure that the next cut would draw blood. Hurt and humiliation drove her rage and she cut deep into her thigh. Blood flowed freely and a sense of relief flooded through Julianne.

The late Princess Diana had bravely admitted to the fact that she was a self-harmer; her explanation had perfectly described how Julianne was now feeling – 'the pain inside finds relief for the hurting on the outside. It lets out the pain'.

Bright red blood flowed from the leg wound as Julianne cut herself again. The razor was sharp; the pain had a delayed reaction. For a few moments she felt nothing, then an excruciating, searing pain – inside. On the outside, the hot water, the brandy and the heightened emotions served to disguise the seriousness of the cuts. Julianne was an expert. She made patterns with the cuts; studying her handiwork, she was pleased.

No one hurts me as good as I hurt myself, she conceded. Lying in the warm bath full of bloody water, a patchwork of deep gashes on her inner thigh, Julianne felt strangely at peace.

Well-practised in the art of self-harm, she knew what she needed to do next. Stepping gingerly from the bath, she reached into her toilet bag and unwrapped a small bandage. From the same mini medicine bag she removed a hand towel, gauze and a bottle of antiseptic. Wrapping the towel around her leg, she made a tourniquet and stemmed the blood. Julianne placed her foot up on the toilet seat and waited. When the worst of the bleeding had stopped, she cleaned the wound with antiseptic and applied ointment; she then wrapped the wound tightly in the bandage.

Lucky I brought the bandage, she congratulated herself. Don't leave home without it. You never know when the pain will start again. Julianne cruelly mocked her vulnerability and the way she had been dealing with the pain for more years than she could remember. Like a smoker who resists throwing away the last pack of cigarettes in case he is one day desperate, Julianne always carried her emergency first aid kit.

It was so long since she had resorted to cutting herself that she had almost forgotten the sense of power it brought. She tried to convince herself. I am in control.

Briskly towelling herself dry and wrapping herself first in her own nightgown and then in the hotel's fluffy, white dressing gown, Julianne lay on top of the bed and held herself tight. Sobbing like a child, Julianne cried herself to sleep. She knew this madness well. Years of therapy and counselling with the rape crisis centre had not completely cured her of the compelling urge to self-harm when the emotional pain became too much to bear.

Drifting in and out of a fitful sleep, she consoled herself with one thought; maybe I won't ever have to wake up again.

★ ★ ★

Heavy damask lined curtains blocked out the dawning of the day. Julianne slept on until the loud ringing of the telephone intruded on her consciousness. Defiantly, she refused to answer the ringing phone, preferring instead to listen to the subsequent voice message. The digital clock on the bedside radio read 08.30.

Frantically trying to clear her head, Julianne waited an appropriate time to check for a message. Dreading the day ahead and shamed by memories of the night before, Julianne reached for the unopened bottle of spring water on the bedside table. She used it to wash down the pain killers that she had already laid out in anticipation of the headache from which she was now suffering.

Sitting up in bed, she carefully pulled back the covers and opened the towelling dressing gown. Like a nurse treating a patient, Julianne observed the bandaged thigh and checked for signs of leaked blood.

No leakage. Good, she could hope her injuries were not too serious. Some of her deeper scars would never heal – they were always there as a chilling reminder of the fragile state of her mind.

Why, why, why? She asked the same question over and

over again. It had been so long since she had taken this drastic step of self-punishment. So long in fact that she had dared to hope it was all over. Now she knew there was no guarantee when, if ever, she would be able to gather the willpower to stop again. Like an alcoholic – once she started – she had no idea when the relapse would end.

Now she had to reluctantly admit that the old ways of dealing with unbearable hurt were still an option for her. Like the alcoholic who can remain abstinent for long periods, he always knows that just one drink can open the floodgates again to uncontrollable drunken behaviour. Julianne had been abstinent from her addiction to physical pain and self-harm, now she had opened the gates again. The monster was awake.

Determined to protect her guilty secret from no one in particular, she jumped when the phone rang again. Avoidance was not an option, she answered it. Paolo was calling to confirm she would be collected by car for the journey back to Rome and Kira Mae's court appearance.

'Ten o'clock, perfect, thank you,' she told Paolo, her voice calm and composed. 'I'll see you when I get to Rome.'

Paolo was already in his office and finalising the paperwork he would need for the court appearance. He had driven back to Rome after having a subdued dinner at the hotel. He had resisted the temptation to call Julianne and say he would stay over at the hotel; instead he preferred to keep things on a business footing. For the time being.

chapter twenty-nine

'Bear with me, I am hungry for revenge.'
Shakespeare's *Richard III*

Directly across the room from her bed, a strategically placed dressing table mirrored her image. Julianne averted her eyes from the revulsion at the sight of herself.

Wave after wave of guilt washed over her.

Fear and anxiety filled her mind. Of course she knew that her daughter should be a priority at this time, but that only made her feel even more guilty. What would become of her darling Kira Mae?

So absorbed had she been by her own problems that she had pushed aside the most pressing matter of her daughter's impending court appearance.

If only she could stop thinking about Romero. If only, if only. How had they all gotten into this pit of blackness? What weird fate had conspired to entwine them in this Greek tragedy?

With an almighty effort of will, Julianne pushed herself out of bed. Whatever else happened today, she had to assume responsibility and remember that she was still the parent in this situation. Capable, in control, making it all better. Padding across the Persian carpet, Julianne drew back the curtains. The view from her bedroom window was spectacular. Muted yellow sunshine was washing over the formal gardens and sparkling off the azure tinted lake. Tripping across the Mediterranean sky, fluffy white clouds formed patterns and drifted across the newly risen sun. Through the open window, Julianne breathed deeply of the early morning air and a glorious perfume of lavender and wildflowers pervaded the room. Filling her lungs, she intoned a mantra between deep inhalations.

Breathe out, fear and doubt. Breathe in, love and faith. Breathe out, fear and doubt. Breathe in, love and faith.

Suitably energised, she made her way to the en suite bathroom. The emotional hangover from last night's drastic actions was replayed as soon as she entered the white tiled chamber.

Thankfully, it was now only a memory. It never failed to impress Julianne how carefully she would cover her own tracks. Everything, including the bloody towel, had been carefully stored away in her overnight bag and no one would be able to detect any signs of the fragility of this particular human being – and her method for coping with the traumas of real life.

Running a bath, Julianne slipped off the monogrammed dressing gown and stepped into the revitalising, cleansing, foaming water. Today the water temperature was just right, but she did not trust herself to sit down. Instead she took the hair washing attachment and made it into a personal shower – nothing too intimidating – a gentle spray, a healing baptism, carefully avoiding the area of the wound and dressing.

Out of the bath, she towelled herself dry and opened the doors of the hand painted distressed wooden wardrobe.

Covering up was a necessity, so she chose a pair of wide-legged Balenciaga pants. Today's outfit needed to be smart, business-like and concealing. The solution was to wear her navy blue pin-striped Balenciaga trouser suit with a pale blue co-ordinating blouse. The blue of the blouse complimented the cornflower blue of her eyes and the sailor leg pants gave Julianne a sense of freedom and, more importantly, comfort. Selecting a silk multi-coloured scarf from her case, Julianne threw it casually over her shoulders and anchored it with an antique cameo brooch. Her freshly washed hair flowed freely.

Almost as a punishment, Julianne decided killer heels were a definite. Julianne slipped into a pair of her favourite Christian Louboutins, with the trademark scarlet soles. To accessorise the daring red shoes, she chose a red Chanel tote bag.

Julianne knew she looked good on the outside, clothes were her salvation. Whatever the circumstances, she always dressed to impress. You don't get a second chance to make a first impression, she reminded herself. No matter how low she was feeling dressing for a part always renewed her confidence. On this important day, Julianne chose to look like a woman who was not going to take 'no' for an answer. One simple psychological trick she had learned was that 'acting as if' allowed her to be the best version of that person that she could be.

'I won't let you down, Kira Mae, my darling girl,' she promised. And to avoid laughing at the irony of the remark she reminded herself, 'Blood is still thicker than water.'

Although Paolo's friend, Victor had kindly arranged for Julianne to stay on at the hotel, pending the outcome of the court case, Julianne decided to decline.

Maybe she would get the opportunity another time – in happier circumstances she could treat herself to the indulgence of such luxury and avail herself of some of the unique and innovative spa treatments that the hotel had to offer. The holistic back, face and scalp massage with hot stones had sounded divine. But not now.

She needed to get away from the scene of her hurtful nocturnal activities. Back in Rome she would find another hotel for her – and hopefully her daughter too.

Carefully packing her Louis Vuitton skipper case, Julianne rang reception and asked for a valet to take down her luggage.

'Of course, Madame,' said the efficient voice on the end of the phone, 'and when you are ready your car awaits.'

The lift was an easy option and Julianne regretted that she had not made more of an effort to study and enjoy the magnificent architecture and splendid decoration of the grand hotel. Somehow though, she did draw strength from the centuries old ambience and she now was convinced she had at least enough strength to face one more day. Julianne asked the smiling receptionist to pass on the hastily penned note of thanks to her host.

On the return journey to Rome, Julianne reclined comfortably in the back seat of the jet black limousine, courtesy of Paolo, closed the connecting window between her and the driver to discourage any friendly chatter – and plotted her next move.

This vow I make, Julianne promised herself dramatically as she gazed out at the glorious Italian countryside. Next time blood is spilled, it will not be mine – it will be Romero's. For what he has done to my daughter and to me – he will die.

Like a force of nature, beautiful and unstoppable Julianne

strode through the police station looking every inch the fashion model. At the front desk she was informed by the desk sergeant that Paolo was already with his client, her daughter.

A policeman guided Julianne down the dark airless corridor to the interrogation room, where Kira Mae was being held. Inside Paolo and Kira Mae sat on opposite sides of the table engrossed in conversation. They gave her a brief nod of acknowledgement, but did not break off their discussion. In whispered urgent tones, they seemed to be forming a plan. Both looked serious and Julianne observed that Kira Mae had been biting her nails – a nervous habit that she had overcome, but now the nails were bitten and the skin around them looked swollen and raw.

'Forgive me,' said Paolo after a few moments. 'There has been a worrying development. The matter of bail may not be as certain as we previously anticipated.'

Kira Mae sat at the table, nervously fiddling with her hair, twisting and untwisting it from her finger. She looked like a frightened little girl and Julianne's heart went out to her. She crossed to the table and, preparing herself to be rebuffed, put her arms around her young daughter.

'How are you bearing up, baby?' she asked.

An answer was hardly needed. Kira Mae looked terrible. Her face was tearstained from all the crying she had done, her eyes were puffy and her nose was red. Her normally bright, healthy glowing skin was sallow and taut. Her long blonde hair was scraped back off her face into a pony tail and the casual gym clothes that Julianne had brought her the previous day looked out of place in the dank, scruffy surroundings. Julianne wanted to scream out in pain at the indignities her daughter was going through.

Fearful that she would lose control, Julianne turned away from her daughter and addressed Paolo.

'Tell me, what is the problem?'

Looking sympathetically at Kira Mae, who had started to cry, Paolo explained, 'It is the defendant, her supposed friend, Romero. He has made very damaging allegations about your daughter's involvement in the criminal actions that led to his and her arrest.

'According to him, she was a willing accomplice. He has told the police, in a sworn statement, that she knew perfectly well what was being carried in the suitcase. In fact he goes so far as to say that it was because of her that the gun was there in the first place.'

Juliana felt a tightening in her chest, she was having trouble breathing. Reaching into her handbag she took out a small bottle of water and dabbed her face. She offered some to Kira Mae who, impatiently, shook her head.

Paolo continued to talk while Kira Mae continued to cry.

'Romero or Jesus Floris, as he is better known, claims that your daughter incited him to kill his fiancée, because she was wild with jealousy. He claims it was a crime of passion. Romero and Kira Mae were going to go away together.'

Pushing back her chair angrily, Kira Mae pleaded with her lawyer and her mother, 'He's lying, it's not true. You've got to believe me.'

Julianne also now reacted with anger, 'Then why the hell did he say it?' she yelled. 'Do you have any idea how much trouble you are in? You stupid, stupid girl.'

In an attempt to calm down the situation, Paolo took control.

'It is unlikely that bail will be granted now. Your daughter may be perceived as a danger to others. We have to be prepared for her going straight from court to the women's jail today; there she will stay until the trial.'

Regretting her outburst, Julianne attempted to comfort her daughter, but Kira Mae pushed her away. 'Even you don't believe me, so why should the judge?'

Julianne had no answer. She lowered herself into the chair which Paolo had placed for her at the table; her leg was throbbing and she was too weak to stand any longer. She sat down and started to massage her thigh under the table. She stared into space. Hopeless and helpless, she felt repulsed by herself. She could not see a way forward. All she knew for certain was that she had turned out to be a lousy mother. No wonder she hated herself so much; she needed to be punished.

Paolo checked his watch. 'It is almost time to go,' he informed Julianne. 'Your daughter will be taken to court with a police escort; you and I will go together. We should be able to see her again before the court appearance.'

Knowing she had now driven a wedge between herself and her daughter, Julianne again attempted to offer a comforting touch. Kira Mae was in no mood for forgiveness, but she did agree to change into the clothes that her mother had brought for her to wear for a court appearance.

The effect was electrifying. Kira Mae was transformed as she stepped into the white shift dress by Chloé and a pair of milky white leather Pied à Terre court shoes with a demure heel. The look was not an accident, it was done for effect; Julianne had chosen well – the all-white image was virginal, a picture of youth and innocence.

Julianne brushed her daughter's beautiful blonde hair – wishing she could have washed it, not just sprinkled some dry shampoo on it in an attempt to make it look less matted – and as she tried to tie a blue satin ribbon, Kira Mae turned on her.

'You don't know what it's like to be in love,' she said cruelly. 'Romero will not let me down. There must be a mistake.'

Wounded, Julianne hit back and unkindly forced her daughter to face reality.

'See if you believe that when you're spending years locked up in a prison cell and they have thrown away the key. Perhaps love will sustain you then.'

Julianne marched to the interview room door, knocked and waited for it to be opened by a guard. Suddenly, regretting her outburst, she burst into tears and turning back to the sad figure of her daughter, she again asked for forgiveness.

'Please, please, don't let us part like this. You know that I love you and I'll do everything I can to get you out of this mess. I'm sorry. Really I'm sorry. I'm just so scared, I'm hardly thinking straight.

'You're still my little girl, no matter what you've done. It's his fault. Not yours. We'll make it okay, I promise.'

The roller coaster journey of emotions, on which they were both travelling, came to rest for a moment and mother and daughter embraced. Both tearful, but relieved that for the moment at least the animosity between them had abated.

Heightened emotions erupted and subsided leaving behind a sense of calm that cloaked mother and daughter, offering momentary relief.

'Blood is thicker than water,' Julianne reminded Kira Mae as she took her leave.

★ ★ ★

Paolo's fears were realised. Bail was not granted.

Kira Mae was transported to one of Rome's half dozen houses of correction close to the shores of the Tiber River, which housed several hundred women and a couple of thousand men. The overcrowding was epic and prisoners were often accommodated six to a cell that had been built for half that number. The painfully slow justice system, lack of money to build new facilities and longer sentencing for drug-related offences ensured that there was always an excess of inmates in ancient buildings, many of which were former monasteries or convents.

The correctional facilities were bursting at the seams with an avalanche of convicted men and women from all nations of the world, many suffering from mental illness or drug and alcohol addiction. The conditions of detention with shared but limited toilets and showers ensured that the clashing cultures and lack of common languages led to regular outbreaks of violence. A basic brutality and every man – and woman – for themselves mentality, meant the hardship of daily existence was pervaded with cruel, humiliating and degrading practices adding to the general levels of lack of dignity. Personal safety was constantly put at risk and being locked in a cell for sometimes over twenty hours a day meant that mental, emotional and physical health quickly deteriorated. Suicides were frequent and the strong soon exerted pressure on the weak. Kira Mae was not street wise, she was going to have to learn some basic survival skills – and quickly. It was highly likely that she would be locked up and forced to wait up to a year until a date was set for her trial.

Having been driven to the prison in a police van with several other men and women, Kira Mae felt isolated and frightened.

She had not heard English spoken since she arrived. An intensive process of registration to her new life of incarceration had involved interminable form filling, cursory but demeaning medical examinations and the removal of all her personal belongings. She was handed an unflattering and over large regulation grey prison uniform; assigned a prison number and handed a slip showing the number and location of her cell.

Her new cellmates ignored her when the prison guard unlocked the door to allow her to enter. The guard nodded towards an empty bunk bed on which there was some bedding and a thin pillow and without further remark, closed and re-locked the door. There were already two women in the cell. One a Muslim, sitting on the floor praying – a ritual she performed five times a day – and the other a young black girl who was busy braiding her own hair.

Kira Mae sat on the empty lower bunk and stared into space. Her eyes were drawn to the only visible reading matter, two faded posters on the cell wall. One offered advice against self abuse, the other suggested ways to protect against sexual abuse. Kira Mae's first night in the notorious prison made her understand those inmates who chose suicide as a way out. Her heart was filled with dread at what prison life would entail and she wondered if she would survive the ordeal.

Wrapping the inadequate bedclothes around herself, she wept silent tears and all through the long night prayed as reverently and frequently as her Muslim cell mate. Kira Mae would learn to live her life regulated by ringing bells and shouted commands. The next morning at the first sound of the wake up bell, after a cursory wash and tying her hair into an unflattering bun, she listened for the subsequent ringing of the breakfast bell and joined the food line. She was relieved to discover that the food served by fellow prisoners looked edible and plentiful. Kira Mae gladly filled her plate and her empty belly.

★ ★ ★

Paolo and Julianne walked sadly, without speaking, down the interminable, marble-floored corridor and out of the courthouse.

'What now?' asked Julianne at last. 'When will I be able to see her?'

Paolo did his best to reassure the distraught mother.

'A few days at most. I will arrange a visit as soon as possible. I promise.'

Julianne nodded and tried to smile her thanks. Smiling was not going to come easy until her daughter was back with her safe and sound.

'Shall I drive you back to the hotel?' Paolo enquired kindly.

'Oh, no, I'm sorry,' said Julianne, embarrassed. 'I didn't get a chance to tell you. I left a note for your friend that I would not be coming back. I had thought I would find a hotel for myself and Kira Mae in Rome.'

Paolo was disappointed with the change of plans, but too professional and too much of a gentleman to let his disappointment show.

'We will take care of the matter of the hotel,' he said briskly. 'But first, lunch.'

Julianne was too deflated to argue. When they were seated at a table in the restaurant, Juliana asked Paolo the question that had been puzzling her.

'Why are you being so kind to me, surely you have plenty

of other clients who need your attention?'

Now it was Paolo's turn to look embarrassed.

'None of them is as beautiful as you,' he admitted boldly. 'Besides I never could resist a damsel in distress – especially a British one. My mother was British. She came from Cardiff. I plan to go there one day.'

Knowing that there was nothing they could do to help Kira Mae, the handsome lawyer and vulnerable English lady decided to make the best of the situation, and enjoy lunch together.

'Allow me to introduce you to some of the house specialities,' said Paolo. Realising that she had not actually eaten properly for several days, Julianne agreed.

They sat outdoors in a small square close to the Coliseum and sipped vermouth and soda while feasting on lobster – a whole one each, the first half being served cold with creamy mayonnaise and the second half hot – thermidor – followed by pistachio and almond ice cream.

This feast was delivered without ceremony in an unpretentious family run trattoria, with its tables covered in cheerful red and white checked tablecloths and small bowls of freshly cut gardenias giving off an intoxicating perfume.

Paolo explained that Rome's ancient downtown skyline was one of the best preserved in the world, thanks to stringent planning regulations that forbid modern constructions over a certain height and mandate buildings are only permitted to be painted in the specified Roman palette.

Julianne realised that her personal map of Rome, like many other thousands of cinema lovers, was forever immortalised by the iconic image of Audrey Hepburn clinging to Gregory Peck being charioted around Rome on the back of a Vespa 150 in *Roman Holiday.* She and Kira Mae had watched it together many times on Turner Classic Movies.

Paolo and Julianne indulged in an Italian style leisurely three-hour lunch, as they ate and drank until late in the afternoon. By the time they chose to leave, Paolo and Julianne were as comfortable in each other's company as old friends, or new lovers. They left the restaurant arm in arm.

Paolo walked her to her modest four star hotel, The Hotel Casa Domus, in the city centre just five minutes' walk from the walls of Vatican City. Paolo had found the hotel for Julianne and thoughtful as ever, had her bags delivered, but when he offered to come up and check that the room was suitable, Julianne declined.

Tender loving care was just what she needed in these worrying circumstances, but Julianne had already promised herself that no professional lines would be breached. Refusing an invitation to dinner, she claimed tiredness, which was patently true and she was sad that this time Paolo did seem to be annoyed with her.

He'll get over it, she told herself. I didn't ask him to spend so much time or energy on me. If he feels that there should be a price to pay – well, he will be disappointed. It's just a complication too far.

Now listening to the convivial sounds of the inhabitants of an Italian city enjoying this seductive, summer evening, she almost regretted her decision. But, no, she forced herself to stay focused. Julianne needed time to be by herself, plan a strategy and prepare herself for what could well be the worst.

She knew there was now a strong likelihood that her daughter would go to prison and the thought put her into a blind panic. How would Kira Mae cope? Would she be badly treated, bullied, hurt? Would she be able to adapt, at least make friends? What would she do all day? Would the authorities make her work? When, oh when, would she be able to go and see her?

Julianne felt helpless, afraid. She wished her Mummy Mitchell was still alive. Well, no she wouldn't have wanted to expose her to all this, but at least she would have provided a strong shoulder to cry on – everything was always okay when she was taking control of the situation.

Thank God that Paolo was on their side. He would take care of the legalities and do everything in his power to make sure that they got a good result.

Julianne was exhausted – she lay fully clothed on the bed and prepared to have a short nap – or maybe even a meditation. It was so long since she had practised her daily routine of meditation and if there was ever a time when she needed to calm her mind it was now. Switching her phone to silent, Julianne realised that she hadn't checked her messages all day. There had not seemed much point as both Kira Mae and Romero were in jail and – although she had heard that there were close to fifty million mobile phone users in Italy – her understanding was that prisoners were not allowed to make phone calls.

Now she collected a voice message from a London art dealer who wanted to talk to her about a Vettriano painting – but I haven't got any Italian paintings, she mused.

He elaborated. 'The one in *La Dama Escalata* shop window.' Now she was completely bemused. Reluctantly she decided to return the call.

Reginald Haverstock was most pleased she had responded to his call. Back at his Chelsea home, he explained that he had just that very day returned from Spain.

'On a family visit to San Juan I saw the watercolour painting in your shop window,' he informed her. 'I can hardly contain my excitement,' he admitted. 'I have very good reason to believe that it is an early, previously unknown, example of the work of one of Scotland's foremost painters. Jack Vettriano also known as Jack Hoggan.

'His most famous work, *The Singing Butler* recently sold for over a million pounds. His work is very collectable and many famous people have his work in their collections.'

Julianne realised that of course she had heard of Jack Vettriano, she loved his romantic stylised brightly coloured paintings, especially the aforementioned *The Singing Butler* and the hypnotic imagery of the lady in a flowing white evening dress in *Dance Me to the End of Love*.

Almost everybody had a Jack Vettriano print somewhere at home – his prints were among the best selling in the world. Now it seemed she might have one of his original paintings. But how could that be?

Reginald Haverstock was eager to explain. In his home county of Methil in Fife, Jack Hoggan had worked as an apprentice mining engineer before being given his first set of watercolours by a girlfriend on his twenty-first birthday.

'Do you by chance have any Scottish connections?' Reginald asked.

The light went on. Julianne remembered the story of her miner grandfather's friend whose son – what was his name Broggan? Or could it have been Hoggan? – had given him the gift of the painting. If the art dealer was right it could be one of a set of paintings called *Blossom Time*. Mummy Mitchell had always told her how convinced her husband and the lad's father were that he would one day be famous.

Julianne hung up the phone promising that she would temporarily remove the painting from the window and that, after she had verified his credentials, she would allow Mr Reginald Haverstock to collect the painting and take it to London to be checked and authenticated.

'But I am not selling it,' she had assured him. 'That painting belongs to my daughter and she would never forgive me.'

Julianne decided to meditate on this new development, but exhaustion overtook her and she passed peacefully into a deep sleep.

★ ★ ★

The sun's rays were shining through the window when she awoke and from far below she could hear the sounds of the small public square coming to life and greeting the morning.

Rested and refreshed, Julianne felt energised to face a brand new day. She did battle with the antique shower attachment above the enclosed bath. Hardly a relaxing experience but Julianne did feel strangely hopeful as she applied a citrus body lotion and vigorously dried her hair.

Without her extensive wardrobe, a restricted choice of clothes meant that the dressing decision was not complicated. Taking a deep blue geometric patterned silk wrap dress from her case, Julianne teamed it with flat ballerina slippers and a large satchel bag. Simple, stylish and uncluttered, Julianne endeavoured to make her mind replicate her clothing.

An early morning call to Paolo's office confirmed that she would not be able to visit Kira Mae for at least another week.

Julianne made a decision. She would fly back to Spain.

No way could she stay in Rome cooling her heels for several days with no possibility of a visit to her daughter. Also, she was determined to put distance between herself and Paolo. In all matters legal she needed to depend on him but personally she was scared of getting too close. God, preserve me from myself, she prayed.

On the flight back to Spain, Julianne was amazed at how calm she managed to stay. It did not make her feel good to admit that, as so often before, the pressure was relieved by the self-harm she had learned to inflict. Since the incident in the hotel, she had felt more in control. However, she was consciously wary of again beginning to see the self-abuse as the solution rather than the problem. Her very sanity and physical well-being was at stake. It had taken such monumental efforts of will to stop her old behaviour; she must not allow it to become an issue again.

Paolo had reluctantly agreed that it was a good idea for her to return home and he promised to be in touch the moment he had anything to report.

chapter thirty

'These words are razors to my wounded heart.'
Shakespeare's *Titus Andronicus*

Julianne had the sense of being reunited with an old and dear friend when she arrived back at *La Dama Escalata* in San Juan. Work had always been her salvation and now she was grateful for the opportunity to keep occupied by resuming the undertaking she had started with such enthusiasm and high hopes.

Making good her promise to the charming London art dealer, Mr Haverstock, Julianne removed the Scottish painting from the window, all the time looking at the simple pastoral scene and wondering, is this really the work of a world famous artist?

If such were the case, she calculated, Mummy Mitchell had again assured the financial security of her darling daughters. Or more rightly, they should this time thank the grandfather they had not even known.

But for now, she had work to do and she desperately needed to keep her mind occupied. Determining to open the premises for potential weekend shoppers, Julianne told herself that even if there were few customers – and only a minimal amount of stock had been delivered – at least the shop could be opened and give the impression that it was a going concern.

Julianne put in a call to her old boss in London, Maria de Angeles and thanked her for allowing her current assistant to help out Julianne with pulling in favours at various fashion houses and having sample stock delivered to her in Spain.

'Let me know when you are up and running and I will pay a visit,' said Maria who had never lost affection for Julianne, one of the best assistants she had ever had. 'And I can always find a way around long waiting lists for designer pieces – you are more than welcome to use my name if you need to pull a few strings. You know we will all do everything we can to help get *La Dama Escalata* established.'

Julianne feigned a delivery emergency and told Maria, 'Sorry must go, the charming bar owner across the street from my shop who takes in packages when I am not here, is at the door. Can't stop.'

It was only half a lie. The owner, Carlos whose bar and street café looked out on to her new shop, had been kind enough to sign for mail and deliveries. His wife, Carla, was not so keen but as she had explained fondly patting her own ample hips, 'I am a follower of fashion.' Julianne smiled kindly and promised to show her around the premises when they were ready for an official opening.

No, the truth was she wanted to get off the phone to Maria because she was avoiding answering the friendly questions about 'darling Kira Mae – is she with you in the shop, how is she enjoying her life in Spain?'

As she said extravagant goodbyes, Maria had one last word for Julianne, 'By the way, love the name of the shop. *The Scarlet Lady*. Suits you!'

★ ★ ★

Julianne kept in touch with Paolo by phone and stressed to him that the minute a window opened that would allow her to see her daughter, even for a brief period of time, she would be there. Also she asked him to check the situation regarding taking or sending goods; food, books, toiletries. Perhaps the fact that she was on remand, not convicted would mean that the regulations governing her would be more lenient

Paolo assured her that if there was an opportunity, even for a lawyer or embassy visit, he would try to get permission for her to go along. Julianne had already started to send daily letters to Kira Mae in jail, though she had no idea whether they would reach her. Paolo also had it on his list to check whether it was permissible to make or receive phone calls.

Julianne found plenty to occupy herself with at the shop; she enjoyed displaying her limited stock to show it off to best advantage and poring over the designer catalogues to make her choices for new merchandise, accessories and footwear. Also the office area she set up for herself was rapidly filling up with paperwork, this being Spain, there was a mountain of administration and bureaucracy to navigate.

Despite her best intentions to keep herself busy, Julianne found that she was tired and lethargic much of the time and was suffering from bouts of nausea. She put it down to the extreme anxiety. Some days it was a struggle just to get out of bed and she knew she wasn't eating properly or taking care of herself.

She did everything in her power to avoid thoughts of Romero – with little success. On the one hand she craved him and became obsessed with reliving every moment of the time they had spent together. She remembered every touch, smile, gesture and term of endearment he had uttered. She longed to see him and hear his voice.

On the other hand, she hated him. She longed to stick a knife in his heart and watch him die for the hurt he had caused her and her daughter. Hatred fuelled her rage and loathing drove her need for justice. Inflict the pain on him, not yourself, she warned. You do not deserve any more punishment. Let him feel your wrath. Let him feel the fury of a woman scorned. Let him burn in hell.

★ ★ ★

It took two weeks before Paolo called and said she was going to be able to see her daughter. She took his advice and again flew to Rome from Alicante via Madrid.

Visiting her daughter in a women's prison was one of the most heart-breaking situations Julianne had ever had to endure. Kira Mae on the other hand was acting very brave; the naive young girl had been forced to grow up fast in the noisy, explosive women's prison, where any sign of weakness was exploited. Julianne sensed these changes and felt reassured that her daughter was taking care of herself and being treated well.

'I want to know everything,' said Julianne. 'What is the food like, do you get on with your cell mates, do they have a library, have you got a job, have you got a friend, what is your cell like, do you sleep alright?

Kira Mae gave the answers but she was aware that time was restricted on visits and she had something more important on her mind than general questions about her welfare.

Kira Mae knew that she was going to have to reveal the

reasons for her new found maturity. She took a deep breath and unburdened herself. 'Please, don't be angry with me,' she said. 'It's too late to change anything.' Julianne waited.

Kira Mae said nothing but glanced over to the corner of the large communal room where the unflappable Paolo sat apart and silently; she was looking for moral support.

'You might as well spit it out,' said Julianne. 'I don't think I'm up to making a guessing game of it.'

Kira Mae bit her lip, took a deep breath and admitted, 'I'm pregnant. I'm going to have a baby.'

Julianne turned sharply to Paolo, 'Did you know about this? Have you been keeping it from me?'

'It was not confirmed,' he said. 'We didn't want to concern you unduly. Kira had indicated to me that she had not been feeling well and I arranged for her to have a medical examination. That's when we found out. The prison system is well equipped to look after pregnant young ladies; it is not an unusual situation.'

'Not an unusual situation?' said Julianne, deliberately using all her reserves of strength to sustain her. Breath deep, don't shout, you have to be the adult in this situation.

'Not an unusual situation?' she repeated. 'Well it is for me. I've never been told before that I'm going to become a grandmother.'

She leaned over the solid wooden table to where her daughter was sitting, pulled her close, hugged her tightly round the shoulders and resting her chin on the top of her head, Julianne cried.

Certain buildings in the complex of the women's prison on the outskirts of Rome were modern and well equipped. Now that it was confirmed that she was pregnant, Kira Mae had been moved to a special section close to the medical centre where she was given her own room with bathroom facilities and access to a library, gymnasium and a small chapel.

'I pray every night and light a candle in the chapel,' she told her mother, 'I have this deep sense that everything is going to be okay.'

After the birth of the baby – if she had not been released by then – the two would be moved into the mother and baby unit. A high quality state of the art facility with nursing staff and nursery workers helping to care for the babies.

Kira Mae's pregnancy had brought some unexpected benefits. Some of the women with whom she shared her cell block, had begun to take her under their wing. Many were mothers and they knew what it was like to be pregnant and need support, encouragement and tender loving care. Also being a first time mum, Kira Mae had many questions about her body changes, mood swings and the scary but exciting prospect of becoming a mum. The milk of human kindness flowed even in the unforgiving regime of a prison and Kira Mae was protected, offered all manner of good and conflicting advice and presented with tiny baby clothes made by some of her fellow women prisoners or passed down from their own babies. While fussing over her, new friends promised to watch over her as did the highly experienced medical team.

In common with practically every other one of the prisoners, Kira Mae protested her innocence. She was determined to present herself as an innocent victim and she managed to convince herself that when her court date came she would not be found guilty. Sadly her confidence was misplaced.

★ ★ ★

Kira Mae had at first retained her belief that Romero would save her. He was to be her knight in shining armour, riding to the rescue. Maintaining this huge delusion seemed to be the way she had chosen to blind herself to the reality of her situation. The walls of denial would have to come crashing down and when they did, her daughter would need Julianne more than ever. Kira Mae resolutely refused to confront the truth about this man she had decided to mythologise.

Until the time of her trial, which took just six months – a surprisingly short time in the Italian judicial system – to come to court. Then Kira Mae had the veil ripped from her eyes as she heard the full facts about the murderous drug dealer she had chosen to love and try to protect.

In partnership with his wife Annabelle the two had made their fortunes dealing in drugs, money laundering and acting as enforcers for those who broke the rules of the cartels. They had started out as opportunistic drug addicts, mules who acted as couriers transporting goods around the world for money. They had climbed up through the chains of command and earned the trust of the lieutenants of the Colombian drug warlords and finally the warlords themselves.

By proving their loyalty and ability to eliminate all who got in their way, Romero and his wife, Annabelle, had worked their way to the top of the supply chain and taken over running their own drug export rings. They ruled with iron fists and those who crossed them or their bosses were subjected to savage violence and often death. The couple lived dual lives and whenever anyone got in their way they killed them. They were remorseless, even a defenceless young woman like Romero's fiancée was disposed of when she was no longer of use to the pair.

Kira Mae finally saw them for what they were, evil and beyond redemption. She accepted that she had been contaminated by her association with Romero and she was sentenced to two years' imprisonment as an accessory after the fact. Even an impassioned plea from Paolo for clemency for this young girl, who was pregnant and in a foreign country, could not save her from a custodial sentence. However, her six months in custody would be counted towards her sentence and with good behaviour it was realistic that she could be out in a little over a year.

Romero was also found guilty and Paolo could not keep the professional pride from his voice as he reported that the career criminal had been sentenced to a hefty fifteen years, because of his many previous convictions. Drug trafficking was his business and the judge made no secret of the fact that he was imposing heavy sentences to send strong messages to others who profited from the deadly trade. His wife Annabelle was sentenced to ten years, though Paolo had heard that she had applied to be allowed to serve her prison time in England.

True to their word, Kira Mae had been assigned a place in the mother and baby unit at the newly built prison facility. There were to be no cells and no bars. Instead Kira Mae was housed in the brightly painted special hospital unit, under medical supervision with special food and medicine.

Mothers awaiting the birth of their babies were encouraged to help with the care of the babies and infants in the baby unit. Visiting restrictions were still in force and Julianne could visit just once a month. On their regular monthly visits she was generally accompanied by Paolo and Kira Mae looked forward to seeing both of them.

Paolo continued to petition for her early release, but Julianne was at least reassured that her daughter was being taken care of properly. It had taken Julianne all her willpower to admit her own secret to her daughter. She was embarrassed and reluctant, but also resolute that there should be no more secrets between the two of them.

She let the facts out as if she was having teeth pulled. 'You remember I told you I hadn't been feeling well? Nauseous. Not eating properly? I was also putting on weight? Well, I've been to the doctor. He recognised the symptoms.'

Kira Mae waited expectantly, and then realisation dawned. 'You're not? Are you?' she said dramatically. 'Pregnant?'

Julianne could deny it no longer. In fact it was a relief that the secret had been revealed. You are as sick as your secret, she had told herself over and over as she cajoled herself into telling her daughter. Her darling daughter did not give her a hard time or even press for the name of the father. For the time being, Julianne was content to let her believe that it was probably Paolo. He was the only man she had seen her mother with and the two certainly seemed to be close.

Now Kira Mae took it upon herself to become her mother's pregnancy buddy. She worried about her mother and urged her to get proper attention and care. 'Don't forget, you are getting on in years,' Kira Mae told her bluntly. And as she pointed out, having become an instant expert from her brief helping sessions in the mother and baby unit, 'Pregnancy in older women needs careful monitoring.'

The terrible shock that she had experienced on first learning that she was pregnant had caused Julianne many weeks of anxiety and stress. At first she had been reluctant to tell Kira Mae about her own pregnancy, but it was not something that could be ignored or hidden indefinitely.

She kept details of her exact dates vague and Paolo was happy for Kira Mae to believe him to be the father. Indeed he had become a close friend and confidant to Julianne though the two were not romantically linked, however much Paolo might have wished that they were.

Diplomatically, he had never enquired as to the identity of the father of Julianne's unborn child. Instead she allowed him to believe it was an on-going romance with an old faithful boyfriend, who had worked in Spain and left Julianne with her forthcoming gift, when he had returned to England.

★ ★ ★

There were many tortured white nights when Julianne lay awake and blamed herself for the terrible predicament, but never did she resort to hurting herself or her unborn child.

Julianne maintained a discreet isolation at the home and business she continued to rent. The local village doctor was brusque but kind. Like Kira Mae, he was aware that older women needed extra monitoring and supplied all the tests and examinations that Julianne required. He suggested that she go to the maternity unit in Alicante for the birth, rather than contemplate a home birth.

Having accepted her situation, Julianne kept in remarkably good health and her pregnancy could have been a time of joy had she not still been tortured by memories of Romero. Thoughts of love had been transformed and now all she felt was the deep desire for revenge.

The months of Julianne's pregnancy became a learning time, reading about what to expect at each stage while new life grew inside her. Strangely she could hardly seem to recall the time of her pregnancy with Kira Mae. All she remembered was the cosy domestic existence, love and support she had received from her beloved Mummy Mitchell. That great lady made sure it was a happy time of preparation when they would knit and sew and crochet for the new baby.

Julianne did remember that she had been scared about the actual birth, but as many mothers had told her since, you completely forget the pain of giving birth; otherwise no one would ever have number two.

Julianne reflected on how history did indeed repeat itself. Here she was again living a secret life, far from anyone who knew her, denying the name of the man who had fathered her child. As she had done with her father, she vowed to find a way to hold Romero to account for his evil deeds.

Fortunately no one in the village knew her history, so she was able to effectively isolate herself with her lack of fluency in the language.

The shop may have been called *La Dama Escalata*, but Julianne was more *La Dama Misteriosa*.

Kira Mae gave birth in the beginning of the year to a beautiful dark-haired, brown-eyed girl; she named her Angel Rose Gordon. Fewer than four weeks later, Julianne gave birth.

For the birth and delivery she took her doctor's advice and travelled to the state of the art maternity unit at Alicante Hospital. She was all alone save for the expert care of the medical staff; she gave birth also to a beautiful baby girl with black hair and brown eyes.

Cultivating an air of secrecy Julianne had just one visitor while she was in hospital. Mr Reginald Haverstock, art dealer and wine connoisseur, an elderly, quaintly old fashioned white-haired gentleman who wore a bow tie and spoke with a cultured and unhurried upper class accent. However, even the usually unflappable Mr Haverstock could not keep the excitement from his voice, as he relayed the good news from the art gallery curator.

'Mrs Gordon,' he said deferentially, 'you are in the most enviable position of owning a rare and most valuable early work by the artist Jack Vettriano. Please promise me that I will be the first person to know if you are ever minded to sell it.'

In honour of the painting, Julianne called her beloved new daughter Isabella Blossom Gordon, after Mummy Mitchell and the name she had given to the painting, *The Blossom Garden*.

chapter thirty-one

'Double, double toil and trouble,
Fire burn, and cauldron bubble.'
Shakespeare's *Macbeth*

Proud new mother Julianne sat in the back of the chauffeur-driven car she had booked to collect her from the hospital maternity ward and make the long journey to her San Juan home. Her tiny baby, wrapped in a white fluffy blanket was asleep in her arms. A study in serenity the baby was perfectly at peace. Her head and miniature face was the only thing visible outside the confines of her swaddling clothes. Downy wisps of black hair had been lovingly brushed and surprisingly thick black lashes shaded dark eyes that could not yet see, the delicate lashes fluttered open for a second and closed again. Her skin was like glazed china, a little red but devoid of discolouration or marks. The most perfect baby in the world. Or so her mother thought.

Julianne had given birth with relatively little pain or fuss even though she was almost twice the age of most of the other mothers in the delivery ward. The child had made its entrance to the world in the middle of the night when all was quiet and dark. A dignified stress-free arrival, the baby already seemed reluctant to expend unnecessary energy in screaming, wailing or protesting her arrival on earth.

'Hello, beautiful,' said Julianne, and kissed her forehead as the nurse handed over the infant. 'Thank you for choosing me to be your mother.'

Julianne had not been able to take her eyes off the precious bundle since that magical moment just forty-eight hours before. Bathing the wriggling infant delighted her and even struggling to manoeuvre doll size arms and legs into size zero baby clothes was a joy. Julianne fed, changed, dressed and softly kissed and stroked the baby with a heart bursting to capacity with love.

Arriving home she lovingly carried the baby inside while the taxi driver brought up the rear carrying Julianne's small overnight case and the baby's large suitcase plus a holdall full of baby supplies.

Paying him off and accepting his well wishes for a long and happy life for herself and the baby, Julianne climbed the stairs to the newly decorated, toy filled nursery and laid the still sleeping baby in its lace frilled Moses basket.

'We are home, baby, safe and sound,' she said. Then as a lump formed in her throat, she tried to stop herself from crying as she said, 'Everything would be just perfect if your sister Kira Mae and little cousin Angel were here.'

★ ★ ★

Kira Mae's conditions were not quite so idyllic but they were comfortable. She hardly remembered anything of the birth having gratefully accepted all offers of painkillers to ease the delivery. However, she quickly came round from a sedated experience when she heard her child cry.

Angel emerged into the light of life in the early afternoon. An alert, excitable baby who was happy to be passed from individual to individual in the prison hospital all the time gurgling and smiling as she settled into each new pair of arms.

As the newest baby on the unit she was spoiled and fussed over and petted and the older babies and toddlers on the unit became companions and playmates. Kira Mae was a patient and loving mother and despite the circumstances, she made the best of her new position in life.

At first she turned down her mother's request to bring her own baby Isabella into the unit to meet Angel but gradually she relented and agreed that it would be good for them to bond. She had also been assured that babies had no memory of their first few months so neither should be able to recall their unconventional start in life.

★ ★ ★

The babies were a few months old when Julianne decided it was time to move into the next stage of growing her business. The fashion boutique had been steadily and surely attracting a regular flow of loyal clients under her expert ownership and the professional services of a local manager.

Julianne was fulfilled and happy to have her beautiful baby girl, Isabella to look after and, despite the sadness surrounding Kira Mae, there were times when she truly felt that she was in seventh heaven. Unfortunately those days were always overshadowed by the knowledge that her other daughter was still in jail along with Julianne's granddaughter.

Babies were allowed to live in the special prison unit with their mothers up to two years of age. Julianne had offered to

301

bring little Angel Rose to live with her and Isabella, but Kira Mae would not hear of it. The best place for her baby was with her, she judged and besides, having her daughter with her made prison more bearable. It was like being in hospital rather than prison. She looked forward to the visits from her mother and was always happy to see little Isabella.

Motherhood had mellowed both women and rarely did bad feeling flare between the two of them. They came to an unspoken agreement that circumstances were difficult enough without recriminations between them adding to their woes.

If there were conflicts, they generally centred on the best way to raise babies. Kira Mae had attended parenting classes in prison and had become a trustee in the mother and baby unit. Instead of being only interested in fashion, she had developed an interest in child care and fancied herself an expert. She kept up to date on all the new perceived wisdom about the best way to bring up a baby and loved passing it on to her mother. Julianne was more like the new mother, having generally relinquished the care and welfare of her first born.

They counted the days until Kira Mae would finish her sentence and be able to return home. 'My new prayer is that Angel will be able to celebrate her first birthday with you and Isabella at home,' said Kira Mae. Already Angel was being introduced to the world outside the prison gates in supervised visits to the local park and gardens. It was essential that everyone remembered the babies in the unit were not prisoners. Kira Mae dreamt that she would be released in time for Angel's first birthday, by then she would have served eighteen months of her two year sentence.

Mother and daughter made plans and talked about all the adventures they would have with their adorable girls. Kira Mae was anxious to ascertain that there was still a place for her at *La Dama Escalata* and she would regale her mother excitedly with ideas for a designer boutique of clothes for babies, toddlers and children.

Julianne listened indulgently, she would deny her daughter nothing, so eager was she to have her home and put the nightmare of the past years behind them and get some closure.

'When you have a loved one behind bars,' she told Paolo, 'a piece of your heart is always there chained to them.'

★ ★ ★

The day of Kira Mae's scheduled release just days before Angel's birthday was an emotional one. Julianne and Isabella arrived at the prison gates, driven by Paolo, even before the early hour release time of 6 a.m. Please God, don't let anything go wrong, Julianne prayed silently. Set her free and I can be free too.

The huge jail gates clanged open and Kira Mae walked out carrying Angel Rose. The two young ones, safe in their mothers' arms, smiled happily at each other. Kira Mae and Julianne hugged each other tightly and sobbed.

'Quick, let's get away from here,' Kira Mae said to Paolo, who as always was standing by. 'In case they change their minds.'

Paolo settled them all into the hired, large black limousine and drove joyfully home.

chapter thirty-two

'Is this a dagger which I see before me, the handle towards my hand?'
Shakespeare's *Macbeth*

Now their new lives could really begin, mother and daughter devoted all their time and energy to their darling little girls. Being almost the same age and looking so alike, the toddlers were often mistaken for twins.

One of the great joys shared by the mothers was to dress the girls in the latest baby fashions such as Dior and Gap. Diligently Kira Mae did her research and sketched, created and schemed to start her own label.

Apart from her baby line she began to garner a reputation for designing one off evening creations for the affluent ladies who visited the boutique.

Kira Mae adjusted well to life outside prison. Though never could her time of incarceration be considered a good thing, she had grown up in a very mature and focused way. She had taken a degree of personal responsibility for what happened and in prison had learned that she had many good qualities and skills that made her popular and successful. Now she was ready to put the past behind her and get on with living a worthwhile life for her, her daughter and her mother.

Work for Kira Mae, like her mother before her, was her saving grace. She embraced a new philosophy learned in jail: you need just three things to be happy – someone to love; something to do; and something to look forward to.

Watching the girls grow and run and play in the lovely warm Spanish sunshine, mother and daughter were in their element.

Life was good.

* * *

There was just one villain of the piece and neither woman could go for long without bringing up the name of Romero.

Julianne had promised her daughter she would avenge the man who had betrayed her – put her in jail and left her with a baby. Never once did Julianne breathe the dreadful truth that she too had been the victim of Romero's cheating and betrayal. If she suspected, Kira Mae never voiced the suspicion.

Instead, she was prepared to believe that her mother's wrath and enduring hatred of Romero was because of what he had done to her daughter. A lioness defending her cub.

Julianne was adamant that she would never forget and she would never forgive. With her friend and ally, Paolo, she plotted her revenge. Paolo was a frequent visitor to the family home in Spain. He loved all four girls, mothers and daughters but for Julianne he always carried a torch. They had been friends and even briefly lovers over the years and now they were the best of friends, never entirely convinced that they would not be lovers again one day.

Paolo had never hidden his love for Julianne and though he suspected she was not in love with him, he was prepared to settle for what was on offer. When Kira Mae was first in jail, Paolo had decided that however long it took for her to agree, Julianne was the woman with whom he wanted to spend his life. Julianne understood their romance was far from the heady passion of her relationship with Romero but it did provide a loving safe environment.

After she discovered she was pregnant, Paolo had made his intentions clear. 'I will ask for nothing,' he promised, 'but let me take care of you.'

Julianne gratefully accepted though she told him, 'I don't deserve you.'

Over the past couple of years they had shared a bed and on occasion their physical and emotional closeness had become sexual. Paolo was a considerate lover and Julianne trusted and respected him. As she had told him frequently, 'I love you and there is no one else with whom I would rather share my life and my bed.'

In their intimacy she had revealed all her darkest secrets and Paolo was aware that when painful memories overwhelmed her she needed to distance herself from him and her past trauma. He loved her enough to accept the situation and explained, 'That's what unconditional love means.'

One night as they lay comfortably together in Julianne's double bed, Paolo asked, 'Do you want me to find out what happened to the men in the Cambridge paedophile ring investigation?' He had heard that arrests had been made and charges brought.

Julianne thought carefully and then told him, 'No, thank you. I played my part when I made my report to the police. Let fate take its course. I don't want to ever have to think about it – or him again. I have closure on that one.'

Paolo was lover and confidant to Julianne, and favourite uncle to Kira Mae, Angel and Isabella. They adored him and he played a huge part in their lives. The handsome lawyer also had access to certain valuable information that was vital to Julianne and her future plans. He took very seriously the vow he had made several years before, to keep her informed of the movements and whereabouts of Prisoner 45691, one Jesus Floris.

Romero had been moved several times to ever more awful prisons in more remote parts of Italy and one of the main reasons was said to be the fact that the authorities believed he would attempt to escape. Julianne consoled herself with the fact that had he known the fate that awaited him outside the prison walls, he would beg to be kept behind bars.

Julianne had cunningly instigated a relationship by mail with Romero. She knew exactly what she was doing, she thought of nothing but her determination to exact revenge. In her first letters she angrily berated him for what he had done to her daughter, though she did not report that he was a father. Her letters were full of rage that he had seduced her daughter, deceived her and betrayed both of them. You are the lowest of the low, she told him. Because of you, my daughter went to jail.

Subtly, after a few months she changed tactics. The tone of her letters altered and she began to remind Romero of the romantic times they had shared. She spoke longingly of their lovemaking, the passion he had awoken in her, the fact she still desired him.

Now that Kira Mae was free, explained Julianne, she was ready to forgive. If only he had been able to read between the lines and know how far that statement was from the truth. Instead even writing the sentence had brought up such fury in Julianne that she had ripped up the first three versions.

What she really wanted to write was: You bastard, I will never forgive you for what you did to us. Every waking minute, Julianne felt the pain of the treachery she had endured. Deep down in her soul she felt the desperation and vowed to avenge the wrongdoing.

Demonically, mercilessly she enticed Romero, the ever-arrogant adventurer, into her web. Like a black widow spider she vowed to devour him – and spit out his bones. The woman who had spent so many years harming and torturing herself was now set to unleash all that rage on the man she had once loved.

Maliciously she lied and encouraged him that if ever he needed a friend on whom he could rely, it was her.

So in love with you am I still, she wrote in one letter. I would do anything for you. Give me a chance to prove my love for you. I pray that one day we can be together again. As artfully as a wicked witch casting evil spells, Julianne intoned her curse and stirred the cauldron of her righteous indignation.

Romero's latest escape plan was taking shape and he had no doubt where he would go to hide out. A beautiful white painted house in a Spanish village awaited him and there a beautiful woman who was crazy about him also waited. Romero did not know just how crazy his English lover was. His own wife Annabelle was still in jail – and would be for many more years.

Julianne enticed Paolo into her web of intrigue. He was by now filled with hatred and jealousy for Romero, the man who had reaped such injustices on the woman he loved and left her filled with such savage bitterness.

When Julianne told him, 'I could murder him. I will never rest as long as he is alive,' Paolo let it be known that if Romero ever escaped there would be plenty of people who were willing to do the job for her.

'He is a marked man,' Paolo told her.

The by now familiar stationery with its prison postmark and prisoner's name and number on the outside arrived from Romero, telling her to expect a surprise visit and Julianne excitedly put her fiendish plan into action.

Anonymously she wrote to the accomplice who had been arrested with her daughter. If you want revenge, she told him, I can deliver your betrayer to you.

chapter thirty-three

'Will all great Neptune's ocean wash this blood clean from my hand?'
Shakespeare's *Macbeth*

Gio Lopez was a small time crook whose hometown was the housing projects on the outskirts of the Eternal City, Rome; though there was little of the internationally famous art, culture or romance where he came from.

He talked big and was always dreaming of running with the top guys but really he was just a pipsqueak who they used when it suited to do their dirty work. He had been in gangs from the age of about twelve when under the cover of being just a harmless kid, he would ride his bike all over the neighbourhood to deliver drugs to his schoolmates and contacts.

With parents who neither knew nor cared where he spent his time and school authorities who had long since given up trying to pursue him through streets which he could run blindfolded, just to return him to a classroom from which he would truant as a matter of principle. Gio was a lone wolf.

As he grew and began to knock up an impressive street cred rap sheet – mostly for small misdemeanours – he served a few short prison sentences, built his reputation and expanded his circle of bigger time crooks who required a willing gofer or Mr Fixit. Gio was their man.

On the side, he made money selling tips and insider information to the police. It was a dangerous game but for Gio, the only game in town. He had never worked a job and the money he made was way better than a regular wage though by no means in the big league.

A fresh-faced, plausible and likeable kind of guy, when still a teenager he had acquired a wife and gradually added a couple of kids. His wife despaired of the life of petty crime he led and the unwelcome dawn raids that were an occupational hazard. However, every now and then, Gio would make a killing, buy her some pretty clothes, pay off debts and promise to turn over a new leaf. They both knew it wasn't going to happen so, every now and then, when the money ran out, his long suffering wife returned with the kids to her mama.

Gio's latest gangland role model and boss had been Jesus Floris, a truly international player in the drug and enforcement trade. Gio was his right hand man – until the day the carabinieri caught him red-handed attempting to bury evidence along with drugs and a gun.

Jesus had gone on the run and Gio went to jail but by acting as a collaborator, selling out his former gang boss and plea dealing, he served less than half his four year sentence. Two years later and he was back out on the streets – literally. His wife had packed up and left while he was in jail and although divorce would not be an option in the strictly Catholic community, she made it clear that she no longer considered herself his wife. She'd had enough of being the wife of a criminal, especially one who kept getting caught.

Gio was enjoying his freedom having already been released

from prison, but his life had been ruined. Unlike Romero, he had not salted away large amounts of money from the drug running, he was a small time crook and addict who had paid a hefty price for his involvement with Romero and his band of criminals.

The arrival of a letter addressed to him at a local bar, puzzled Gio. He did not receive many letters. In fact he tended to avoid them like the plague; they usually brought demands for money from the tax man or some other authority or collection agency.

However, this particular piece of mail looked like it might be interesting.

He first looked for a signature but there wasn't one. The writing was neat, all capitals and probably disguised. It simply stated, IF YOU WANT REVENGE, I CAN DELIVER YOUR BETRAYER TO YOU. The only other information was an address in a small village in Spain. Gio knew the story of Julianne and her daughter's imprisonment and though he had no intention of trying to find out the truth, he had his suspicions who had written to him.

'Revenge is a dish best served cold,' Gio laughed to himself. 'The only thing that kept me going in prison was the thought that one day I'd make him pay.'

Now by some kind of divine intervention, he was being offered Romero's head on a plate, he was not about to refuse such an invitation. On the criminal grapevine he had already heard that Romero was planning an escape and there had been a strong rumour that he would return to Spain, his homeland, where he had been living before his latest imprisonment.

It seemed that the letter held the key to his exact location and Gio knew some powerful operators who would pay handsomely for the address. Gio could get access to at least one top Mafia gangster who would be grateful to know where Romero was hiding out.

Gio relished the opportunity to set up an ambush and even offered to be the one who wielded the murder weapon.

Alongside the address on the letter was a series of numbers – Gio had previously overlooked their significance. Now he deciphered the code and realised they were time and date. PM 10-10-10 stood for 10 p.m. 10th October.

The place and time was set, the deed would be done. Julianne had plotted the end game with devastating precision.

Romero was being lured into a deadly trap and when he received the instructions to proceed after his escape to a small empty farmhouse near to his former home in the mountains of Murcia, he did not hesitate. Nor did he stand a chance.

Normally he insisted on checking and rechecking all arrangements. His meticulously planned escape had been paid for and organised with the help of prison guards and compliant court ushers. During a scheduled early morning court appearance in Genoa, a city in the far north of Italy, escorted from his police cell and handcuffed to officers, he would be allowed to walk free from the bathroom after the officers uncoupled his cuffs to allow him to go to the toilet. A small window inside the cubicle was unlocked and an accomplice waited in a fast car yards from the sidewalk.

The officers might be reprimanded for their stupidity – that would be nothing new – but what did they care? They had been well paid.

The escape went like clockwork and once settled in for a long ride across Europe, Romero made a crude remark to the driver of his getaway car and assured him that his desperate need for sexual relief would be top of the agenda – even before a decent meal and bottle of wine. Expecting to meet his lover, the woman who had forgiven him and now was fool enough to want to help him start a new life, he saw no need for caution or to protect himself.

Romero sped ever faster towards to his death – as far as he was concerned a moving target was harder to hit. He would be glad to be out of Italy and on his way back to the land of his birth, Spain.

The journey would take the best part of a day but the wait would be worth it. Sentiments echoed by his waiting assassin. The wait would be worth it. Gio had let himself into the small farmhouse, the address of which had been provided in the initial letter he had received. He was amused by the fact that the door was not even locked. This was a safe and trusting neighbourhood. Gio settled down with a bottle of wine and large plate of bread and cheese which had been thoughtfully provided in the store cupboard.

He almost wished that whoever had organised this most civilised of killings could be here to watch the conclusion of the plan.

Despite the wine, Gio was aware that he must stay alert and ready to complete his mission. He had been well paid by the gang bosses who had already split up territory and had no intention of meekly stepping aside now that Romero was here to reclaim ownership. He sat in an armchair beside an unlit fire with no light on, lovingly polishing the double edged eighteen inch steel dagger with the buffalo horn handle that he had brought specially to kill his target. It was the weapon of choice on many Italian streets and he knew how to use it – one downward strike carrying the full power of the elbow and sticking the cruel blade in up to the hilt hitting the bull's eye – the vital organs. Gio One Strike was his well earned gang nickname.

Years of housebreaking had taught Gio how to prevent being identified. He had been careful to avoid leaving fingerprints, now he stuffed the half empty wine bottle into his holdall. He had used his trusty dagger to cut the bread and cheese and his own handkerchief as a plate.

First he saw the headlights of an approaching car and then it slowed to a halt on the dirt track outside the farmhouse. A door slammed and Romero and the driver engaged in friendly banter as they said their goodbyes. 'Give her one for me,' said the driver. 'You got it,' Romero called out raucously.

There were no other houses nearby and a bold Romero was not afraid of being heard or seen. He had just one moment of apprehension when he thought that a waiting lover would have kept a light on – but his suspicions were not aroused so sure was he of a loving welcome. As he walked up the gravel path in the dark a light went on in an upstairs room and he smiled to himself. Pushing open the door he realised it was not locked. Indeed he was expected.

Stepping over the threshold of the rough-hewn wooden doorway, Romero dropped his small travel bag, which had been delivered via the car driver, courtesy of his friends on the outside.

Pumped up with excited anticipation and pent up sexual fever he followed the source of the light. Stepping into the small bedroom at the top of the stairs with a wicked smile on his face, he fantasised that a naked Julianne would be stretched out on the bed awaiting his pleasure. Instead the room was bare.

Suddenly he heard a tell tale squeak and the bedroom door

swung closed. Romero turned to be confronted with the sight of his one time friend Gio, poised, knife in hand raised up to his shoulder. Having ambushed his victim he wasted no time in plunging the razor sharp blade into Romero's heart. He cheered as the dying man's blood poured out. Gio felt no guilt.

To add to Romero's pain and visible distress, he cruelly twisted the dagger, tearing the lacerated and bleeding skin. Gio was pleased with his work.

Why should he feel guilty? He was an Italian and proud of it – he had been taught from birth to avenge those who betrayed you – or your friends – or your family. Gio observed the fear in Romero's eye as he feebly tried to raise his hand to ward off another deadly blow. Too late. Gio had struck with devastating accuracy and as he pulled his precious dagger from the bleeding skin, avoiding the viciously splattering blood, the traumatised victim went into shock and fell to the floor lying helplessly on his back, blood soaking his white shirt.

Gio was a true professional, his first and only blow fatally wounded Romero but that did not mean he would die immediately. Gio intended to make him suffer. The wound would spurt and erupt guaranteeing a certain but slow and painful death. Romero's eyes were wide open, enlarged and silently screaming as if asking 'Why?' He knew he had been betrayed, but only when Gio bent over his body as the life force drained away and stuck the razor sharp thorns of a long stemmed rose into the gaping wound, would he die knowing the answer. Gio always left a signature on his work – the rose was a gift for a beautiful lady.

Gio was sure, with all his street smarts, he had worked out exactly who had set up this whole scene – a lover's revenge. Finally, Romero was the one with a fatally broken heart.

Before his dead and mutilated body was even discovered, Gio would be on the highway back to Rome. He closed and locked the door. There was just one job left to do, he pulled from the back pocket of his trousers the letter that he had received only a few short days ago giving the address and the coded date and time. His blood-stained hands left bright scarlet lipstick-like smudges on the letter.

Now he checked the last set of figures on the bottom of the letter, and tapping the digits into his cell phone, waited for a reply. As a woman's voice answered he confirmed: 'The roses have been delivered.'

Mother and daughter rejoiced. The Gods had been avenged. The final act was ready to be played out. Triumphantly they made plans to attend his funeral – and dance on the grave.

WITH GRATITUDE

Wherever I am in the world, my heart is always at home—be it London, Miami, or Spain. My books are brought to life—and the bookshelf—by an excellent creative and production team.

Thanks go to graphic designer Gary Rosenberg of The Book Couple in Boca Raton, Florida, line editor Lori Lewis in Vermont, USA, and Jo Ware of Type It Quick in Brighton, West Sussex. Always by my side, to cheerlead and guide, Doctor Michelle Ruger.

My thanks, as ever, to those loyal readers who challenge and inspire me to write and share my stories. I am grateful for a blessed life. Love really *does* make the world go round.

ABOUT THE AUTHOR

ELLEN FRAZER-JAMESON is a professional communicator working in media, print, and theater. A former BBC broadcaster and Fleet Street journalist, Ellen is a published author, producer, theater director, and performer. She co-presented the largest late-night audience show in Europe on BBC Radio 2. Ellen lives in London and Miami Beach, and to relax dances Argentine tango.

Ellen has written several non-fiction books and six novels. Ellen's round-the-world travels provide her with research, inspiration, and adventure—*An Invitation to the Captain's Table* is an amalgamation of several ocean-going cruises.

All her current titles are available on www.Amazon.com and www.Amazon.co.uk:

Love Trilogy: The story begins with *Love Mother Love Daughter,* the love affair continues with *Love Refuses to Die,* and reaches its thrilling conclusion in *Love Kills with a Kiss.*

Set in New York and Miami, *Dark Hole in My Soul* is the first edition of the retitled *Flame Island.* Ellen's novel *Once Upon a Lie* takes place in Spain and England.

Seven Steps to Fabulous and *Seven Steps to Cruising Fabulous* are Ellen's two must-read nonfiction life-style guides.

Travels with Otto and *Slim with the Stars* are now available for the first time on Amazon.com.

Contact Ellen at ellenfrazerjameson@gmail.com or visit www.ellenfrazerjameson.com

www.ingramcontent.com/pod-product-compliance
Lightning Source LLC
Chambersburg PA
CBHW070914260626
47162CB00007B/2671